SPACE TEAM

SONG OF THE SPACE SIREN

SPACE TEAM: SONG OF THE SPACE SIREN
ISBN: 978-0-9956233-3-0

Published worldwide by Zertex Books.
This edition published in 2017

1

Copyright © 2017 by Barry J. Hutchison

www.barryjhutchison.com

SONG OF THE SPACE SIREN

BARRY J. HUTCHISON

ZERTEX

For Mr T, and all his pitied fools.

CHAPTER ONE

Dogan Murt was not, by any stretch of the imagination, a brave man.

He wasn't technically a 'man' at all, in fact. He was a Talpan – a race of wide-eyed humanoid, yet somewhat mole-like creatures who traditionally lived deep underground, and smelled ever so faintly of kitty litter.

Not content with spending the entirety of his adult life in a dark cave (or overly keen on the kitty litter thing), Dogan had struck out on his own, determined to make his way in the world. That had been several years ago. Of late, things had not been going well.

Dogan looked down at the scrap of paper he clutched in his shaking hands, then up at the flickering neon sign above the door. His reading ability was low at the best of times, and a full third of the letters in the sign were in darkness, but he was pretty sure this was the place.

He pushed open the door. Sweat and smoke and noise and movement all rushed out through the gap.

He closed the door again, alarmed by the brutality of it

all.

"Do it, Dogan! Do it, Dogan!" he whispered. It had become a sort of personal mantra of his over the years, and he called on it whenever fear threatened to thwart his attempts to better himself.

'Do it Dogan,' had even been his nickname for a while back in the caves, although it was usually said in mocking tones, and followed swiftly by a sharp punch to the testicles. He had no nicknames now, of course. To have a nickname, first you needed a friend. Or an enemy who knew you well enough.

Siphoning some air in through his sharp front teeth, Dogan pushed the door all the way open, clenched his fists down at his sides, then stepped into the bar.

Even before getting the measure of the place, Dogan knew he didn't approve. The Talpan were fiercely moral, and public venues where people got into fights, drank excessively and did the sort of things the three-legged gentleman on stage was doing were very much frowned upon.

Despite himself, Dogan looked more closely at the man on the stage, and came to the conclusion that the third appendage wasn't actually a leg at all.

Horrified, Dogan turned away, blinked several times to try to erase the images he'd just witnessed, then headed for one of the bar's empty booths.

"Sorry. Pardon me. Can I just squeeze... thanks," he mumbled, weaving his way through the crowds. He reached the dimly-lit booth, only to find a hulking green figure lurking in the corner, nursing a drink.

"Oh. Sorry," said Dogan. "I just... I didn't..." He smiled hopefully at the booth's occupant. "Would you mind?"

The creature stared impassively at Dogan for several seconds, its eyes glassy and black. At last, it waved a clawed hand at the bench across the table, and Dogan slid gratefully onto the ripped and threadbare padding.

"Thank you," said Dogan, nestling into the shadows. The lizard-creature nodded once, but said nothing.

Now that he was out of the crowds, Dogan took a moment to scan the place. A horseshoe-shaped bar took up around a quarter of the floor space, with the raised stage over by the far wall taking up a much smaller chunk. Clearly people came for the entertainment, but stayed for the booze.

The lights were low, the volume was high, and while there were a few groups hanging out together, most of the clientele seemed to be in pairs or on their own.

Dogan felt the lizard-creature's eyes on him, and smiled shakily. "I'm looking for someone," he explained. "I was told I might find him here."

He glanced around the bar again, anxiously picking at his black fingernails. "I need his help. I am in trouble," he explained, his voice dropping to a whisper.

Dogan caught himself just in time. He regarded the green-skinned alien cautiously. "You are not with the Xandrie, are you?"

The creature shook its head slowly.

"Zertex?" asked Dogan, eyeing up the exit. "Are you law enforcement? Because I'm not allowed to talk to them, the Xandrie made that very clear."

The creature shook its head again.

"And you have to tell me if I ask you. It's the law," Dogan insisted.

The creature growled deep down in its throat, then shook its head again.

Dogan nodded, relieved. "Good. Good. I apologize. I had to ask, you understand?"

The creature said nothing.

"You understand," said Dogan, answering on its behalf. He rubbed the tabletop that stood between them, feeling every scratch with the pink, wrinkled skin of his fingertips.

"The problem is, I do not know what he looks like," said Dogan, gazing out across the bar again. The genetically blessed young man had been joined on stage by two alarmingly supple women, and many of the bar's occupants had started to gravitate towards that end of the room.

Dogan clicked his tongue against his teeth in disapproval, then angled himself for a better view so that he could *really* disapprove if things went the way he thought they were probably going to go.

"But I am in trouble, and I believe he can help me," Dogan said, tearing his eyes from the stage. "The Xandrie, they want money from my business. In return, they have offered to 'protect' it. 'It's a nasty part of town,' they tell me. 'Wouldn't want anything happening to you,' they say."

The mole-man's eyes moistened, and he lowered his head for a moment, composing himself. "I paid. For a long time, I paid, but now the cost has gone up, and I can no longer afford to do so. Besides," he said, getting angry. "It is *my* business. *My* money. *My* hard work. Why should I pay these... these... gangsters?"

He banged a fist on the table. It very clearly hurt, but he tried not to let on. He glanced around nervously, and the anger left his voice in a long outward breath. "I just want someone to make the Xandrie understand that I cannot be pushed around. That they cannot continue to do as they please."

Dogan's eyes swept the bar again, searching for someone he didn't know, but on whom he'd pinned all his hopes. "I am told this man and his crew may help me. I was told he might be here." He sighed. "It appears my information was incorrect."

Drumming his hands on the tabletop, Dogan met the gaze of the lizard-creature and had another attempt at a smile. "My apologies. None of this is your concern. Forgive me for bothering you."

As Dogan spoke, one of the alien's clawed hands fumbled at a spot halfway up its scaly throat. Dogan watched in amazement as the claws dug into the spongy flesh, then blinked in surprise as a square flap was peeled aside, revealing a sweat-soaked human face inside.

"Holy shizz, it is fonking hot in there," gasped the man. He grabbed for his glass, shut his eyes, then tossed his drink in his face. "Oh, yeah. That's the stuff," he sighed. "Wow. That's better."

Dogan's face crumpled in confusion. "I... I do not understand. Who are you? *What* are you?"

"Oh. Yeah. Forgot that bit. Sorry. Name's Cal. Cal Carver," said the man in the suit. He gave a rubbery thumbs up. "And, mister, you just hired the Space Team."

Cal swept the clawed hand across his face, wiping away his drink. "I mean, technically it's just 'Space Team' not 'the Space Team' but, well, there was this TV show where I came from, and every week the leader, Hannibal, would..." He shook his head. The rubbery lizard head shook, too. "Know what? It doesn't matter. The main thing is, you've got a problem, no-one else can help, and you've found us."

"Uh... 'us'?" said Dogan.

The back of the bench behind Dogan shook as someone

moved in the next booth over. There was a *whirr* and a series of *clanks*, then a scuffed and dented metal figure stepped into view.

Cal looked the cyborg up and down. "Mech! I thought I told you to find a disguise?"

"I did," said Mech. He ducked a little and pointed to the top of his head.

"A tiny hat," said Cal. "That's your disguise? A tiny hat."

"I'm a seven foot tall cyborg. What the fonk should I have disguised myself as?"

"I don't know, maybe a *different* seven foot tall cyborg?" Cal suggested. "One who *isn't* on a list of the galaxy's most wanted."

Dogan looked between Cal and Mech, his mouth hanging open. A sudden movement at the edge of the booth caught his attention, and he almost screamed when a wolf-like creature in a tightly-fitting leather outfit slid onto the seat next to Cal.

"Hey," she said. "Who's the wrinkly pink guy?"

"Uh, D-Dogan," the wrinkly pink guy stammered, silently adding the "Please don't eat me," part in his head.

"Miz! Why aren't you disguised, either?" asked Cal, turning to look the wolf-woman up and down. Because of his costume, this wasn't easy, and it took several attempts before he could twist his body enough to let him see her properly.

Miz shrugged. "I don't know. Seemed kind of lame. Besides, look at me. Blending in? Totally not my thing."

Cal tutted and shook his head. "How hard would it have been to pop on a pair of glasses or something? You know? A fake nose. A mustache! You couldn't even give me a mustache."

"Why are you disguised?" Dogan asked.

"Because we're wanted by the government for a crime we didn't commit," said Cal. He caught the looks from Mech and Miz. "OK, OK, we're wanted by the government for a crime we *did* commit. A number of crimes, actually. Mainly, abducting the president, ejecting him into space, and stealing an experimental ship, but it's a pretty big list."

Cal pointed a clawed finger at Dogan. "But we're not here to talk about us. We're here to talk about *you*."

He leaned across the table, but it made his costume ride up and forced his cheeks up into his eyes, so he leaned back again. "Tell us more about these Xandrie guys. And, more importantly, just where we might be able to find them."

Cal, Mech and Miz stood in a darkened doorway, watching the building directly across the street. Cal had ditched the lizard costume in an alleyway behind the bar, and now wore the black shirt, cargo pants and scuffed brown boots he'd picked up on their recent trip back to the Bug-infested wasteland that was now the planet Earth.

"So, if I had to say who was who," said Cal, rubbing his hands together to drive away the cold, "I'd be Face, because, you know, I'm the smooth-talking one who always charms his way out of trouble. But – and here's the thing - I'd *also* be Hannibal, because I'm the leader."

Mech raised an eyebrow. "Leader? You ain't the leader. We ain't got no leader."

"Well, we do, obviously, and it's me, but that's OK, because you're B.A., and everyone loves B.A.!" Cal said, patting Mech on the chest. "'I ain't goin' on no plane, sucka!' You know?"

Miz wrinkled her nose. "What is he talking about?"

13

"I have no fonking idea," Mech admitted.

"Loren's Murdoch, because they're both pilots, not because she's got undiagnosed PTSD or whatever Murdoch had, and Miz…" His mind raced. "Miz is the sexy werewolf lady they rarely spoke about."

He shoved his hands in his pockets and turned his attention back to the doorway across the road. "I mean, we're not *exactly* the same, but there are broad similarities is the point I'm trying to make."

It had been over a month since Cal had been abducted from his prison cell and whisked into outer space, and while lots of it was all still new and exciting, there were a few parts which were already losing their novelty.

Streets like this, for example. He knew he couldn't have seen this street before – they'd only arrived on the planet a few hours ago – and yet there was something tediously familiar about it. The shadowy nooks. The grimy windows. The flurries of litter tumbling along it on the whims of the breeze.

There were streets just like it back on Earth. Streets you didn't walk down if you valued your wallet, your kneecaps or your life. Cal had seen more than his fair share back on his home planet, and was amassing quite the collection on other worlds, too.

"Think that's the place?" he asked.

Mech tapped the screen on his forearm and scanned the doorway opposite. "Door's heavy. Reinforced. Take a tank to knock that thing down."

"Can you do it?" Cal asked.

Mech snorted and *clanked* his way across the street. "Just watch me."

Cal hurried to keep up, with Miz stalking along behind

him.

"OK, so let's just go in there, throw our weight around a little – well, your weight, mostly," Cal said, looking from Mech to Miz in turn, "and give them a warning. Let's try not to kill anyone this time, if we can avoid it. Mizette, I'm looking at you here."

"Fine," Miz sighed. "But what if they deserve it?"

"If they *genuinely* deserve it, it's totally fine," said Cal. "But you said that last guy deserved it because he was wearing yellow pants."

"He totally did deserve it," said Miz.

"Girl's got a point," agreed Mech. "Those were some nasty pants."

A car blared its horn at them as it hovered past. Miz gave it the finger, and Cal felt a swelling of pride that he'd taught her the gesture. They stepped onto the sidewalk and positioned themselves by the reinforced door.

"We should have brought Loren on this," Cal whispered, drawing a blaster pistol from the holster on his belt.

"Why, so the two of you could hold hands?" asked Miz, the fur on her neck sticking up ever so slightly.

"How many times do I have to tell you?" Cal whispered. "There's nothing going on between us."

"Oh, *please*," said Miz, then she jabbed a thumb towards the door and glowered at Mech. "Are you going to kick this thing down or not?"

"Get ready," Mech said. He adjusted the dial on his chest, just a fraction, diverting additional power to his hydraulics. Then he raised a leg and thrust it out in front of him like a battering ram.

The doors flew apart with a screech of tearing metal.

"Oh, man," Cal whispered. "That was *so* B.A."

He took cover behind Mech as the cyborg ducked through the doorway and stomped into the starkly gray hallway beyond. A fluorescent strip light flickered on the ceiling, sending shadows dancing over the gloss-painted walls.

"Attention, uh, the Xandrie," Cal began, but his voice trailed away when he spotted the blood. It pooled on the vinyl flooring and dribbled down the walls. It dripped from the light fitting and seeped from below the door at the far end of the hall.

And, perhaps most significantly of all, it oozed from the quivering, gelatinous remains of what had presumably once been a living creature, but was now nothing more than gristle and flesh.

Cal's grip tightened on his blaster. "Uh… hello?" he said, poking the fleshy lump with his shoe. He backed off a little and waited.

"Nope. I think it's dead," he announced.

"What do you…? Of course it's fonking dead!" Mech growled. "Look at it."

"Well I don't know, do I?" said Cal, pointing to the bleeding meat. "I saw someone who looked almost *exactly* like that back on that last planet. The guy giving out the parking tickets. Remember?"

"That was the planet before," said Mech.

Cal tutted. "Whatever. My point is, how am I supposed to know it's dead if I don't gently kick it, say 'hello,' and wait to see if it responds?"

Mizette's nostrils flared. "It's worse in there," she said, nodding towards the door.

"Worse?" Cal squeaked. "There's blood pouring from the ceiling and, I don't know, a fonking *hip* lying on the floor.

How can it be worse?"

Miz met his gaze and held it. "Trust me," she said. "It's worse."

Cal took a deep breath. It tasted like pennies. "Fine. I'm sure it's nothing we can't handle. Let's go check it out."

"Why?" asked Mech. "Let's just turn around and get back to the ship. This shizz right here? This shizz ain't our problem."

Cal shook his head in disgust. "And you have the nerve to call yourself B.A. Baracus," he said.

"I don't! You called me that," Mech pointed out. "I don't even know who that is." He threw up a hand. "Come on, man. Where are you going?"

Cal had about-turned and now strode purposefully along the hallway, doing his best to look like the man in charge. This was marred slightly by him slipping in the blood puddle and skidding several feet along the corridor, while waving his arms in a panicky flap.

He stumbled the last couple of feet, then steadied himself against the doorframe. "Totally meant that," he said, then he turned the handle, opened the door a fraction, and poked his head inside.

A moment later, he took it back out again. He turned to Miz, all color draining from his face. "I take it back," he said. "It's waaaay worse."

CHAPTER TWO

If Cal had been asked to describe the scene beyond the door in one word, he would have mumbled something high-pitched and incoherent, before immediately throwing up in his mouth.

Unlike the featureless hallway, this room had been decorated to excess. There were gold drapes over the barred and shuttered windows, a delicately intricate chandelier hanging from the patterned ceiling, and various sideboards cluttered with what Cal would describe as 'space antiques' were he not currently wrestling with the vomiting-in-mouth situation.

Because worse than the décor – worse than the hideous wallpaper, the zig-zag patterned carpet and the enormous framed prints of alien dogs playing space pool – was the gore.

There were no body parts in this room, but Cal would almost have preferred it if there had been. You knew where you were with a body part. Admittedly, it was rarely anywhere good, but at least you knew.

Instead, there was a general sort of lumpy red puree covering every surface. It clung to everything like crimson moss, and reeked of things Cal was trying very hard not to think about in too much detail.

"And in case you're wondering," said Mech, indicating the mulchy wet redness. "Also dead."

"Maybe we *should* get out of here," said Cal. "This is…" He swallowed. "I don't know what this is, but I get the feeling it's not something we want to get caught up in."

"What did I tell you?" said Mech. "What did I say not twenty fonking seconds ago?"

"Yeah, yeah," said Cal, spinning on the spot. There was a *squelch* as the pressure of his heels sprayed blood-slush over the sodden carpet. "Let's all just run back to the ship as fast as we can and agree never to speak of this again."

Miz's hand clamped around his forearm. "There's someone here," she whispered.

Cal pointed to the red mush on the ceiling. "What, besides…?"

Miz nodded. She raised her ears and flicked them as her eyes took in the room. "Heartbeat," she said. "In there."

Cal followed her gaze. Another door stood just to the right of one of the shuttered windows. It was, given the state of the rest of the room, remarkably clean, with only a few red dots marking the otherwise crisp white paintwork.

"What kind of heartbeat?" Cal whispered, adjusting his grip on his gun.

Miz frowned. "What do you mean?"

"Well, you know. Is it, like a big *boom-boom-boom* elephant heartbeat, or a *brrrrr* hummingbird heartbeat or… what is it? How big a thing is in there, is what I'm asking, and is it going to come jumping out and bite my head off if

I open the door?"

Cal shook his head. "In fact, why am I the one opening the door? Mech. Open the door."

"Fonk you, man. I ain't opening the door," said Mech.

"Well, I'm not opening it," said Cal.

Mech shrugged. "Fine by me. I'm all for just turning around and getting out of here."

Mizette crossed the room in six big steps, huffing like the Big Bad Wolf. "Here. Look. *I'll* open the door."

Cal screamed and raised his blaster as Miz tore the door off its hinges. Through the now gaping doorway, they saw several coats, a plastic basket, and what looked from where Cal was standing to be an ironing board.

And tucked in amongst it all was a woman. A girl, maybe. It was hard to tell with the cloth bag over her head. Between that, the ropes around her bare ankles and the way her hands were pulled behind her back, Cal got the impression she hadn't put herself in there on purpose.

"Is she dead?" Cal whispered.

"No," said Miz.

Cal looked at her. "How can you tell? Kick her and say 'hello'."

Miz pointed to one of her ears. "I can hear her heart beating."

"Oh. Yeah," said Cal. "Gotcha."

He squelched across the carpet and squatted down in front of the hostage. She drew in a ragged and panicky breath, like she was about to scream, and Cal moved quickly to intercept.

"Hey. Hey, miss? Are you OK?" he asked, softly.

The scream snagged at the back of the woman's throat.

"We're here to help. We're not going to hurt you,"

Cal assured her. "I'm going to take the bag off your head. Now, you might see an enormous wolf-woman, but she's harmless."

Miz growled.

"*Mostly* harmless," Cal corrected. "But she won't hurt you. We're the good guys."

The woman didn't resist when Cal's fingers brushed against her neck. The bag was tied on pretty tightly, and it took several seconds of fumbling before he could get the knot undone.

"OK, bag coming off now," Cal said. "Please don't, you know, bite me or spit acid in my face or anything. Good guys. Remember? Keep that in mind."

The bag was removed, revealing a shock of bright red hair. It had been cut in a way that suggested the girl had done it herself with a pair of blunt scissors and no available reflective surfaces. If the hairstyle was a statement, that statement was almost certainly: 'I've recently lost a bet.'

She looked maybe twelve or thirteen, based on Earth ages. He'd discovered those didn't mean much out here in space – Miz, for example, was six years old, but part of a species that matured much faster than humans – but something about the girl told him she was young.

Her skin was a pastel green, with hundreds of raised white bumps dotted like freckles across her nose and around her eyes. The eyes themselves were wide ovals with piercing blue irises and curved lashes the same color as her hair.

A purple bruise flowered on one of her sharply-defined cheekbones, and her dark green lips were swollen on one side. Her gaze flitted anxiously from Cal to Miz to Mech, before returning to Cal again.

She closed her mouth tightly and sobbed at the back of

her throat, her body vibrating violently as tears rushed to fill her eyes.

"Hey, shh, it's OK, it's OK," Cal said. He gestured to the restraints around her ankles. "Miz."

Mizette flashed her claws and the ropes fell away. The girl drew her knees up to her chest, her breath whistling in and out through her nose.

"What's your name, sweetheart?" Cal asked, but the girl didn't answer. She looked so terrified, Cal wasn't sure she'd even heard him. He backed away a little and gestured for her to shuffle towards him. "Come on, out you come. Just try not to look at the walls or carpet. Or, you know, anything else in the room."

Miz's ears flicked. "Sirens," she said.

"Zertex?" asked Cal.

Miz listened, then shook her head. "Local cops, but four or five squads."

Mech was hurriedly tapping the screen in his arm. "They're coming here," he announced. "Someone heard screaming and shooting. Called it in a few minutes ago."

"Well they're annoyingly efficient," said Cal, straightening. He motioned for the girl to stay where she was. "It's OK. The police are coming. They'll sort out this…" He looked around at the blood-slush. "…whatever this is, and get you back home. We'd stick around but, well, they might think we did this, and that would be problematic."

He gave her one of his best smiles – a lips together, eyebrows raised little number designed to make his face as comforting as possible – then backed towards the door. "You take care of yourself, OK? Stay in school. If, you know, that's a thing where you come from. Eat your vegetables, respect your parents, try not to dwell too much on the whole being kidnapped and locked in a closet thing…"

"Cal," Miz urged. "We need to go."

Cal nodded, but hesitated just inside the door. He met the frightened gaze of the girl among the coats. "You're safe, kid. You're going to be just fine."

Mech shoved him through the door and Cal skidded along the hall. He slid out onto the sidewalk, and his boots immediately found their grip on the slabs, snapping him to a jerking stop.

Outside, Cal could hear the wailing of the approaching cops. They didn't sound like any cop cars back home, but he'd heard enough of them to know a police siren when he heard one. The sound was different, but the intent it suggested was the same.

"Come on, we should get back to the ship," said Mech.

Cal nodded. "Just one sec. Look over there."

"Over where?" Mech asked. "What you talking about?"

"Just fonking look somewhere over there!" Cal yelped, then he opened his mouth and an eruption of vomit splattered across the ground. "Too late," he groaned.

"Aw, man. That's nasty," said Mech.

"Like, *ew*. That totally stinks," agreed Miz.

"I tried to warn you!" Cal protested. He spat a few times and rubbed his stomach. "That does feel better, though. I guess it's true what they say, better out than…"

He stopped talking when he saw the girl peeking out from behind one of the broken doors. "Hey. Uh. You should go back inside."

The girl glanced back over her shoulder, then shook her head and stepped out onto the sidewalk.

Cal put a hand on her upper arm. She flinched, but didn't quite pull away. "No, listen," he said. "Hear that? The police are coming. You'll be safe with them."

"Shizz. Cal!" Miz barked, just as the street became a red and blue lightshow and several wedge-shaped black vehicles skidded around the corner on cushions of air or magnetism or whatever alien science was keeping them hovering above the ground like that.

The beam of a powerful spotlight hit Cal full in the face and he hissed in shock. "Jesus. That's bright. What is that, the fonking sun?"

He turned away from the light and realized he was still holding the girl by the arm.

The handcuffed girl.

With the bruises.

"Oh, shizz," he said, pulling away. "That wasn't what it looked like," he shouted towards the oncoming cops. "This is nothing to do with us! Honest. We're the good guys in this situation."

"Come on, man, this way," Mech urged, clanking a few paces in the opposite direction.

A heavy rectangular armored vehicle rumbled around the corner, blocking the road that way, too. A set of double doors opened at the back, then a dozen or more black-clad figures jogged down a ramp and formed a line across the street from one side to the other.

On some hidden signal, they all tapped switches on their left forearm, and a wall of crackling blue energy shields spread out from their wrists. Riot cops, Cal guessed. That wasn't good. Back on Earth, at least, riot cops weren't exactly renowned for their willingness to listen to reasoned debate. These guys didn't look like they'd be any different.

The cars had come to a stop around sixty feet away from Cal and the others. Litter swirled beneath them as the vehicles lowered to the ground, their sirens screaming as if the end of the world was chasing right behind them, and closing fast.

The sides of all four vehicles swung upwards like the doors of an Italian sports car. Mech and Miz both tensed as eight more of the darkly-dressed figures emerged. Where the riot cops had shields, this lot carried blaster rifles. Seven of them took cover behind the cars, while the eighth – the leader, presumably – stood his ground.

"Just leave the talking to me," Cal said, gesturing in the direction of the cops. "I'll have this sorted out in—"

A blast of laser-fire scorched the air by his head. Cal yelped and ducked, clamping a hand to his ear. When he took it away, his palm was slicked with blood. "Ah! Jesus! My ear! They shot my ear! Why did you shoot my ear?"

"Maybe because you're waving a fonking gun at them," Mech hissed.

Cal looked at the hand he'd pointed to the cops with. Sure enough, his blaster pistol was clutched in it. He quickly lowered the weapon and offered an apologetic smile. "Sorry! Didn't realize. I can see how that might have looked."

Miz's ears twitched. "They're going to shoot us."

"What? Why?" asked Cal.

"Guy in front's got an earpiece. Someone just gave the command."

"Aw, fonk. Get behind me," Mech said, but before anyone could move, the girl stepped forwards, putting herself in front of Cal.

"Hey, uh, miss? You might want to get back inside," said Cal. "This isn't really the place for…"

The girl opened her mouth. A note rang out. It was piercingly high-pitched, but was over so quickly Cal would almost have believed he'd imagined it, had it not been for the ringing in his ears.

The lone cop in front of the cars flipped violently backwards, his head practically touching his heels as his body looped back on itself.

The cars went next, rolling across the ground in a shower of shattering glass and a tangle of twisting metal. The other cops – the ones who had been taking cover behind the vehicles – became seven explosively colorful stains on the tarmac, before those, too, were swept away as if in the path of a raging tsunami.

The girl turned to Cal, who gawped at her as if she were an unexploded nuclear bomb. "What the fonk was that?" he asked, but she just clamped her lips shut, then angled herself so her bound wrists were pointed towards Mizette.

Miz looked to Cal. He deliberated briefly, then gave a nod.

"Do it. Cut her loose." He glanced in the other direction along the street, where the assembled members of the riot squad were advancing behind their shields. "Then get ready to run, because we are getting the fonk out of here!"

CHAPTER THREE

Miz bounded ahead, leading the way through the warren of back streets and alleyways. She heard sirens coming from several blocks away, smelled cops before they got too close. Sure, they had to duck behind the odd trash can and sprint across the occasional wide open street, but the going had been pretty easy, considering.

Cal would almost have felt relaxed, were it not for the girl. She jogged along beside Mech, slowing down and speeding up in time with his clanking mechanical steps. She kept her mouth shut the whole way, breathing through her slender nose as they navigated back to the landing pads.

It took Cal a few moments to spot the ship. He was looking for the *Shatner*, but it had been destroyed after they'd plunged through an anomaly he'd come to think of as 'a big space hole'. The new ship was better in pretty much every way, but Cal couldn't help missing the old one.

The *Currently Untitled* – because Cal hadn't as yet come up with a name for it – stood dead ahead, sticking out like a sore thumb among the other ships around it. It was completely spotless, that was the problem. The other ships looked like they'd been around the galaxy a few times, and the *Untitled* looked forecourt-new by comparison.

It was also, Cal was happy to report, the coolest looking of the ships around it. The others looked home-made at worst, boxy at best, but the *Untitled* was a collection of sleek curves, with a hull that was either black, gray, dark green or a sort of chrome-color, depending on how the light happened to be reflecting off it at the time.

"So what, we're just leaving?" asked Mech. "What about our money?"

"What money?" asked Cal.

"You know. From the mole-guy. He wanted us to stop them gangsters shaking him down. Well, I reckon they ain't going to be shaking him down any time soon. We should get paid."

Cal jabbed a thumb back the way they'd come. "So… you want to take credit for that, do you? You want to take credit for painting the inside of that house with people puree? With the cops looking for us?"

Mech shifted on his big metal feet. "I just think we should get paid, is all."

Miz raised an eyebrow. "Seriously? It was, like, fifty credits. If you care that much, I'll pay you myself."

"Not the point," said Mech, crossing his arms. "Ain't the point. It's the principle of the thing. We did a job, we should get paid."

"But we didn't do the job, did we? We were going there to talk to those guys. Did any of us do that? Do you recall walking in there and saying, 'Hey, please stop taking money from our friend, oh and by the way, did you know you're currently dripping from the ceiling?'" said Cal.

"Fine. Whatever," said Mech, begrudgingly. "But next time, we're getting paid."

"Good. Well, I'm glad that's sorted," said Cal. He turned to the girl. "Which just leaves you. And we *are* going to leave now, sweetheart. You should stay here. OK?"

The girl didn't respond. Cal smiled. "OK. She gets it. Come on."

He strode towards the *Untitled*. The girl followed. He stopped.

"No, you can't come with us," said Cal. He pointed to the girl, then the ground at her feet. "You, stay. Capiche?"

He strode towards the *Untitled* again. The girl followed. Again.

Cal sighed. "Look, what part don't you—?"

A laser blast screamed from the shadows at the far end of the street. It left a shimmering heat trail in its wake as it raced towards Cal's face, and the goofy expression of surprise currently plastered across it.

Mech thrust up an arm in front of Cal's head, and grimaced as the blast exploded against his wrist. "Ow. That actually hurt."

A mechanical voice rolled along the street like thunder. "This is the police. Put down your weapons. This unit is authorized to use lethal force."

The ground trembled beneath Cal's feet as something enormous emerged from the shadows. It looked like a cheap Chinese knock-off of one of the *Transformers*. And not one of the friendly ones. Each leg alone had to be eight feet high, and the body that sat atop it looked to be part robot, part tank, and another part tank for good measure.

"Mech?" Cal whispered.

"What?"

"I think your dad's here."

"Shut the fonk up."

A red and blue beacon began to flash way at the top of the towering robo-tank.

"Aw, look, they gave it a little light on its head," said Cal. "Is it weird I think that's kinda cute?"

"Repeat. This is the police. Put down your weapons. This unit is authorized to use lethal force," boomed the mechanoid.

Mech's fingers went to a button on his wrist.

"Wait, you're not going to shoot at it, are you?" said Cal. "No offence, Mech, but that thing could pick you up and use you like a toothpick."

"OK, *one*, I'd like to see it try," Mech grunted. "And two, no, I ain't going to shoot at it. I'm opening the landing ramp."

Cal glanced over at the *Untitled* just as a ramp lowered smoothly beneath it. "Ah. Gotcha."

"OK," Mech whispered. "On my mark, we…"

But Cal and Miz were already off and running. The walking tank swiveled to track them, and Mech hissed with rage. "They couldn't have waited three fonking seconds," he muttered, raising his arm and pumping out a few laser rounds. They ricocheted harmlessly off the police robot's chest, but they got its attention. Mech beat a retreat towards the *Untitled* as the tank opened fire.

A blast slammed into his shoulder. Another tore into his thigh, staggering him in a shower of sparks. "Shizz," Mech spat, as the hydraulics in his left leg twitched and spasmed. He limped on. The ramp was less than fifteen feet away, but a warning on the HUD behind his eyeballs suddenly flashed up in red.

"Missile lock?" he yelped. "Aw… *fonk*!"

Mech heard the *paff* of the rocket launching. There was nothing he could do but cover his head with his hands, grit his metal bottom teeth against his organic top ones, and hope there was a Cyborg Heaven.

BRRRRRRRRRRRRRRRP!

The staccato screech of a blaster turret burst into life right beside him. The missile erupted a hundred feet behind Mech. He raised his head to see Cal standing at the bottom of the ramp, the turret hooked over his shoulder, his face a mask of excited glee as he sprayed thirty blasts of concentrated firepower a second along the street.

"Woo-hoo! This thing is *awesome*!" Cal announced, but his voice was drowned out by the turret's din.

Despite the barrage of laser blasts current slamming into its upper body, the tank-cop advanced. "Hurry up, Mech!" Cal bellowed. "Get in."

Mech struggled forwards, *clanking* onto the ramp just as the *Untitled's* lift-thrusters painted the underside of the ship in shades of brilliant blue.

Miz caught Mech by the arm and helped him aboard. Cal backed towards the ramp, still raining blaster fire on the approaching mechanoid. He hopped on and released the trigger as the ramp raised, and the ship lurched into the air.

Cal unhooked the turret from his shoulder and blew on his hands. Even through the grips on the handles, the metal had become uncomfortably hot. "Remind me to wear gloves next time," he muttered.

And that was when he spotted the girl. She stood behind Mech, half-hidden by his hulking frame. "Wait. Why's she here?" asked Cal. "How did…? You're not supposed to be here."

"Guys!" called a voice from up front. "Get up here. We've got a problem."

"Well, like, isn't *that* a surprise?" Miz muttered. "Surely even she can't have crashed already?"

Cal pointed to the girl. "You. Follow me. We'll drop you off somewhere once we're out of whatever mess we're currently in. But for now, just don't touch anything."

On the bridge, Teela Loren sat at a horseshoe-shaped bank of controls, gazing grimly at the star-filled sky ahead. Miz flopped down and slouched into her chair, while Mech took up his usual standing position to the right of the viewscreen and activated the magnets in his feet. His damaged left leg *fizzled* and spat angry-looking sparks onto the floor around him. Loren glanced at the leg, just briefly, then turned her attention back to the screen.

Cal noticed the look. "You think that's bad? Check out my ear," he said, bending beside Loren and pointing to the side of his head.

"What about it?" asked Loren, irritated.

"I got shot."

Loren turned back to the screen. "Looks fine."

Cal felt his ear. It seemed to be intact, and the blood was no longer flowing. "Huh, that's weird."

He turned to the girl, then pointed to a row of three chairs fixed to the bridge's back wall. "You, sit there."

"And I'd put on your seatbelt, if I were you," Miz suggested. "We've got, like, the worst pilot in the universe."

"Aww. Don't listen to her," said Cal, rubbing Loren's shoulders. She shrugged him off.

"Quit messing around. We've got a big problem," said Loren. She pointed ahead. "There."

Cal squinted at the viewscreen. He could see mostly

black, with lots of white dots and very little else.

"What am I looking at? The stars? What's wrong with the stars?"

"Not the stars," said Loren. "They've closed the planetary shielding. Whole planet's sealed shut."

Cal narrowed his eyes and stared harder. "Where?"

"Well you can't *see* it," said Loren. "It's an invisible shield."

Cal tutted. "Well why did you point then?" he asked. "Why point at something I can't see?"

Loren opened her mouth, but hesitated. "OK, you're right, that makes no sense," she admitted. She glanced back over her shoulder at Cal, and spotted the girl for the first time. "Who's that?"

"Hmm? Oh. Loren, hostage. Hostage, Loren," said Cal. He caught Loren's shocked expression. "No, not *our* hostage. She *was* a hostage, but we rescued her, and now she won't leave us alone."

"Oh. OK," said Loren, then she shook her head and turned her attention back to the screen. "Anyway, visible or not, the shielding is up, and we are stuck in here."

Cal backed up and lowered himself onto his seat. It was much more comfortable than his chair on the *Shatner* had been, and didn't make embarrassing farting noises when he turned too quickly, but he missed the old one all the same.

"Can't we just shoot our way through?" he asked.

Mech answered before Loren could open her mouth. "Look, I told you, man, the weapons systems on this thing are complex. It's gonna take me a few more days to fix them."

"It was just a suggestion," said Cal.

Mech sighed. "No it wasn't. It was a jibe about me not

getting the weapons fixed yet. You know it, I know it, let's call it what it is."

"Besides, sir," chimed a stiff, elderly voice from somewhere overhead. "Even with weapons systems online – advanced as they are – they wouldn't allow us to penetrate a planetary shield of this magnitude."

Cal spun in his chair to find the girl gaping upwards in surprise. "That's Kevin," he explained. "He's a living computer."

"I am an artificially intelligent synthesized construct," the voice corrected.

"Which is a fancy way of saying 'a living computer,'" Cal reasoned.

"And my name is K-Seven-Zero Dash Nine-Three-Three-Zero-Seven Dash Zeta."

"But we call him 'Kevin' for short," said Cal.

"Cal!" Loren barked. "The shield. What do we do?"

"Why are you asking me? I thought you knew about this stuff?" He looked from Loren to Mech. "One of you must know a way through it." He smiled hopefully. "Right?"

"Can't be done, man," said Mech. "When the shields are up, nothing gets in, nothing gets out."

A series of red dots appeared on a display near the bottom of the viewscreen. "Shizz," Loren spat. "Incoming pursuit ships. Local law enforcement and a couple of Zertex fighters."

"But we can outrun them, right?" said Cal. "We're faster than they are."

"Yes, but there's nowhere to go!" Loren reminded him. She realized she was pointing at the invisible barrier again, and stopped. "What do you want me to do, just circle the planet over and over again until they give up and go home?"

Cal chewed his lip. "Think that'd work?"

"No!"

"If I may be so bold as to make a suggestion, sir?" said Kevin. "I have analyzed the shielding and it appears to be a now mostly outdated piece of Zertex technology, model number BFS-Zero Dash Y Dash Three Seven Four Six Dash—"

"OK! Great. What about it?" interrupted Cal.

"*Nine*," Kevin concluded. "As I'm sure we're all only too painfully aware, sir, this model was plagued by reliability issues, and replaced almost immediately by the upgraded BFS-Three Dash—"

"Kevin!" Loren barked. "We're about to be swarmed by fighters. What's your point?"

The AI paused very deliberately before continuing. "My point is, ma'am, the frequency modulation on this model was an unmitigated disaster. Embarrassing, actually. Hitting the shield at exactly the right velocity and precisely the correct point in its modulation cycle allowed ships to pass through unscathed. Smugglers took advantage of it all the time, I believe. I see no reason why we cannot do the same."

"Fly straight into it," said Mech. "That's your plan?"

"Indeed, sir."

Cal puffed out his cheeks and looked around at the others. "OK, somebody *please* tell me they've got a better plan. Mech? Miz?" He turned his chair and looked hopefully at the girl. "You?"

"We're being hailed by the Zertex fighters," said Loren.

"Ignore them. If it's important, they'll leave a message," said Cal, spinning back to the front. "Kevin, do what you've got to do. Get us through that shield."

"Very good, sir," said Kevin. "Although it will require

Ms Loren's help."

"Great," huffed Miz. "We're all going to die."

"It is quite simple, ma'am," Kevin continued. "On my command, engage warp at zero-point-eight-one thrust. I shall handle the rest."

Loren's fingers danced across the controls. It had been a few days since they'd acquired the ship, and while there was still a dazzling number of buttons, switches and holographic displays which she had no idea the purpose of, she had at least got to grip with the basics.

"OK, keyed in," said Loren.

Mech studied the display at the bottom of the screen. "Those ships are gaining. Whatever we doing, we need to do it fast."

"An excellent point, well made, sir," chimed Kevin. "Ms Loren, kindly engage zero-point-eight-one warp... now."

Loren punched the warp drive. The *Untitled* lurched towards the stars, forcing everyone back in their seats. For a moment, Cal thought he saw a shimmer stretching all the way across the sky. Dead ahead, and getting rapidly closer.

"Or was it point-*nine*-one?" Kevin wondered, and everyone with an arm rest gripped it tightly, and opened their mouths to scream.

The stars rippled. The ship shook. But then they were through the shielding and speeding off into the depths of space.

"Sorry," said Kevin, practically sniggering. "Just my little joke."

"Good one, Kevin," said Cal. "I mean, I almost shizzed my pants and died, but... you got us."

"Yes, I rather did, didn't I, sir?"

"Going to full warp," Loren announced. The stars

became long strings of light as Loren put distance between them and the planet. By the time the shielding was lowered to let the pursuing ships through, they'd be far beyond the range of even the Zertex fighters.

Which left only one problem.

Cal spun in his seat. "So, what do we do about you?" he wondered. The pale spots around the girl's eyes darkened slightly, and she shuffled nervously as everyone turned her way. "We can't bring you back there, for obvious reasons."

"We could put her in a suit and throw her out," Miz suggested.

"OK, well that's one idea," said Cal. "Anyone else have any that don't involve her dying alone in space?"

"We wouldn't just, like, leave here there," said Miz, scowling. "We'd call someone and tell them where to find her, obviously."

"Right. *Better*, but still not great," said Cal. "Anyone else?"

"There's a mining station a couple of hours away," said Loren, bringing up a star chart on the right-hand third of the screen. "We could drop her there."

"Aha!" cried Cal. "That's more like it. We take her there, drop her off, then head off into the sunset like champs. What could be better?"

"Alternatively, sir," began Kevin. "You could return her safely to her parents on her home world and claim the rather substantial reward."

Cal looked at the girl. She twirled a strand of her bright red hair around a finger, looking anxious, but saying nothing.

"Reward, eh?" said Cal. "Now *that*, I like the sound of."

CHAPTER FOUR

Two different three-dimensional images of the girl – one a full-length body shot, the other head only – slowly rotated in the middle of the bridge. The hologram was ever so slightly transparent, giving the girl a ghostly quality. The non-ghostly version gaped at the images in wonder, then touched her face as if checking she was still herself.

"Soonsho Sooss," announced Kevin. "Went missing from her home world of Cantato Minor some three weeks ago. The authorities believe she ran away. Her parents insist she was abducted."

"Score one for mom and dad," said Cal.

"Quite, sir," agreed Kevin. "However, all parties are united in their desire to see her safely returned home. The reward is one million credits."

Mech's metal jaw dropped open with a *squeak*. "Say what?" he muttered. "You got to be kidding me."

"Oh no, sir, I never joke," said Kevin. "It is not in my programming."

"Uh… what about the speed thing? With the shield?"

said Cal. "That was a joke."

"Was it, sir?"

"That's what you said," Loren agreed.

Kevin hesitated. "Oh. I'm afraid the entire exchange appears to have slipped my mind," said Kevin.

This was not new. As a highly experimental artificial intelligence, Kevin could be unstable at the best of times. When the ship that had been carrying the *Untitled* plunged through a wormhole and crashed, resulting in Kevin spending several years in forced solitary confinement, his quirks had gone on to develop quirks of their own.

"However, I shall take your word for it, and reassure you that, in this instance, I am being quite serious. There is a one million credit reward on offer to anyone who safely returns Soonsho Sooss to her parents on Cantato Minor. These are the facts."

Cal looked from the hologram to the girl. He smiled, but she didn't smile back. "Do we know anything else about her?"

"Oh, yes, sir," said Kevin. The viewscreen was suddenly flooded by reams and reams of text. It scrolled upwards in a blur of digital print. "Would you like me to read it aloud?"

"Christ, no," said Cal.

"We're doing this, right?" said Mech. "We're going to get the reward?"

"And, more importantly, reunite a kidnapped girl with her parents," said Loren, shooting Mech an accusatory glare.

"Yeah, I mean, that, too," said Mech. He looked to Cal. "We are, right?"

"Uh, does a bear shizz in the woods?" Cal asked. The others looked at him blankly. "The answer to that is, 'yes,' by the way. We're going to take her home."

"Alright!" Mech cheered. "We're gonna be rich!"

"And *do a good thing*," said Loren.

Miz snorted. "I'm with him. We're totally going to be rich."

He spun in his chair. Soonsho was still transfixed by her hologram. The hair was different – same color, but longer – and she dragged her fingers across her scalp, as if comparing the two styles.

"Hear that, kid?" said Cal. "We're taking you home."

Soonsho eyed him silently.

"Don't look so happy about it," said Cal, then he spun and looked around the bridge. "Talking of people who don't say anything – which I appreciate we weren't, but I was thinking it – where's Splurt?"

"He's hiding," said Loren.

"This again, huh?" said Cal. He slouched down in his chair and used his feet to slowly turn it. "Is he that control panel?"

"No."

"Is he on the floor?"

"No."

"Is he that bit there, with all the wires sticking out of it?"

"I told you, man, I am working on fixing that," grunted Mech. "It's a complex system."

"No."

Cal shrugged. "Then I give up. Come out, come out wherever you are."

For a moment, nothing happened, then the chair on Soonsho's left transformed into a gloopy green jelly. The girl let out a gasp, and the lights on the bridge flickered, just faintly, and barely enough for anyone but Mech to even register.

Splurt collapsed into his usual ball-shape, and rolled towards Cal, his bulbous, oddly human-looking eyes spinning around inside him like balls in a bingo machine.

"There's my little buddy!" Cal grinned as Splurt circled his chair a few times, then rolled beneath it and wrapped himself around the base. "You got me again, Splurt. But I'll find you next time."

He looked across to Soonsho, who was even more shocked by Splurt than by the hologram, which faded away as Cal turned. "That's Splurt. He's a shapeshifter," Cal explained. "If you think his chair was impressive, you should see his Dorothy out of *the Golden Girls*. You'd swear Bea Arthur was right there in the room."

He sang the first few lines of *the Golden Girls* theme, realized that neither Soonsho, nor anyone else, had the faintest idea what he was doing, then stopped and turned his chair to face front again. "OK. Did we do the 'plot a course' bit yet?"

"No," said Loren.

"OK. Loren, plot a course for... whatever that planet was called. We're taking this girl home!"

Loren keyed the details into the controls. The *Untitled* hummed gently and the stars shifted sideways as the ship began to change direction.

"Should I notify the authorities on Cantato Minor, sir?" asked Kevin.

"No!" said Loren, before Cal could open his mouth.

Cal frowned. "No? Why not?"

"She's right," said Mech. "We got a million credit bounty aboard. You do not transmit that information through the whole of space. Not unless you want all kinds of

41

trouble."

"Makes sense," Cal said, nodding. "Good catch, Loren."

"Ah," said Kevin.

Cal raised his eyes to the ceiling. "'Ah?'"

"Well, you see, the thing is, sir, I was so confident that you would answer in the affirmative, that I – and you'll laugh at this, sir – I had already transmitted the information prior to asking the question."

"You did *what?*" Mech barked.

"In hindsight, it may have been an error of judgement on my part."

"Oh, you *think?*" said Miz.

"Although, in my defense, I believe there are lessons we could all take away from the situation," Kevin said. "Were we to look hard enough."

"Loren, how long until we get there?" Cal asked.

"Just under sixteen hours at full warp."

"Can we go faster?"

"Faster than *full warp?*" said Loren, heavily emphasizing those last two words. "No. It's full warp. That's as fast as we can go."

"Wait," said Cal, frowning. "Isn't there, like, a 'fuller' and 'fullest' warp?"

Loren looked back over her shoulder. "What?"

"Full, fuller, fullest. That's how it works," said Cal. He looked to Mech and Miz for support. "Right?"

Mech glared back at him with an expression that didn't just border on contempt, but full-scale invaded it. Mizette picked at her fingernails and didn't even acknowledge the question.

"OK, well what about the bendy space thing?" Cal asked. "Any closer to figuring that out?"

When Cal and the crew had returned through the wormhole aboard the *Currently Untitled*, they'd found a whole armada of Zertex ships waiting for them. A holographic button had appeared in the air right in front of Cal which, once pressed, had turned the space around them into something resembling a giant blister, and catapulted them fifty or so light years across the galaxy in the blink of an eye.

Unfortunately, Kevin was now denying all knowledge of any such button, and all other attempts to activate the system again had failed.

"Kevin still insists we're making it up," said Loren. "So, no."

Cal sighed and wriggled into a more comfortable position in his chair. "Fine. Full warp it is. But sixteen hours is a long time if we're going to have bad guys coming after us. Mech, we're going to need those weapons up and running."

"I gotta fix my leg," replied Mech, indicating the damage to his thigh.

"Oh. OK, cool," said Cal. "Then we'll be able to use that to fight off any space pirates and bounty hunters who attack us. Good thinking. Yeah, concentrate on your leg. That's totally the priority."

Mech muttered below his breath, then made a show of limping to the door at the rear of the bridge. "Fine. I'll go work on the fonking weapons."

"Whatever you think is best," said Cal, smiling innocently.

"Yeah, yeah. Fonk you, man," Mech grunted, then the door slid open and he stumbled out into the corridor beyond.

Cal waited for the door to swish closed again, then got up from his chair and crossed to the rear of the bridge. Soonsho watched him as he took the seat beside her, her movements twitching and jerky like a frightened rabbit.

"Hey, it's OK. Good guys, remember?" Cal said. "We're taking you home."

The girl didn't respond, or show any sign she'd even heard.

"Can she understand me? Can you understand what I'm saying?"

Soonsho nodded, just a fraction.

"Oh, OK, great!" said Cal. "And can you talk?"

A pause, then another nod.

Kevin made a sound like he was clearing his throat, despite the fact he didn't have one. "I'd strongly advise against pursuing this particular line of questioning any further, sir."

"What? Why?"

"Had you permitted me to read you the information I was able to compile on Ms Sooss," Kevin began, with just the faintest hint of accusation in his voice, "you would be aware of her abilities."

Miz lifted her eyes from her nails long enough to glance at the girl. "Abilities?"

"Her voice," said Cal. "She flipped those cop cars with her voice."

"Indeed, sir," said Kevin. "All female Cantatorians are gifted with a remarkable vocal range. Their songs can enthrall and captivate even the hardest of hearts. Their screams have been known to reduce entire buildings to rubble."

Soonsho lowered her head and wrung her hands in her

lap.

"She could kill you all with a single word," Kevin concluded.

"That must've been what happened to those guys in the house," Miz realized.

Still holding his smile in place, Cal slowly leaned away from the girl. "OK, great," he croaked. "That's really good to know, Kevin, thanks. I mean, a little earlier might not have gone amiss…"

"The information was readily available on screen, sir," Kevin pointed out. "Oh, and on an unrelated note, I have picked up a signal."

Cal jumped to his feet. "Pirates? It's pirates, isn't it?" He ran to his chair. "Mech! Pirates!"

"It isn't pirates, sir," said Kevin.

"Oh," said Cal. He lowered himself into his seat. "Bounty hunters?"

Loren's fingers tapped a series of keys. "It's a distress signal." A star map slid in from the right of the screen. A red light blinked on and off. "There. It's a Symmorium Thresher. It's being attacked by Scrivers."

"Threshers are war ships, right?" said Cal. "Then it can defend itself?"

"Ordinarily, sir," said Kevin. "However, the distress signal indicates they have taken substantial damage, and are in no condition to fight back."

"Cal, it's the Symmorium," said Loren. "There are kids on that ship."

"Uh, hello?" said Miz. "No weapons, remember? What good can we do?"

"Scrivers don't like a fair fight," Loren reminded her. "They pull passing ships out of warp and scramble their systems so they can't fight back. If we turn up, we might scare them away just by being there."

"Or they might tear us to pieces, too," Miz argued.

Cal drummed his fingers on his arm rests and clicked his tongue against the back of his teeth as he watched the red dot blink on and off.

"Or it could be a trap," Cal pointed out. "We've got a million credit bounty aboard, and someone – naming no names, but it was Kevin – announced that to the whole galaxy."

He watched the blinking red dot a little longer. Finally, he turned his chair. "Miz, go tell Mech we need weapons online now. Even just one fonking gun would be a start."

Miz scowled and gestured to Loren. "Why can't she do it?"

"Uh, maybe because I'm the pilot?" said Loren.

"*Maybe because I'm the pilot,*" Miz mimicked. She sighed huffily and got to her feet. "Fine, whatever. I'll do it."

"That's the spirit!" Cal cheered.

"Should I acknowledge the distress signal, sir?" asked Kevin.

"No. We don't want the Scrivers to know we're coming."

"Ah," said Kevin. "It's funny you should say that…"

Cal looked up in despair. "Seriously, Kevin. Again?"

"Lessons shall be learned, sir."

"If the Scrivers tear you a new one, it'll be your own fonking fault," Cal scowled, then he wrapped his fingers around the end of his arm rests and braced his feet on the floor. "Loren, plot a course. Let's go save that ship."

"On it," said Loren, as the *Untitled* banked steeply and Cal swallowed back the urge to vomit. "Arriving in three… two…"

The ship snapped to a jerking stop, almost throwing Cal out of his chair.

"Oh, *shizz*," groaned Loren.

There, on screen, where she had expected to see a damaged Symmorium Thresher, was a fleet of fierce-looking pirate ships. Dozens of warning lights illuminated on screen as a wide variety of weapons systems locked on.

"It's a trap."

"Oh," said Cal. "You *think*?"

"Incoming transmission, sir," announced Kevin. "Should I put it on screen?"

"Why bother?" Cal sighed. "I mean, I assume you've already replied, anyway."

"No, sir. Should I have?"

Cal dropped his head into his hands for a moment, then straightened up. "No. On screen. Let's talk to them."

A black square appeared in the top right corner of the viewscreen. A little camera icon flashed up, disappeared briefly, then flashed again.

"Is this... Is it on?" asked a voice over the speakers. "I can't see nuthin'. Hello?"

Cal's stomach tightened. That voice. He recognized that voice.

"Oh shizz," Loren whispered. "Is that...?"

The camera icon blinked off and the black square was replaced by an extreme close-up of what looked like a cliff face with eyes. "Hold up. I can see them. It's him. Hoo-ya! It's him!"

The craggy gray expanse pulled back, revealing a figure who appeared to have been hewn from solid rock. He wore a black pinstripe suit which looked to be *exactly* the wrong size for him, and an expression of utter glee.

Kornack, Warlord of the Remnants, Slayer of the Sh-in'tee, Lord of the K'tubboth and destructor of countless planetary systems fixed his gaze on Cal and rasped his sandpaper tongue across his diamond-edged teeth.

"Eugene Adwin, the Butcher of Planet Earth!" cried Kornack, in that voice he had that suggested he was channeling the ghost of the (presumably) dead Al Pacino. "Hoo-ha! You are *not* an easy man to find."

CHAPTER FIVE

Cal and Loren both stared at the screen in horror. Their history with the Remnants warlord was brief, but eventful. It had started with a trade deal, rapidly deteriorated into Kornack's fetish for cannibals, swung wildly into Cal being pressured to cut off his own arm and eat it, before ending when Cal had buried an axe in the skull of Kornack's butler, and everyone had run like fonk.

"Do you know how long I've been looking for you, Eugene?" asked Kornack. "Do you have any idea how much effort I've put into tracking you down. And now – BOOM! – there you are. What a day. What a day! Am I right? Ha!"

Kornack threw a couple of punches at thin air. "Pow-pow! Whoo! You and me, we're gonna have some fun, Butcher."

"Uh, hi there!" said Cal. "So good to see you again, Kornack. Have you lost weight?"

Cal's chair creaked as he shifted around in it. "But, you see, well the thing is… I'm not actually Eugene Adwin. It's a pretty funny story, actually…"

"*Excuse* me?" said Kornack, his smile falling away. "What are you talking about?"

"I mean, I'm not the Butcher of Planet Earth," said Cal. "See, there was this mix-up during the abduction. I was sharing a cell with Eugene when—"

Kornack held up a piece of torn cloth. On it was part of the portrait he'd painted of Eugene Adwin to celebrate his arrival. It showed the Butcher's chubby baby-like face and wispy white hair. "Are you seriously trying to tell me this ain't you?" Kornack demanded.

"Well, I mean… it looks nothing like me," Cal pointed out.

Kornack's face darkened. "You ungrateful son-of-a-bedge," he hissed. "That took me weeks."

"No, I mean, it's great. Very accurate – you're really quite the artist," said Cal. "It's just… that's not my face. It's not even close to my face. Is it Eugene's face? Sure! But it's, like, fifty pounds heavier than my face, and completely bald."

Kornack examined the painting. He looked back at Cal on his screen. He repeated this several times. "I don't see any difference," he said, then a broad grin broke out across his face. "Wait a minute, wait a minute," he laughed, pointing to Cal. "The Butcher of Planet Earth avoided being caught for years on account of being a master of deception. Hoo-ha! You're the Butcher, alright, and you and me, we got an appointment."

"Uh, yeah, no," said Cal. "Loren, punch it!"

Loren jammed the throttle forwards. The *Untitled* whined and vibrated, but the stars and the other ships remained fixed in place.

"We're not moving," said Cal. "Why aren't we moving?"

"I think… Tractor beam. We're caught in a tractor beam!"

Kevin's voice crackled from his speakers. "It appears we are about to be taken rather roughly from behind," he announced. "If you'll pardon the expression."

The left side of the screen swapped from showing the view ahead to the view behind. The enormous gaping maw of a destroyer-sized ship unfolded like a set of jaws behind the *Untitled* and moved in to swallow it whole.

"What the fonk is that?" Cal whispered.

"I have no idea," Loren admitted. A shadow crept across the viewscreen, inching its way from the top to the bottom. "But we're about to find out."

Kornack leaned forwards until only his eyes and grin filled the comm-screen. "See you inside, Butcher. I got everything set up and ready. Hoo-ha!"

The camera icon returned, but Kornack's voice continued. "How do I…? Is it off? I think… hello? Why's that light still—?"

The sound cut off and the comm-screen square slid upwards off the screen. The view of space ahead was narrowing rapidly as the jaws of the much larger ship closed around the *Untitled*.

"Was that Kornack?" asked Miz, striding onto the bridge. She stopped when she saw what was happening on screen. "Like, what is going on?"

Cal spun in his chair. "To answer those questions in order, one: yes, that was Kornack. He still thinks I'm the Butcher and has apparently been hunting me for quite some time. Yay! And two: I have no idea. But let's assume it's nothing good."

He stood up and shot Soonsho the most reassuring smile

he could muster. "This is nothing for you to worry about, OK? It's just… a hiccup. This sort of thing happens to us all the time. Seriously, it's pretty ridiculous. I was inside a giant worm a few weeks back. This is actually one of our better days. Everything is going to be just fine."

The jaws shut around them with an ominous *clang*. The *Untitled* shuddered as a pair of enormous mechanical pincers clamped onto it and lowered it onto the darkened deck of the larger ship.

"Probably," Cal added. "Miz, get Mech. Tell him what's going on. The weapons will have to wait."

Mizette tutted. "Like, I literally just came from back there," she said, but she left without any further argument, but had the door not been automatic, she'd almost certainly have slammed it behind her.

"Splurt."

The little green blob poked out from under the chair, his eyes gazing up at Cal.

"Best if you stay here, buddy. As far as Kornack's concerned, you belong to him." He glared at Loren. "After *someone* – again, naming no names, but it was Loren – traded you for… whatever it was. I don't even remember."

"OK, OK, I've apologized," said Loren. "How many times do I have to say it? I was following orders."

"You know who else was just following orders, Loren?" asked Cal. "The Nazis."

"Who are the Nazis?" Loren asked.

Cal sighed. "Forget it. Splurt, stay out of sight. Hide and Seek, OK?"

Splurt *boinged* happily from under the chair, rolled around in a circle a few times, then rocketed off into the corridor. He passed Mech marching in the opposite

SPACE TEAM: SONG OF THE SPACE SIREN

direction.

"Say what now?" Mech barked, stomping onto the bridge. "Kornack's got us? I turn my back for five fonking minutes and…" He looked at the viewscreen. "Wait. Where are we? Who turned out the lights?"

"Hey, breathe big guy, breathe," said Cal, soothingly. "In through the nose, out through the mouth. Let's not freak out here."

"Me? I ain't freaking out," Mech grunted. "I ain't the one he wants to watch eat his own arm."

"Ha. Yeah. Good point," said Cal. He thought about this for a second, then breathed deeply in through his nose and out through his mouth for several increasingly panicked seconds.

"I'm going to get my jacket," he said, shoving his way past Mech. "Maybe the leather will stop the axe cutting through. Or, you know, at least make me look stylish while I'm tucking in."

Darting along the corridor, Cal tapped the button on the wall outside his sleeping quarters. The door slid aside, revealing an unmade bed, several different piles of dirty laundry, and a number of half-empty takeaway containers strewn across the floor.

The tan leather jacket he'd picked up during a space station stop lay abandoned in the corner of the room. It wasn't technically 'leather' in that the material almost certainly didn't come from cows, but it was close enough.

Cal tapped the touchscreen beside his opaque window as he pulled the jacket on. The glass turned wispy, then transparent, but there was only darkness beyond.

Once he'd finished adjusting his collar, he reached for the controls again. Before his fingers found them, the

53

darkness outside was pushed aside by a series of powerful overhead lights. They switched on in rows, marching their glare in stages across the vast deck of the ship that had swallowed the *Untitled*.

Kornack had been busy. Through the small window alone, Cal could see four other ships, all pinned to the deck by robotic clamps. He could probably have seen more, were it not for the fact that the fourth ship was a bulky freighter, easily twice the size of the *Untitled*. The wall was some distance beyond, and there could easily have been half a dozen other ships lined up between it and the freight ship.

Tapping the touchscreen to darken the window, Cal emerged into the corridor to find Loren slamming a battery pack into a sizeable handgun. Mech held up two other weapons – a blaster rifle and something resembling a portable rocket launcher.

"Take your pick," he said.

Cal looked the weapons over, but didn't commit. "Where's Soonsho?"

"We told her to stay on the bridge," said Loren, aiming along her gun's sights, then tucking it into the belt of her pants. "Thought it was best."

Cal gestured for Mech to lower the guns. "The first thing they're going to do is take any weapons we've got on us," he said. "The next thing they'll do is search the ship. Miz, go get Soonsho."

Miz, who had been leaning against the wall checking her nails, threw back her head, let out an annoyed, "Gah, seriously?" then shouldered past everyone as she stomped in the direction of the bridge.

"They've turned on the lights, so they'll probably come get us soon," said Cal. "For now, we'll keep the landing hatch closed and see how it plays out."

"Ah."

Cal, Mech and Loren all looked up. "You didn't," Cal groaned.

"We had landed, sir," said Kevin. "Lowering the landing ramp seemed like an eminently sensible option."

"Then close it!" Mech barked.

"Very good, sir," said Kevin. "However, I feel I should probably warn you…"

Two heavy-set figures stepped into the corridor. Each one held an assault rifle bigger than Cal.

"Kornack's men are already aboard."

Cal gave the gunmen a resigned wave, then raised his eyes to the ceiling again. "Kevin, you've got to promise me never to use your initiative again, OK? I want you to swear to that."

"Very good, sir."

The corridor was suddenly filled by the sound of chittering, as dozens of little round critters swarmed along it. They stood between one and three feet high, with most of them towards the bottom end of that scale.

They wore lengths of tatty green rope over their shoulders, which trailed down past their knees, yet did very little to protect their modesty. Pointed hats made of something resembling wicker – space wicker, Cal guessed – were pulled down over most of their faces, affording only glimpses of their wide yellow eyes beneath.

The hat-things scurried around, standing atop one another to open doors, then falling inside. A pair of Cal's dirty shorts were ejected from inside his room, followed by a half-eaten carton of something orange and congealing.

"Hey, be careful in there!" Cal protested. "It took me all

week to get that place just the way I want it."

Soonsho stumbled into the corridor from the other direction, with Miz emerging through the doorway behind her. The girl's eyes were wide and staring and she was biting her bottom lip, digging her teeth in until the skin around them turned white.

"Ladies. Just in time," said Cal. "We have guests."

The larger of the two gunmen – which was really saying something, because the other guy was fonking enormous – gestured at Cal with his rifle. He looked, Cal thought, like someone had taken DNA from the top ten percent of the food chain, blended it all together, then dressed what came out it in an unflattering beige jumpsuit.

His partner wore much the same look. Maybe the mix of apex predators wasn't exactly the same, but he gave the same impression that he might devour you whole at any moment as his partner did.

"You will follow us. Kornack awaits," growled the bigger specimen. "Leave your weapons."

One of the tiny minions chittered excitedly as it leaped up and yanked Loren's blaster from her belt. "Hey!" she protested, but the critter was already lost in the sea of hats that bustled along the corridor.

"Hey, cut that out," Mech warned, as another of the minions dug its baby-sized hands into the hole on Mech's leg. Dropping the guns, Mech tore the hat-thing free. It squealed as it went hurtling along the corridor. Soonsho and Miz both ducked and the hat-thing hit the bridge door with a satisfying *thwap*, before tumbling to the floor.

Cal adjusted his jacket collar. "Right, then," he said, wading through the minions towards the gun-toting beast-twins. "Let's go see what our old pal Kornack has to say."

CHAPTER SIX

Kornack sat on his ornate throne, his slab-like fingers steepled in front of him, his eyes fixed on a cinema-sized screen on the room's far wall.

He didn't turn when Cal and the others were shoved through the door, but gestured to the screen and to the familiar face projected across it.

Hayel Sinclair, head of the Zertex Corporation and president of much of the galaxy, did not look happy. Of course, he rarely looked genuinely happy, but he was usually smiling, at least. Now, though, his salesman grin was nowhere to be seen. It had been replaced, instead, by an expression of well-calculated solemnness.

"You believe this?" said Kornack, still not turning.

Sinclair's voice rumbled from the speaker system. "… my grave duty to inform you that within the past few hours, Zertex and the Symmorium have officially declared a state of war."

"Oh my God," Loren whispered.

"We did not want it to come to this," said Sinclair. "For

years now, I have personally been brokering a treaty with the Symmorium. A treaty I believed would lead to lasting peace. However, it appears I was misguided. My judgement was incorrect. For that, I owe you an apology."

The screen changed to show a planet. No, not a planet, Cal realized. A moon. "Hey, wait. That's... what was it called? With the zombie virus?"

"Pikkish," said Loren, her voice suddenly flat. "He isn't. He can't be."

On screen, the camera flew across the moon's surface, showing hundreds of thousands of pinpricks of light on the land masses below.

"The moon of Pikkish, located just within Symmorium space," Sinclair's voiceover continued. "Home to some thirty billion people."

"Thirty-*five* billion," Loren mumbled.

"No longer."

On screen, the moon erupted like the galaxy's biggest firework, spraying debris in all directions as its atmosphere was consumed by towering walls of fire.

"Hoo-ya!" cheered Kornack, bouncing excitedly on his throne. "That's what I'm talkin' about!"

"The Symmorium destroyed it. Thirty billion innocent civilians wiped out in the blink of an eye," said Sinclair. "If they will do this to their own people, what might they do to ours?"

Pikkish was already little more than a memory on the screen. Where it had been was now nothing but debris-filled space.

"And that was just the beginning," Sinclair continued. The shot of space lingered for a moment, then the president's face returned. "When challenged, the Symmorium destroyed several of our ships, killing everyone on board."

"OK, well *that's* bullshizz," said Cal.

"Since then, all attempts at negotiation have broken down. They have no desire to listen, and no interest in peace." Sinclair took a breath and fired a solemn stare down the lens of the camera. "And so, it is with a heavy heart, that I must take us once more into war.

"Our way of life – the Zertex way of life – is in peril. We must retaliate, and we must retaliate swiftly. Without mercy. Without regret. For we have done all we can to avoid this… terrible situation, but we cannot – we must not – stand back while murderers run amok. And so, I say to you…"

Kornack waved a hand and Sinclair's face froze, mid-sentence. It was an unfortunate look – eyes half open, mouth pulled to the side like a fish caught on a hook – and Cal wished, more than anything, he'd had a camera with him to capture the moment.

With the screen frozen, Kornack finally stood and turned to the door. He practically groaned with pleasure when his eyes fell on Cal, and he spent a full five seconds looking him up and down.

"So, *war* huh?" he said, once he'd finished appraising Cal. "How about that?"

"He's lying," said Loren. "About Pikkish and the Symmorium. That's not what happened."

Kornack shrugged. "Meh. What do I care? Me? I love me a war. Wars are good for my business, and anyone who knows me knows I'm all about two things."

He held up a thumb. "One. My business."

He held up the index finger of the same hand, then pointed it at Cal like a gun. "And two. You, Eugene Adwin. You."

Cal swallowed. "I'm not that interesting, honestly. I'd put me at like, number twelve, tops."

"Shut your mouth," Kornack warned, all hints of amusement draining from his voice. His granite lips parted into a sinister grin. "Until I tell you otherwise, anyhow."

He clapped his hands together twice, making a sound like an earth tremor. The two henchmen who'd escorted Cal and the others from the ship were joined by a veritable freakshow of other guards. They spread out behind Cal's crew, each of them tooled up with guns or sharp things.

"Everyone but you," - Kornack pointed to Cal – "and you," – he pointed to Loren – "on your knees."

Miz tutted. "Seriously?" A gun pressed against the base of her neck. She flashed her claws, but Cal caught her arm.

"Easy," he said. "It's OK."

Miz glared at him angrily, then her eyes softened. She nodded, almost imperceptibly, then dropped to her knees.

Mech looked over his shoulder and glowered at the gunman behind him. "That peashooter ain't gonna do squat against me, son."

Three different guns all took aim at the back of Mizette's head. "Not against you, maybe. But against her? That's a different story," said Kornack, grinning. "So what's it to be, big guy? Hoo-ha! Moment of truth."

Mech ground his teeth together, eyeballing the henchman directly behind him. Then, with a series of *whirrs*, he knelt on the carpet.

Kornack's smile faded when he looked along the line to Soonsho. "Hey. Princess. Get on your fonking knees."

Soonsho didn't react, just kept chewing her lips and squeezing her hands down at her sides.

Kornack's eyes narrowed. "Wait a minute. Wait a

minute. Do I know you?"

The warlord lumbered slowly towards her, each thudding footfall shaking the room. "I do. I definitely seen you before somewhere." He tapped the side of his head. It made a tiny spark. "See, I never forget a face, and your face is *awfully* familiar."

A tear rolled from one of Soonsho's eyes, and began the process of trying to navigate through the barnacle-like white lumps on her skin.

"She's no-one," said Cal. "She's just…"

"She's my cousin," said Loren. "You know… distant, but, she's my cousin. I'm showing her the sights."

Kornack clicked his fingers. That, too, made a tiny spark. "No she ain't. I got it. I knew I knew you, princess. I know *exactly* who you are." He leaned in until his grimace was all Soonsho could see. "You're a fonking dead girl walking if you don't get down on your knees right now."

"If I were you," said Miz. "I'd *totally* scream in his face right now. Just really belt it out."

"Uh, nooo, let's not do that," said Cal. "It might make the nice people behind us upset, and we wouldn't want that now, would we?"

He placed a hand on Soonsho's shoulder. She jumped in fright, and Cal's breath caught in his throat as she snapped her head towards him and opened her mouth.

"Wait, wait! Easy!"

She clamped her mouth closed again before any sound could emerge. Cal gestured to the floor and smiled encouragingly. "You'll be fine. Nothing bad's going to happen to you. Right, Kornack?"

Kornack rocked on the heels of his expensive yet poorly fitting shoes. "Her? No. I see no reason why anything bad should happen to her, long as everyone does as they're told."

"See?" said Cal. He upped the encouragement factor on his smile a couple of notches. Soonsho chewed on her lip for a couple more seconds, then fell onto her knees and hung her head.

"Attagirl," said Kornack. He raised a hand and pointed two fingers – one at Cal, one at Loren. "You two. With me."

"Ladies first," said Cal, motioning after Kornack.

"Such a gentleman," said Loren.

"I know, right?"

They followed Kornack over to his throne. He lifted the enormous chair with a grunt of effort, then moved it aside to reveal a small table that had been set for dinner. It had a large round plate, a silver knife and fork, and even a little napkin folded into the shape of a swan. Assuming your definition of 'swan' was a very loose one.

"This is right, right?" asked Kornack, indicating the place setting. He almost looked nervous as he waited for Cal's response. "I mean, this is how they do it on Earth, ain't it?"

"Yeah. Pretty much," said Cal. "I mean, I'm more of a Styrofoam cup, eating out of a foil tray kind of guy, but yeah. You nailed it. Good job."

He gave a thumbs up which seemed to make Kornack very happy. "I wanted it to be just right, you know? I wanted to get it just perfect."

"You did great. Although, I must say the axe is an unusual addition," said Cal.

Beside the place setting was a short-handled hatchet, the blade rusted and blunt. Kornack ran his fingers down the wooden shaft and grinned. "Ha! But then it's gonna be an unusual meal, am I right, Eugene? Well, not for you, maybe.

You do this shizz all the time, you crazy fonking cannibal!"

Kornack leaped into a boxing stance and laughed as he pretended to duke it out with Cal. Cal tried to laugh, too, but between one thing and another, his heart wasn't really in it.

"So, just so I'm clear," Cal began. "You still think I'm the Butcher, and you still want me to chop my arm off and eat it while you watch? I just want to make sure we're all on the same page here."

"Yes and no," said Kornack.

Hope fluttered in Cal's stomach. "You *don't* want me to cut my arm off and eat it?"

"No," said Kornack.

"Oh, thank God," Cal panted. "Wow. That is a relief. You have no idea."

"I want *her* to chop your arm off. *Then* you're gonna eat it."

"What?" Loren spluttered. "No! I'm not doing that."

Kornack shrugged. He gestured over to one of his apex-predator-blend henchmen. "Then Marvin there, he'll shoot your hairy friend through the spine. Make it so she can't walk. After that… after she can't move – after she's helpless, like - who knows what he'll do to her? See, Marvin – he is one sick son-of-a-bedge. Ain't that right, Marvin?"

Marvin flicked a tongue against his raptor-like teeth. "That's right, boss."

"And then he'll do your little cousin. Maybe even your robot friend. He has… eclectic tastes."

Cal cleared his throat and leaned closer to Kornack. "For the record, he's not a robot. He's a cyborg. I know. I made that mistake all the time. Often on purpose."

"Shut your fonking mouth," Kornack warned. He pulled

a wooden chair from below the table. "And take a seat."

Cal looked across to Loren. She shook her head but, annoyingly, offered no alternative course of action. With a resigned sign, Cal lowered himself onto the chair. His eyes fell on the napkin.

"Nice duck."

"Pick up the axe," growled Kornack, shoving Loren forwards. She stumbled to the table and her hand found the hatchet's wooden shaft. Her knuckles turned white as she gripped it, and Cal slapped his hand on top of the blade just in time.

"Don't," he warned. "There's no point."

If asked, Cal would generally have described himself as something of an optimist. He was able to see the good in most situations, often spotting the silver lining where none even existed.

The deaths of pretty much everyone on Earth – and Hollywood actor, Tobey Maguire in particular – had come as a blow, and yet he'd quickly bounced back, throwing himself into his new life in outer space, instead.

When Splurt had been brainwashed and the others had written him off as a lost cause, it was Cal who persevered, convinced his little blobby pal was still in there somewhere, just waiting to emerge. And he'd been right.

Without his natural optimism, Cal would have checked himself out of existence several years before - the same day he'd watched his wife and daughter be lowered into the ground. It had saved him then, although arguably just barely, and it had continued to save him on a near-daily basis since.

Now, though, that optimism was gone. Last time, he'd buried the axe in the head of Kornack's butler, and they'd all run for their lives back to the ship. There was no soft, easily breakable butler-skull in range, though, and the route back to the ship was blocked by a wall of ugly armed bamstons. One wrong move from Cal, and the others were dead. In the face of all that, even *his* optimism had slunk off to sit in a corner, and declared he was on his own.

It felt… strange, not having that urge to look on the bright side. It was oddly liberating, in fact. Accepting there was no way out of the current situation meant he didn't have to waste energy trying to figure one out.

This was happening.

His arm was coming off. And then he was eating it.

And that was that.

Despite what the next few minutes held, Cal felt calmer than he'd done in years. Possibly calmer than he'd ever felt. All the uncertainty had been removed. All the options were gone. There was just him, the axe, and most literal finger buffet in history.

Cal gently pushed Loren's hand aside. "I'll do it," he said.

"No. No, you will not," said Kornack. "You had that chance, but you chose to kill Dtgadston, instead. You know how hard it is to get good help? I still haven't found a replacement for that uptight old fonk."

He caught Cal by the wrist and pulled his hand away, then took Loren's hand and slammed it down on the axe's handle instead. "She does it. That's the deal. And you'll notice the axe, it ain't as sharp as the last one. That one would've taken the arm off clean. This one? This one's gonna hurt."

"I can't," Loren whispered.

Cal smiled up at her. "Hey. Hey, it's OK. This is how it has to be. You can do this."

"I can't," she said again. "I can't."

She pulled her hand away, but Cal lunged across the table and caught it. "Loren, look at me," he said. "There are two ways out of this, and while neither of them is what you might call ideal, one of them is way better than the other."

He turned to Kornack. "If I do this – if *we* do this – everyone gets to leave, right?"

"I'll even give you a bandage and a fonking lollipop," said Kornack. "Now, please, hurry up." He grinned. "Or should I say… *chop chop*?"

Placing his arm on the table, Cal pulled up the sleeve of his leather jacket. It dragged the sleeve of his shirt up with it, revealing his bare skin.

"Higher," said Kornack. His tongue rasped across his teeth. "Below the elbow."

Cal pulled the sleeves up further. "Jesus. There. Happy?"

"Oh yeah," Kornack said, his voice a scratchy whisper of anticipation. "I'm real happy. Hoo-ya! Let's get chopping!"

Cal nodded to Loren. Her hand trembled as her fingers wrapped around the axe. "Cal…"

"It's OK," Cal said, although he had to admit the feeling of calm from earlier was rapidly being replaced by a rising sense of panic. Any second now he was going to grab the fork and try to ram it in Kornack's eye, dooming them all. "Just do it. Hurry."

Loren's pale blue skin was almost white. Her eyes shimmered and her breathing came in shallow gulps as she lined the axe up with Cal's arm. The blunt metal was cold against his skin.

"Ooh, this is happening," Cal grimaced. "This is actually happening. OK. OK. It's like taking off a Band-Aid. Nice and quick. That's the way to do it. Nice and quick." He puffed his cheeks out, taking several rapid breaths. "Loren, go!"

Loren raised the axe. Cal closed his eyes and gritted his teeth.

Several seconds passed.

Cal opened one eye. Loren still had the axe raised, but couldn't bring herself to swing it down.

"I swear, you'd better hurry the fonk up, or my guys turn nasty," Kornack warned.

"Loren. Do it!" Cal barked.

"You got three seconds, sweetheart," Kornack growled. "Three."

"Loren!"

"Two! Marvin, get ready to put a hole in that hairy bedge."

Marvin pressed his rifle against Miz's back.

"*Loren, now!*"

Screaming, Loren brought the axe arcing down towards Cal's exposed arm. Kornack's face lit up with glee as the weapon *whummed* through the air. Instinctively, Cal tried to pull his arm away, but the warlord had caught his wrist the moment the axe had begun to swing, and Cal could only watch, transfixed, as the blunt metal blade raced down to meet his second favorite arm.

CHAPTER SEVEN

As the blade *swished* down, Cal felt a wriggling sensation by his elbow. A split-second before the axe split him into two unevenly-sized pieces, his jacket moved to intercept.

The leather clamped around the blade, stopping it with an inch to spare. Loren and Kornack both stared at the jacket sleeve in confusion. After a few seconds of relieved sobbing, Cal joined them.

"What the fonk?" Kornak muttered, then Loren yelped as the axe was wrenched from her grip. The sleeve parted along the seam and slid over Cal's arm. It rose from his shoulder like a snake, curved hypnotically in the air for a moment, then snapped suddenly, filling the room with a sound like a cracking whip.

The axe buried up to the hilt in Marvin's forehead. The hulking henchman's eyes crossed as he attempted to survey the damage, then he slowly toppled backwards and hit the floor with a crash.

Cal shot Kornack a sideways glance, then laughed, nervously. He swung with his left hand, smashing a fist against the warlord's head. Pain exploded through his knuckles and up along his arm.

"Ow, ow, bad idea! What was I thinking?" Cal yelped, tucking the hand under the opposite armpit and hopping around on the spot.

Kornack lunged, his face twisting in fury as his granite hands grabbed for Cal's throat. Across the room, Miz spun on her knees, claws flashing, teeth bared. The unlucky henchman behind her found his insides becoming his outsides, and dropped his weapon while he frantically tried to keep all his purple knobbly bits in the right place.

One of the other guards opened fire on Miz, but a bulky mechanical hand blocked the blast. The hand clamped down on the gun's barrel, collapsing the metal with one effortless squeeze.

"I told you. Peashooter," Mech grunted, then a single punch sent the henchman crashing through the wall.

Kornack's hands wrapped around Cal's throat and jerked him into the air. Cal kicked and struggled, but the warlord's grip was literally rock solid.

"Leave him alone," Loren roared, jumping onto Kornack's back. She wrapped her arm around his neck in a sleeper hold, but Kornack barely seemed to notice.

"Be with you in a second, sweetheart," he growled. "First, I gotta murder this no-good piece of shizz, then you can have my attention."

Cal felt his jacket wriggle and squirm again. The sleeve oozed down along his arm, changing shape and hardening as it coated his clenched fist.

With some difficulty, Cal raised his hand. It was now encased in a spiked metal mace. Despite the crushing pressure on his windpipe, he managed to grin. That would do nicely.

He swung his arm wide, then slammed the spiky ball of metal hard against Kornack's shoulder. Once. Twice. The warlord hissed as his rocky skin chipped and cracked.

Roaring, he tossed Cal across the room. Cal flipped through the air, rocketing towards a worryingly solid-looking wall.

Around him, the rest of the leather jacket inflated, becoming something not a million miles away from a car airbag. It took the brunt of the blow as he slammed into the wall, then he dropped, upside-down, to the floor.

Over by the door, Miz pirouetted on the spot, her claws eviscerating the three closest guards, and making a fourth seriously reconsider his choice of career.

Mech rose slowly on his injured leg, his gun-arm turning two more guards into abstract wall art. His top half spun like a tank turret, taking aim at another of the henchmen. He stopped when he saw the terror on Soonsho's face.

She was on her feet, a skinny copper-colored arm across her throat, a gun to the side of her head. "Stop!" warned the guard. "Everyone stop, or I kill this bedge."

Miz drew back her gums and growled, then lowered on her haunches. Mech grabbed her tail, catching her before she could lunge. She hissed angrily at him, her brown eyes now so dark they were almost black.

"Don't," Mech warned her.

"You heard him," the gunman warned. He had the look of a goldfish about him, with his rusty-looking scales and boggle-eyed expression. "I swear, I'll shoot her right now."

Cal heaved himself to his feet. His jacket was... well, it was a jacket again. Nothing more.

Loren was still gamely trying to throttle Kornack into

submission, but the warlord simply reached up over his shoulder, caught her by the arm, then tossed her over his head. She hit the ground awkwardly, but managed to recover into a half-decent forward roll that almost made Cal want to applaud.

Kornack surveyed the room. Aside from the one currently holding Soonsho hostage, his guards were all various shades of dead. There were a couple of holes in the wall, several small piles of intestines on the carpet, and the napkin swan was now barely recognizable.

Things had not, it was safe to say, gone according to plan.

Without a word, Kornack pointed to Cal, then over to the others, indicating he should join them. The warlord grimaced in pain as he bent to retrieve a fallen blaster rifle. The weapon looked cartoonishly small in his oversized hands, but with a bit of effort he managed to squeeze his finger through the trigger guard.

"Look. Kornack. The girl is nothing to do with any of this," Cal said. "We literally just met her today."

"Oh?" said Kornack. "That's interesting. So I can blow her brains out and you won't mind?"

He raised the gun to Soonsho's head. She bit her lip so hard a thin line of blood oozed from where her teeth met her skin.

"Wait! Don't!" Cal protested, holding up his hands. "She's just a kid!"

"Like I give a fonk," Kornack growled. Keeping the gun trained on Soonsho, he turned to Cal. "Take off the shapeshifter."

Cal hesitated, then sighed. "Splurt."

The jacket squirmed, becoming a gloopy green goo

across Cal's upper torso. Splurt fell to the floor in a long string of slime, then rolled himself into a ball. His eyes went from Kornack to Cal and back again.

"Thank you for bringing back my property," Kornack said. "It's much appreciated. Pick one."

"One what?"

"Pick one of your friends who's gonna die," Kornack explained.

Cal looked along the line at his crew. "Jesus, OK, I'll eat the arm."

Kornack nodded. "Oh, I know you will. But before that, I got to teach you all a lesson. About respect. So pick one. And be quick about it."

"And if I don't?"

Kornack lunged forwards, grabbing Soonsho by her hair and yanking her towards him. He jammed his gun against her stomach and gnashed his diamond teeth. "Then I take this bedge apart piece by piece until—"

Soonsho's scream lasted less than a second, but that was all it took. Kornack disintegrated in an explosion of flying rubble. It peppered the screen at the far end of the room, punching holes through President Sinclair's still-frozen face.

The goldfish-guy stood frozen in shock, his bulbous eyes blinking slowly. Loren drove a side kick into his stomach, doubling him over just as her other knee came up. His nose, which had already been pretty flat, became infinitely more so, and he dropped to the floor in a sniveling mess of snot, tears, blood and regret.

Cal stared at Soonsho.

He stared at the stone fragments scattered across the room, and at the rockery of larger chunks on the floor at Soonsho's feet.

He whistled quietly through his teeth. "OK. That was…"

"Painful," said Miz, her ears flat against her head.

"Just be glad you weren't in front of her," said Mech.

Cal nudged the rubble with the toe of his boot. "I mean, I don't think anyone can argue that he didn't totally deserve that."

He jumped back as one of the boulders wriggled free of the others. It was the size of a large grapefruit, and rose up on two stick-thin stone legs. Kornack's face was perfectly reproduced in miniature on the front of the rock.

"Hol-eee shizz," Cal mumbled.

The mini-Kornack raised a tiny pebble fist and shook it angrily up at Cal. "I'll fonking get you for this, Eugene," he said, his deep, gravelly voice now a high-pitched squeak.

Kornack darted across the floor, kicked Cal on the toe of his boot, then scurried through a hole in the wall and out into the corridor.

Cal blinked. "Well," he said. "There's something you don't see every day."

"Want me to go after him?" asked Miz.

"What? No," said Cal. "That's the most adorable thing I've ever seen."

Down at his feet, Splurt rippled. Cal winked at him. "OK, *second* most adorable thing I've ever seen."

Splurt hopped up onto Cal's back, transforming into the leather jacket as he wrapped himself around Cal's back.

"Thanks, buddy. You are *awesome* at Hide and Seek," Cal whispered, then he snapped up the collar, took a final look around the room, and gestured to the door. "Now, who wants to get the Hell out of here?"

*   *   *

It took Mech almost twenty minutes to locate the controls that opened the ship's jaws, then another ten for him to patch himself into the interface.

Several more minutes of limping later, he was back aboard the *Untitled*, where everyone else was strapped in and ready to go.

"Well, this was all quite exciting, wasn't it?" said Cal, flashing his grin from one end of the bridge to the other. "But let's never do it again."

"Agreed," said Loren, her voice clipped and short. "Mech, we good?"

Mech tapped the controls on his arms. The *Untitled* rocked gently as the docking clamp disengaged. Ahead of them, the ship's vast doors slowly inched apart.

"Just a reminder," chimed Kevin's voice. "A number of vessels loyal to Kornack are currently assembled outside. They will almost certainly seek to engage us."

"Good point, Kevin, well made. Loren, be ready to get us the fonk out of here as soon as that door's open."

"We can't warp from in here," Loren said, engaging the forward thrust and lifting the *Untitled* off the deck. "We have to get outside and clear of the ship first. If we're lucky, they won't be on us right away."

"Yeah. Remind me when we've ever been lucky," said Cal. He turned his chair. "Mech, don't suppose you'd be able to fix the weapons in the next, oooh, twelve seconds?"

Mech's only response was a raising of one eyebrow.

"Yeah, thought not," Cal said, spinning back to the front. "Then I guess we're back to our default position of crossing our fingers and hoping for the best."

"Shouldn't we wait until the mouth thing is all the way open?" asked Miz, gesturing ahead to the eye-lid shaped doorway ahead of them.

"Why?" asked Cal.

"Uh, because *she's* flying," said Miz. "You just know she's totally going to fly us straight into the wall."

"Hey, come on! Have a little faith," said Cal. He leaned forwards and whispered to Loren. "Please don't fly us into the wall."

"Totally heard that," said Miz.

"Here goes. Everyone hold on," Loren said, guiding the throttle forwards. The *Untitled* lurched forwards, did a series of kangaroo-hops in the air, then rocketed towards the lower half of the still-opening doors.

"Pull up, pull up!" Cal yelped.

"You're gonna hit!" cried Mech.

"See? I told you," Miz snorted.

The ship banked smoothly upwards and passed cleanly through the gap. Loren turned and smirked. "Seriously? I could have fit ten ships through there. Have a little more faith, in future."

Cal's eyes widened and he jabbed a finger to the screen. "Uh, Loren…"

Loren turned. Her smirk withered and died. Dozens of fighter ships approached on an attack run, their weapon systems glowing with soon-to-be-unleashed power.

"Oh, *shizz!*"

"I had a thought, sir," said Kevin from the speakers.

"Not now, Kevin!"

"Very good, sir."

The first three ships unleashed searing hot beams of cannon-fire at the *Untitled*. Cal felt his stomach *boing* around inside him like a rubber ball as Loren sent the ship into a spin, weaving between two of the blasts. A third struck a glancing blow off the hull, and warning lights illuminated all across the control panels.

"We got no shields," Mech realized. "Why ain't we got shields?"

"As I was saying, sir, I had a thought about raising the shields," intoned Kevin. "But then I remembered Master Carver's instruction about not using my initiative, so I felt it best if I didn't—"

"Raise the fonking shields!" Cal cried. He was lifted up until his seat belt went tight, then slammed back down into the chair as Loren threw the *Untitled* into a dive. Two of the ships turned in time to give chase, but the third overshot the turn, banked too sharply, and exploded against the side of Kornack's capture-ship.

"One down!" Loren cheered.

"Dozens to go," added Miz, helpfully.

Two laser blasts streaked past from behind. Loren yanked back on the stick, sending the ship into an agonizingly steep climb. The *Untitled* was the most responsive ship she'd ever flown, able to turn at near ninety-degree angles without slowing. From a pilot's point of view this was great. From the point of view of a human skeleton, not so much.

"Ow. Jesus. A bit of warning, next time," Cal winced. "I think I just shrunk an inch and a half."

"What? Where?" asked Miz, suddenly concerned.

"Height, I meant, not... not... Forget it."

"Six more coming in high," Mech warned, studying the scanners. "Looks like they're warming up torpedoes."

A blast of cannon-fire clipped one of the *Untitled's* wings. More warning lights illuminated. "What the...?" Mech yelped. "Why ain't we got any shields yet?"

"No-one specified, sir," said Kevin. "And I didn't want to take any liberties."

"No-one specified *what*?" asked Cal.

"Precisely which shields to raise, sir. The ship has several."

"*All of them!*" bellowed Cal, Mech and Loren at the same time.

"Very good," said Kevin, sounding ever so slightly taken aback. "Raising all shields."

The sky ahead shimmered, just for a moment, as the shielding wrapped around them like a bubble. The knot in Cal's stomach loosened a fraction. "OK. Good. Soonsho, you OK back there?" he asked, then he remembered what happened the last time she opened her mouth. "Wait! On second thoughts, don't answer."

He half-spun his chair to check on her. She had her eyes closed and her head back and was gripping her seatbelt so hard her knuckles were white. "I know *exactly* how you feel," he said, then he turned back to the front in time to see a torpedo explode against the shielding.

"I think I'd like to get out of here now," said Cal, gripping his armrest as the aftershock of the torpedo strike trembled through the ship.

"Give me a second," said Loren. "I need to calculate our heading."

"Well hurry up and do it!" said Cal.

"I'm trying!" Loren snapped. She threw the ship into a spinning dive, dodging a hail of cannon-fire. "But it's not easy with everyone shooting at us!"

"Then just hit the fonking button!" Cal yelped. "Take us anywhere that isn't here."

"We could end up somewhere worse."

Another torpedo slammed into the *Untitled's* belly. "I doubt it!" said Cal. "Go!"

"Fine!" Loren hollered. "But don't say I didn't warn you!"

CHAPTER EIGHT

"You know your problem, Loren?" Cal asked, spinning in his chair as the stars streaked past on the viewscreen.

Miz enthusiastically raised a hand, but Cal gestured for her to put it down.

"I'm sure you're about to tell me," Loren said.

"You worry too much."

Loren sighed and shook her head. "For the fifth time, we could have warped straight into a ship, a space station – maybe even a planet. You can't just pick a random direction and hope for the best."

"And yet – and correct me if I'm wrong here – that's exactly what we just did." He looked around the bridge. "And we're all still here to tell the tale."

He drummed his fingers on his arm rest and puffed out his cheeks. "Now, what were we doing before we were so rudely interrupted? Oh!" Cal spun his chair to face Soonsho. Her terror levels had dropped a little, but she still looked a few stressful moments away from a complete nervous breakdown. "We were taking you home."

Miz, who was lying sideways across her chair, her legs hooked over the armrest, reached one arm down to the floor and turned the seat so she could see Soonsho. "That was pretty awesome, by the way. You know, the way you took care of Kornack? That totally rocked."

"Ha!" said Cal. "'Rocked'. Good one."

Miz shot him a withering glance that suggested she had no idea what he was talking about, then turned her attention back to Soonsho. "She looks like she's freaking out. Want me to, like, go help her get cleaned up, or whatever? She's got bits of dead guy all over her."

"Great idea, Miz, thanks," said Cal. "Because if being scrubbed clean by a seven foot tall talking wolf-woman doesn't calm her down, I honestly don't know what will."

Miz tutted. "Whatever," she said, then she got up and slouched towards the door, motioning for Soonsho to follow. The girl shot Cal a look that suggested she had very deep reservations about this, but then unclipped her belt and followed Miz off the bridge.

"And you say Miz is never nice," said Cal, turning to the front.

"No, I said she's never nice *to me*," Loren clarified. "Not the same thing."

Cal sat back in his chair, watching her for a while. Once they'd gotten clear of Kornack's fighters, she'd done all her stuff with headings and co-ordinates, and pointed them towards Cantato Minor, Soonsho's home planet.

As far as Cal knew, there was very little to do now but wait, and yet Loren's fingers passed over the same three sets of controls again and again, like she was stuck in some endless loop. As her fingers brushed against the levers and dials, Cal could see them trembling.

He looked over to Mech, who stood with his arms behind his back, gazing blankly into space. He looked a million miles away, and the fact he'd stop complaining about his leg suggested something was weighing on his mind.

Cal nudged Loren's chair with his foot. This required him to slide down in his own chair until his shoulders were barely touching the seat part, and stretch his leg out as far as it could go.

The moment his foot touched Loren's chair, he lost his balance and fell to the floor. He quickly rolled onto one side and raised himself onto one elbow, like a young Burt Reynolds on a bear skin rug.

Loren turned, looked briefly confused by Cal's empty chair, then spotted him on the floor. "What are you doing?"

"Just chilling," said Cal. "Just, you know, chilling here on the floor."

Loren blinked. "O-K," she said, stringing the letters out.

"Care to join me?"

"Not really."

"No, don't blame you," said Cal. "It's surprisingly uncomfortable."

He clambered back into his chair. "That's better."

"Uh, good," said Loren, then she started to turn back to the front again.

"Hey, Loren, wait," Cal said.

Loren stopped, but didn't turn back.

"You OK?"

"Fine," said Loren.

"Good," said Cal. "Good to know. It's just… that stuff with Kornack. And the axe."

"What about it?"

"You were just doing what you had to do." He raised his

hand and waggled the fingers. "See? No harm done."

Loren didn't say anything for a while, then she turned her chair all the way front. "Yes," she said, her fingers instantly looping between the controls again. "I know."

"Loren…"

"I told you, I'm fine," said Loren, and the tone of her voice suggested the conversation was over.

Cal clicked his tongue against the back of his teeth, then turned to Mech. "And how about you, sparky? You're quiet."

Mech didn't move. "I'm just thinking, is all."

"What about?" asked Cal. He grinned. "Be honest – is it about me?"

Mech sighed. "No. It's about what Sinclair said." He turned away from the view of space, his leg *fizzing* and *popping*. "We're at war."

"No, *they're* at war," Cal corrected. "We're just bumming around, doing our own thing. Our own *space* thing," he added, hoping for a reaction. None came. "Seriously, don't worry about it. Nothing to do with us."

"For how long?" Mech asked. "Because I remember when Zertex and the Symmorium were at war last time. Really at war, I mean, not these past ten years of bickering and name-calling. Man, that thing spread through half the galaxy. Whole planets – Hell, whole *systems* – were wiped out. A lot of good people died. Lot of good people."

Mech turned back to the screen. "And the rest of us… well, we were changed." He *clanged* a metal finger against his chest. It made a hollow, empty sort of sound. "Some of us more than others."

He sighed loudly and shook his head. "We might not be on the front lines yet, but I know how this plays out. We'll get drawn in. Sooner or later, we'll get drawn in." He looked back over his shoulder at Cal. "And then everything's gonna change."

"Hey, come on, guys!" said Cal. "Enough with the long faces. We're going to reunite a kidnapped girl with her parents, then we're millionaires! We can go where we want, do what we want. This war stuff, it doesn't need to affect us."

Mech nodded slowly. His reflection nodded back at him from the screen. "Funny. That's what I said last time." He regarded his mirror image. "Now look at me."

"You, sir, are gorgeous," said Cal. "Unconventional? Sure. Mildly terrifying? Certainly. Partially magnetic? You betcha. But gorgeous, all the same."

Mech grunted. "Point is, sooner or later, we're gonna have to pick a side."

Cal made a weighing motion with his hands. "The Symmorium consider us, like, folk heroes and have given us the freedom of Symmorium space," he said, raising and lowering one hand. He turned his attention to the other. "Zertex are hunting us like dogs, and want us dead. Hmm. Decisions, decisions..."

Loren gently cleared her throat, but didn't take her eyes off her controls. "I have brothers in Zertex," she said.

A silence hung there for a while, until Cal couldn't stand it any longer.

"Jesus, this is the most depressing conversation I've ever had," he said, slapping his hands against his thighs. "And believe me, I've had some fonking depressing conversations in my time. We need to lighten up here, come on, guys."

Loren and Mech said nothing.

"Kevin, how about you? You're a positive kind of guy. Tell us some funny shizz."

"The thirds have harvested the Tuesday, sir," Kevin

announced.

"See? There you go!" said Cal. He laughed, before realizing the words made absolutely no sense whatsoever. "Uh, by which I mean, 'what the fonk are you talking about?'"

"Elbows are in the history. Oh, my."

Cal, Loren and Mech all looked up. "Say what now?" asked Mech.

"My apple-pies, sir," said Kevin, his voice slowing and speeding up like a wonky tape recording. "It appears crab shells have infiltrated m'lady's central pums-pimser."

Cal blinked. "What the Hell's a pums-pimser?"

The stars stopped stretching and snapped to a stop. Cal was jerked from his seat, flipped twice in the air, then slammed against the viewscreen, face first. As he slid to the floor, the bridge's lighting flickered and went out.

"Please tell me it's dark for everyone," Cal wheezed. "Otherwise I've gone blind."

A series of panels in the floor illuminated in an ominous shade of emergency red. "Oh, thank God," Cal whispered, clambering back to his feet. He shot his leather jacket a disappointed look. "Well, thanks for the save, buddy."

The jacket inflated like a giant marshmallow around him.

"Maybe just a smidgen earlier, next time," Cal said. The marshmallow turned green and gloopy, then Splurt dropped to the floor and rolled under Cal's chair.

"What happened?" Cal asked. "Did we hit something?"

"Controls are dead," said Loren.

Mech gestured to the now black and lifeless wall in front of him. "Screen's down. We got no visuals."

"Like, *please* tell me you didn't break the ship again,"

84

groaned Miz, striding onto the bridge. Soonsho slunk along behind her, holding onto the wall to steady herself. "I almost took the new girl's eye out."

"It wasn't me!" Loren protested. "I didn't do anything."

"Oh, like we haven't heard *that* before," Miz snorted.

"It's berries uncle that you attain m'lady's central pumps-pimser," said Kevin. His voice was a full octave higher now, and rising sharply. "Befronk all my dates are corrugated."

Cal pointed to the ceiling. "Has he had a stroke?"

"Could be a virus, maybe?" said Loren. She tapped some keys and waggled a lever. "Nothing's responding."

Cal groaned. "Not another virus. We barely survived the last one."

"Negativity, ma'am," Kevin said. His voice was uncomfortably high-pitched now, like *Alvin and the Chipmunks* covering *The Bee-Gees*. "No voices infraction de-ta-ta-ta-ta in m'lady's frong."

"Well, at least *that's* something," said Cal. "You know, I guess." A thought struck him. He jumped to his feet. "Hey, wait a minute!" he said. "What happened to all those little hat guys?"

The door to one of the many rooms aboard the *Untitled* Cal was explicitly forbidden from setting foot inside slid open, revealing a scene of absolute carnage within.

"Holy shizz, it's *Gremlins 2*," Cal groaned. "Specifically, there's this scene in a cinema when they're all going 'rrraaaa' and smashing the place up, or whatever," he explained, for the benefit of those who hadn't seen it. Which was everyone.

If anything, the scene inside the room was even worse than the one Cal had described. For one thing, the cinema in *Gremlins 2* didn't contain life support systems vital for keeping the cinema's occupants alive. This room, on the other hand, contained exactly that.

A hat-creature dangled from a recently exposed knot of brightly-colored wiring which hung from the back of the life-support terminal like an upside-down rainbow. It tugged furiously on the wires, trying to wrench them free, for reasons best known to itself.

The reason Cal wasn't allowed to enter this room under ordinary circumstances was because everything inside it – literally every panel, console, and cylindrical metal thing that went *whrum* – was important to the running of the ship. Vital, even.

And now most of it was in pieces.

Hat-things pulled on cables, jumped on pipes, hammered buttons and clawed at circuit boards. They chittered excitedly whenever they damaged something, *cooing* in wonder whenever a spark or a *bang* was produced.

"Hump me," Kevin implored, his voice now slow and drawn out. "Hump me, pleebs."

Mech charged into the room and brought his foot down on the hat-thing that was currently up to no good with the life support. It glanced up just in time to see the foot racing towards it, chattered briefly in panic, then exploded like a paint-filled balloon across the floor.

"Jesus," said Cal. "Was that strictly necessary?"

Part of a control panel *whanged* against his forehead. Across the room, one of the critters giggled.

"Ow! You little shizznod," Cal grimaced. "Mech, forget I said anything. Stomp them all!"

Miz shoved Cal aside and bounded into the room, her claws extending from her finger-tips. One of the creatures charged at her, waving its tiny fists in the air. Miz's foot pinned it to the floor, and her tongue flicked hungrily across her exposed teeth.

She looked back over her shoulder. "You might not want to watch this part," she said.

Cal swallowed. "Uh, yeah," he said, backing out of the room. "Loren, why don't you and I leave them to it and check the rest of the ship?"

Mech picked one of the hat-critters up in both hands, then pulled it in two with a sharp, sudden tug. The blue tinge drained from Loren's face. "OK. Yes. Let's do that."

They hurried along the corridor and stopped outside another room. Loren glanced back in the direction of the bridge as Cal listened at the door.

"Think Soonsho's OK?" she asked.

"Splurt's with her. She'll be fine," Cal said. "I mean, you know, the conversation's unlikely to be sparkling, but she'll be safe."

He closed his eyes and concentrated, trying to pick up any sounds beyond the door. "Can't hear anything," he decided, then he tapped the button and the door slid open.

This room was another of those that had been declared off-limits for Cal. It wasn't that he would ever deliberately mess with any of the equipment, it was more that – given his history – there was a good chance the equipment might just spontaneously explode with him around.

During the lengthy discussions about which parts of the ship Cal could and couldn't set foot in, Loren had described him as "a magnet for trouble." Mech had gone a step further, declared him "a fonking jinx" and made it quite clear that he'd personally shoot Cal himself if he ever found him near the *Untitled*'s core systems.

That had seemed a bit harsh to Cal, but he had to admit

that misfortune seemed to follow him around pretty closely, and that perhaps not venturing into areas that might make the ship implode probably wasn't such a bad idea.

As a result, he had no idea what the room they entered was for. It had flashy lights, gurgling pipes and more of those cylinders that went *whrum*. It was also, Cal was happy to note, completely intact.

Although…

Cal nudged Loren and gestured to the floor near the corner of the room. A hat-critter stood at the base of a console, trying to prise open a metal access hatch on the front. It grunted and squeaked as is struggled with the metal, and hadn't, as of yet, noticed it had company.

Placing his fingers to his lips, Cal crept into the room, his hands out in front of him like he was ready to receive a chest pass. The critter heaved and tugged on the panel, its little hat wobbling around on its head.

Cal closed in. Five feet. Four feet. Three feet.

The critter stopped pulling on the panel, raised its head and let out an inquisitive chirp. Cal dived for it, arms outstretched. It darted sideways and Cal slammed into the console, clonking his knees on the floor.

"*Budatie!*" squealed another of the hat-critters, as it hurled itself from behind a ceiling-mounted duct and dropped onto Cal's back. More of the creatures rained down from above, shrieking and squeaking as they threw themselves in Cal's direction.

"What the fonk?" Cal yelped, then he hissed as two of the creatures tugged his ears in opposite directions. "Ow! Cut that out!"

He grabbed for the ear-pullers, but two more critters caught his sleeves and wrestled with his arms. A flood of warmth trickled down over the back of his neck, and several of the creatures erupted into high-pitched laughter.

"Are you... are you *peeing* on me?!" Cal cried. The stench of hat-thing urine answered the question for him. "No! Bad little space midgets!" Cal wailed. "Cut that out!"

It took all his strength to roll over onto his back. Most of the creatures scrambled clear, but one gave a satisfying *crunch* beneath his shoulder as he slammed his weight on top of it. Jeering, the creatures raced to pin him down again. Cal raised a foot to kick out, but before he could, one of the smaller hat-things dived into the bottom of his cargo pants, and began scrambling up Cal's leg.

Cal howled in panic as the creature headed north. Backhanding one of the larger critters away, he grabbed for the moving lump which was already at his knee and moving fast. It scampered around the underside of his leg, its tiny hands tickling at the back of his thigh.

"Don't you dare! Don't you fonking dare!" Cal yelped, wrestling desperately with his belt.

Loren, who had been watching the scene unfold with - she had to admit - some amusement, raised her blaster and fired ten shots in rapid succession. The chittering of the other creatures stopped, leaving only the frantic squeals of Cal as he undid his button and kicked his pants down around his ankles.

He caught the little creature just as it dived for his junk, and tossed it towards the ceiling. Loren whipped up her blaster and shot it in mid-air. Cal sighed as a drizzle of smoldering guts fell on his upturned face.

"Thanks, I guess," he wheezed.

"No problem," said Loren, sliding her blaster back in its holster. She smirked. "Oh, and by the way... nice shorts."

CHAPTER NINE

It was taking almost all of Cal's concentration not to throw up, but he did his best to pretend he was listening.

Mech had been listing the damage to the ship's systems for several minutes now, apparently oblivious to the inch-deep puddle of guts and gore that currently sloshed around on the floor. Miz sat on what must once have been a console, but which now more closely resembled a modern art installation, picking chunks of meat from her teeth with a piece of wicker.

"Uh-huh, uh-huh," said Cal, trying very hard to ignore the knobbly chunks of bloody innards which currently clung to the wall directly behind Mech's head. What the Hell even was that purple thing, anyway? A spleen? A liver? Did the hat-things even have those?

"So, what are you saying, Mech?" Loren asked, cutting the cyborg's list short. "Can we fix it?"

"I was getting to that part," said Mech. "Short answer? No."

Loren grimaced. "And the long answer?"

"Also no," said Mech. He gestured around them to the gut-splattered tangle of wires and broken equipment. "I don't even know what half of this stuff does, let alone how to fix it. That thing over there? That's life support. Totally fonking destroyed, and yet we're still here. So, I don't know, maybe it *isn't* life support."

He shook his head. "That's the problem with experimental prototypes. Ain't no instruction manual on how to fix them when shizz goes wrong."

"Sugar content creator," warbled Kevin.

Cal glanced up at the ceiling and sighed. "Whatever you say, pal. Whatever you say."

A hand touched him on the shoulder and he whipped round, fists raised. "Wah!"

Soonsho drew back in fright, and Cal quickly lowered his hands in case she screamed. "Hey, Soonsho. You probably don't want to see this," he said, blocking her view of the room. "God knows, I don't."

Soonsho stepped back into the corridor and raised an arm. A finger extended, pointing back towards the bridge. Cal leaned around the doorway and looked in that direction. The corridor was still painted red by the emergency lighting, but there was another light, too. A flickering, dancing blue and white mosaic on the walls near the flight deck's open door, as if someone had left the TV on in there.

"Uh. OK," he said. "Guys?"

He stepped out of the room and crept along the corridor. The others followed behind, employing various shades of stealth. Loren moved silently, her feet making no sound on the smooth vinyl floor. Mech's hydraulics *hissed* and *whirred* with every step, but at least he made the effort. Mizette, on the other hand, just plodded along, making no attempt whatsoever to stay quiet.

Soonsho stuck close to Cal. She had a hand clamped over her mouth, as if she was expecting to scream at any moment. Considering she was the only one who knew what was making the lightshow on the bridge, this didn't exactly fill Cal with confidence.

The leather of Loren's holster creaked as she drew her blaster. Cal pressed himself against the wall outside the door and gestured for her to go ahead. She nodded once, made a complicated series of hand gestures that not even Mech fully understood, then dived into the room, rolled into a kneeling position and snapped up her weapon.

"Uh, you might all want to come in here," she said, lowering the gun again.

Cal gasped as he stepped around the doorframe and onto the bridge. There, standing in front of the viewscreen, was an angel.

At least, that was his first thought, thanks to the man's ethereal white glow and kindly features. Cal soon realized he probably wasn't an angel, though. He had no wings for one thing. He was short and stockily built, for another, with a chubby face that – even through the white glow – Cal could tell had rosy red cheeks.

He wore a long apron that clung to his portly belly and flapped around loosely near his knees. He looked less like an actual person, Cal thought, and more like the mascot for a family-owned chain of baker's shops.

"Greetings. I am Dorid Tarkula," he announced, his voice emerging from the speaker system overhead. "Or a holographic representation of Dorid Tarkula, at least," he continued with an amused chuckle. "This vessel's core systems have been damaged."

"You don't say," Mech muttered.

"Who is this guy?" Cal asked, but Loren *shushed* him.

"This recording is activated only when damage levels have become catastrophic, and the vessel is beyond any possibility of space-based repair," the hologram continued. "Life support systems are failing, or have already failed." He chuckled again. "In fact, there's a very good chance you may already be dead."

Cal shot Loren a sideways glance. "We aren't are we?"

Loren nipped his arm through his shirt. "Ow!" he yelped.

"Seems not," she confirmed.

"Fortunately, because of the vessel's experimental nature, I took the liberty of adding a 'recall' function, for just such an emergency," Dorid informed them. "This functionality is not connected to any of the other systems, and is encased in a galvanized neutronium alloy for protection. It should, theoretically, enable you to return to me, so that I may assess the damage for myself."

The hull of the *Untitled* began to creak and groan. Cal glanced around at the metal walls. "OK, those noises are troubling."

"I suggest you take a seat," the hologram continued. "You know, assuming anyone is still alive on there!"

A vibration rose through the *Untitled*'s floor. Cal and the others hurried to their seats and frantically strapped themselves in. Even Mech, whose magnetic feet usually clamped him in place, grabbed onto a control console for additional support.

"I'll see you soon!" Dorid said. He winked, then the image vanished, leaving them with just the red emergency lighting to force back the gloom.

"H-h-he s-s-seemed n-n-nice," Cal stammered, the shuddering of the ship rattling him all the way up to the vocal chords.

"Emulsion rewind in ploffle," announced Kevin, delivering each word at a slightly different speed and pitch. "Knuckle up."

The ship dropped. That was what it felt like, at least. Like that first step off a bungee jump, or an elevator cable snapping on the thirteenth floor. The ship plunged through space, spinning like a yo-yo on a down stroke. Or Cal thought that's what was happening, anyway. The lack of visual input from the screens made it impossible to confirm. All he could rely on was the sloshing in his inner ear and, to a lesser extent, the rising feeling of nausea in his belly.

"H-how long is this going to k-keep up for?" he managed to grimace, despite the G-forces currently attempting to make his eyes meet around the back of his head.

"D-don't know," Loren hissed.

And then it happened. It started with a pinprick of light in the center of the room. The light doubled in size, then doubled again, flowering open like petals as it bloomed to become a series of tumbling loops and whorls painted onto the air itself.

Somehow, without apparently changing, the light stopped being a light and became a sound instead. It bypassed Cal's ears and implanted itself straight into his head. The sound was indescribable. It was beautiful and terrible and every shade in between. It was the sound of angry babies and angels falling. It was the sound of true evil discovering truer love, and of Santa Claus having his heart broken.

It also, Cal decided, sounded a bit like a goose choking on a tiny bell. But you really had to use your imagination for that one, and it seemed less poignant than the others, anyway.

And then, as suddenly as it had started, it stopped.

Cal and the others sat (except Mech, who stood) in the half-dark, gulping down shaky breaths (except Mech, who didn't breathe) bracing themselves for what might happen next. The ship no longer felt like it was falling or spinning, which was a relief, but it could start again at any second, so no-one dared move.

"You know, now that I think about it," said Miz. "I totally should have just stayed at home and been queen this whole time. I bet this kind of stuff *never* happens to queens."

White and blue light flickered up the walls as the hologram reappeared on the deck. Further back in the ship, there was a *clang* as the landing hatch dropped open.

"And you're here," announced the image of Dorid. "If capable of doing so, please exit via the landing ramp. I assure you, you will not be harmed."

He smiled, making his red cheeks even rosier. "Welcome," he said, "to Castle Tarkula!"

Through the open hatch, lightning flashed and thunder rumbled. Somewhere, in the distance, something howled.

"You know," said Cal, unclipping his harness and getting to his feet. "Suddenly, I have a very bad feeling about this."

CHAPTER TEN

Castle Tarkula itself did little to allay Cal's fears. It rose from a hilltop of black slate, its dark, twisting spires stabbing upwards at the cloudy night sky.

A wall that went all the way past 'imposing' and deep into 'psychologically troubling' territory surrounded the collection of towers that made up the castle proper. It was lined along the top with thousands of rusted metal spikes. Gargoyle faces grimaced out from the gray brickwork every ten feet or so, as if watching for trespassers.

A portcullis blocked the only visible route in and out of the castle grounds. From a distance, Cal thought it was your standard wrought iron number, but as they drew closer the surface shimmered and flickered erratically, and made all Miz's fur stand on end with static electricity.

"Well, this is homely," Cal whispered. Another flash of lightning flickered inside a bank of black clouds, briefly turning it shades of purple and blue.

It was rare that Mech allowed Cal to bring a gun, but after walking down the ramp and spotting the castle, Cal had insisted. He had the pistol tucked into a holster for now, but his hand was tightly gripping the handle, and his trigger finger itched so badly it was developing a rash.

Mech and Loren stood either side of Soonsho, shielding her from whatever might come leaping out of the darkness. The only light in the area, besides the thin glow of the half-covered yellow moon, flickered in a few of the tower windows, and Cal couldn't shake the feeling something was watching them from the shadows.

They stood at the portcullis and waited for it to open.

It didn't.

"Hello?" Cal called. "Anyone home?"

A sudden screech of moving metal made him jump. He half drew his blaster, then lowered it back into the holster when he realized the sound hadn't been the scream of a vampire, banshee, or anything else along those lines.

It had been the sound of the ground beneath the *Untitled* twisting as it rotated downwards, lowering the ship into an underground cave.

"Hey!" Cal cried. He tried to rush back to the ship, but a set of doors clanged closed above it. The sound they made was of metal hitting other metal, but the ground once more looked like a patch of flat slate, with nothing to suggest the ship – or doors – had ever been there at all.

"Great. So now we lost the ship," Mech grunted.

"To be fair, it wasn't like it was going to get us anywhere," Loren pointed out.

"Yeah, but Splurt's still on there!" said Cal.

Mech sighed. "How come you always do that, man?"

"Do what?"

"Splurt."

Cal held up his hands in protest. "I have never 'done'

Splurt, and I resent the accusation that—"

"I mean leave him behind. He can handle himself better than any one of us."

"Speak for yourself," Miz muttered.

"Because," said Cal, launching into an explanation despite the fact he didn't actually have one prepared. "I mean… because he's a beautiful innocent creature, that's why. Yeah, that'll do. Can he handle himself physically? Yes. But emotionally? Is he mentally prepared for…" He gestured up at the foreboding castle. "…whatever fresh Hell this is? I honestly don't know."

Cal smiled sadly. "They grow up so fast. Why can't you just let him be a child for a little longer, Mech? Hmm?" He grabbed Mech by the arms and tried, without success, to shake him. "Why won't you just let him be a child?"

"When Zertex was studying him they figured out he's roughly eight thousand years old," Loren told him.

Cal stopped attempting to shake Mech. "Oh," he said. "I shall keep that in mind."

He turned back towards the gate. The portcullis was gone. The archway was clear. A grotesquely misshapen gargoyle with a skull like an exploding pineapple eyed the crew from the top of the arch as Cal drew his gun and slowly approached.

"Looks like we've been invited in," said Cal, as another rumble of thunder rolled across the sky. "Stick close together, no wandering off, and if anyone happens to be carrying any garlic, crosses or holy water, feel free to pass them around."

The moment they were all inside the castle grounds, the portcullis reappeared, as if by magic. Beyond the outer walls, where they'd just come from, the terrain was bleak and uninviting. Inside, it was even worse.

Several trees stood around the otherwise empty courtyard, their trunks blackened, their branches bare, as if they'd all been the victims of some deranged horticultural arsonist. Bird-like shapes – also black – hopped from branch to branch, their beady eyes glinting in the pale moonlight as they tracked Cal and the others all the way to the castle's front doors.

The doors were serious-looking metal things, with hinges as thick and as long as Cal's arm riveted across the front of each. There was no handle that Cal could see, and when he brushed his fingertips across the metal, a shock of electricity jolted through his hand and up his arm.

Cal stepped back and looked across the gray brickwork surrounding the door. "Anyone see a bell?" he asked, then he took a further step back as the doors swung inwards with a predictably sinister *creeeeak*, revealing a candle-lit room beyond.

"This would be the point in the movie where a creepy villager warns us not to go inside," Cal whispered. He looked back, almost hopefully, over his shoulder. "Guess not," he muttered, then he raised his blaster pistol in front of him and quietly stepped into the castle.

"Hello there!" called a cheerful voice.

Cal screamed and spun in the direction of the sound, hurriedly raising his blaster. He closed his eyes and fired twice. Both bolts hit Dorid Tarkula at point blank range in the chest, splattering the wall behind him with blood, flesh-chunks, and sizzling blobs of fat.

With a gasp of horror, Cal lowered the gun. "Ooh shizz. I am *so* sorry," he said. "You came at me out of nowhere, and it just went off in my hand."

Dorid, who had remained standing throughout, looked

down at the holes in his upper torso, gargled something bloody and damp, and then toppled backwards onto the polished wooden floor.

Everyone stared at Cal in silence as he shuffled closer to Dorid's body, nudged it with his foot, and very tentatively said, "Hello?"

When no response came – not even after a slightly louder, "You OK, buddy?" to double-check – Cal made the diagnosis.

"Nope. He's dead."

"You think so?" said Mech.

"Argh! I don't believe you, sometimes," groaned Loren.

"What? It's not my fault! Mech gave me the gun."

"Never again," said Mech. "That's the last time. No more guns for you."

"Although, you have to admit," said Miz. "It was kinda hilarious."

"Not really seeing the funny side," Mech growled. "Now what do we do?"

Cal rolled his tongue around inside his mouth as he thought. "I don't know. Bury him in the garden?"

"Bury him in the garden?" said Loren, flatly. "Not 'inform the authorities'? Not 'notify his next of kin'?"

"Yeah, well *obviously* we'll do those, too," said Cal. "Just, you know, from the safety of outer space."

"Hello there!"

Cal screamed. Again.

Cal spun. Again.

The shots took out half of another Dorid's head, ruining an expensive-looking oil painting hanging on the wall behind him.

"Shizz. I did it again!"

The body slumped forwards onto the floor. This time, Cal didn't feel the need to nudge it with his foot. It was about as dead as it was possible to be.

"Seriously, man, give me that fonking gun," said Mech, snatching the weapon from Cal's hand. He passed it to Loren, who tucked it into the back of her belt.

"So… what? There are two of him?" drawled Miz. She flicked her eyes to Cal. "You just murdered twins."

"I didn't *murder* them," protested Cal. "They just… got in the way of the shots I accidentally fired."

"Oh, so it's *their* fault?" said Loren.

"No! I'm not saying it's their fault," Cal insisted. "I'm saying we're all partly to blame here. It's everyone's fault, collectively."

Throughout all this, Soonsho stood with her back against a wall, trying very hard not to make a sound. While the others argued, she spotted movement in a narrow doorway at the top of a small set of curving stone steps. Clamping a hand over her mouth to be doubly sure she didn't scream the place down, she tapped Cal on the shoulder and gestured towards the door.

The left side of a podgy, rosy-cheeked face edged around the doorframe. "Uh… hello," it said. "Please, don't shoot."

"We won't," said Cal, holding up his hands to show they were empty. "These other two gentlemen surprised me, mistakes were made on both sides, but… Relax. We're not here to hurt you."

The man in the doorway sensibly chose to emerge slowly, with no sudden movements. Once in the open, Cal and the others recognized him right away.

"Hey, it's you!" said Cal.

"So… what?" Loren frowned. "You're triplets?"

Dorid Tarkula smiled, but there was an anxiousness to it, like he was worried it might get him killed. "Goodness, no. Those are – *were* – clones. I created them to help with my work, and with the running of the castle. It's a big endeavor to manage by oneself. Always something needing cleaned up."

"I'll bet," said Cal. He looked down at the two corpses. "Speaking of which, we can help move these somewhere, if you like? It seems… I mean, that seems only fair. You know, considering."

"Considering you shot them through the chest and face?" said Mech. "I'd say it's a pretty long way from 'fair.'"

"Oh no, please, I won't hear of it," said Dorid. "The others will tidy those two away."

"Others?" said Loren. "How many of you – of them – are there?"

Dorid had to give that some thought. "Oh my. Now there's a question. A hundred, perhaps? It varies. As high as two, maybe?" He smiled, more confidently this time. "I'm afraid I don't actually know. Less than four hundred, I'd estimate, but possibly a few more working in the lower levels. I lose track."

"Jesus," said Cal. "That must be some queue for the bathroom." He shrugged. "But speaking of lower levels. The ship – your ship, I guess – got swallowed by the ground with a friend of ours on board."

"Say no more," said Dorid. "I shall send someone to collect your friend at once, before they begin work on the repairs." He clenched his fists and waved them excitedly beside his head. "We cannot wait to get working on it again, after all these years. How is K-Seven-Zero Dash Nine-Three-Three-Zero-Seven Dash Zeta, by the way? Was he damaged?"

"Kevin?" said Cal. "He's... well, I mean, he's..."

Dorid held up an open palm. "I understand. We'll assess the damage and discuss the best course of action with you then."

"Uh, with us?" said Cal. "Why?"

Dorid's face lit up. "Why, because it's your ship, of course!" he laughed. He waddled down the stone steps and clapped his calloused hands together. "Now, is anyone hungry?"

"Dorid," said Cal, putting an arm around the smaller man's broad shoulders. "I thought you'd never ask."

CHAPTER ELEVEN

Twenty minutes later, Cal sat at one end of a long wooden table, eating soup with a sponge. The trick, Dorid explained, was to dip the sponge an inch or two into the liquid, quickly raise it while tipping the head back, position above the open mouth, then squeeze.

The first time Cal had tried it, he'd missed his mouth completely, and almost drowned as half a sponge full of scalding hot gumbo had shot up his nose. His face, clothing and a foot or two in every direction around him looked like the aftermath of a toddler's dinner-time tantrum, but he was starting to get the hang of it now. Still, he couldn't shake the feeling a spoon would have made life much easier.

Loren had mastered the technique immediately, and was now confidently sponging soup into her mouth around the table on Cal's left. On his right, Soonsho was bent low over the bowl, the sponge practically a blur as it moved back and forth from the bowl to her lips. Cal realized he had no idea when the girl had last eaten and that, all things considered, he should probably have offered her a sandwich when she'd first come aboard.

Next to Soonsho, Mizette was licking the bowl clean. The chair across from her was empty. Mech didn't eat, and so Dorid had offered to have one of his clones take him to a repair station, and help patch up his damaged leg.

Dorid sat at the head of the table, directly opposite Cal. He had finished his soup, and was delicately dabbing the edges of his mouth with a napkin.

"This is good," said Cal, licking the last of his broth from his chin. "What is it?"

Dorid looked blankly down at his empty bowl. "You know, I don't have the faintest idea," he admitted. "Some sort of vegetable, I expect. The kitchen – food preparation and whatnot – is handled by one of my others. Possibly more than one, actually."

"Pretty sweet setup," said Cal, nodding appreciatively. "Maybe I should get a clone to help with all my jobs."

"What jobs?" Loren snorted.

Miz raised her eyes from her spotlessly clean bowl and licked her lips. "Oh, please *do*," she said. "I can think of a few jobs two identical versions of you could do."

"Miz, please, children present," said Cal, glancing deliberately at Soonsho, who he was immensely thankful was sitting between them.

"Cantatorian, correct?" said Dorid, nodding in Soonsho's direction. She looked across to him, just briefly, then back to her bowl.

"That's right," said Loren. "We're taking her home."

"Fascinating people. Fascinating," said Dorid. "Their vocal range – the women, at least – incredible. Just incredible. They can hypnotize with their song, you know?" He smiled warmly along the table. "What's your name, my dear?"

"She doesn't talk," said Cal. "Or make any sound at all, generally."

"Oh." Dorid looked taken aback. "A mute Cantatorian? That is a cruel irony."

"She's not mute," said Loren. "I mean, we've heard her make sounds before, it's just they've been... destructive."

"You've never heard her speak?"

Cal shook his head. "No. We thought if she said anything, made a sound or whatever, she'd blow shizz up. Isn't that how it works?"

"Not usually, no," said Dorid. "Even the more powerful Cantatorian females can speak, although they have to be careful of their tone, obviously." He tapped a finger on the wooden tabletop. "When you say 'destructive,' just how destructive are we talking?"

"Destroyed a rock guy, killed a load of gangsters," said Cal.

"Flipped those cop cars," Miz added.

"Yes. Flipped a load of cop cars. Big ones."

"I see," said Dorid. He leaned forwards on his elbows. "And how much effort did these incidents require on her part?"

"Well, we only saw the cop cars and the rock guy," said Cal. "But not much. She just sort of, I don't know, *cheeped* and that was that."

"Oh," said Dorid, suddenly sounded excited. "Oh, now that *is* interesting."

Before he could explain what was so interesting about it, two other Dorids entered through a side door, bowed steeply to the guests, then began clearing the table.

"Thank you, gentlemen," the seated Dorid said, smiling

warmly to the others. "Most appreciated."

"Yep," Cal muttered, watching the clones at work. "I have got to get me some of those."

While they waited for the table to be cleared, Cal took in the dining room. Being in there felt a bit like being inside a storage crate, thanks to the wood-covered floor, walls and ceiling. An enormous window took up most of the room's narrow end. At least, Cal presumed so, but a heavy pair of crimson curtains had been drawn across it, making it impossible to be sure if there was actually a window there at all.

Along one of the longer walls were dozens of shelves, each one loaded with trinkets and nick-nacks. Cal had no idea what any of them were, although he thought one might be some kind of space clock, and a pretty ghastly-looking ornament could have been three duck-like things, but might equally have been one monster-like thing with three duck-like heads.

The other long wall was far less cluttered, boasting just two stuffed animal heads, a painting of a woman who looked suspiciously like an older version of Dorid, and a suit of armor fit for a king. Assuming he was a king who had recently been in an industrial accident involving a chainsaw, some superglue, and several other much smaller kings.

The mounted heads weren't from animals Cal was familiar with. One appeared to be made almost exclusively of thin black spikes, while the other roughly broke down as twenty-percent zebra, ten-percent slug, and seventy-percent teeth.

The whole castle, inside and out, would have been more suited to an old black and white horror movie than the lair of a jovial space scientist. Cal was about to say as much, but Dorid caught the thought before he'd had a chance to vocalize it.

"I know," Dorid said, looking around as if seeing the place for the first time. "My great grandparents built the castle originally, and it was just sort of passed down. I used to hate the place when I was younger. Used to scare the life out of me. Still does, sometimes!"

He leaned back, allowing one of the other Dorids to take his bowl. "Truth is, this is the first time I've set foot in this room for... Oh, I don't know. Years, probably."

He interlocked his fingers and leaned forwards, as if sharing some big secret. "But, well, the thing is, it keeps the riff-raff away. Half this planet has been scavenged. Picked clean. But this place, particularly once I'd sown the seeds of superstition and planted some rumors about the horrors that go on within its walls, has remained remarkably untampered with."

He chuckled. "Of course, I also have a one-of-a-kind security system to defend against attack, but I rarely have call to use it."

"So, these rumors," said Cal. "Just what do they say?"

Dorid's chair *creaked* as he leaned back again. "They tell of beasts and mutants and other monstrous things," he said. "Nightmares, made flesh."

"I see," said Cal. He held Dorid's gaze, watching for a reaction. "And tell me, *doctor*, just how much of that is true?"

"Uh, I'm not a doctor," said Dorid.

"Oh," said Cal. "Right. Really? That's a shame, because it sounded really dramatic when I added 'doctor' in there." He turned to Loren. "It did, didn't it?"

Loren rolled her eyes and shrugged.

"Suit yourself," said Cal. He looked along the table to Dorid. "The question still stands, though, doctor or not. How much of that 'nightmares made flesh' stuff is true?" He gestured around them. "Exactly what goes on here in Castle Tarkula?"

Dorid tapped his finger on the tabletop. His smile widened slowly as another peal of thunder rumbled above the castle. "How about you all come downstairs and see for yourselves?"

Cal, Loren, Soonsho and Miz *clopped* down a spiral stone staircase, following the glow of Dorid's fiery torch. A warm wind wafted up from below, moaning ominously as it rushed past, as if in a hurry to get away. The torch's flame danced and flickered, scurrying misshapen shadows up the narrow stone walls.

"So, uh, I'm guessing you haven't heard of elevators," said Cal. Something about the acoustics of the place made his voice come straight back to him as a scratchy whisper.

"Oh, we have elevators. Several, in fact," said Dorid. "But – and please forgive me – taking you in one of those would grant you access to the whole facility, and I don't yet know you well enough to allow that. Please understand."

He glanced back over his shoulder and the shadows twisted his face into a mockery of a grin. "Besides, Mr Carver, I thought you'd enjoy the scenic route."

Cal stopped, then was almost knocked down the stairs when Loren, Soonsho and Miz all bumped into the back of him, in that order.

"Hey, wait a minute. Wait a minute. I never told you my name."

Loren tutted. "Yes you did. You told him all our names

almost immediately after he offered us dinner."

"I think you even gave him your date of birth," said Miz from the back of the line.

"Oh. Oh, yeah. So I did," said Cal. He continued walking.

"Almost there," said Dorid. "Won't be long now."

The flickering torchlight, creepy castle and general *Hammer House of Horror* vibe of the whole experience were combining to give Cal a serious case of the heebie-jeebies. As they arrived at the heavy wooden door at the bottom of the steps, he found himself reaching for his gun, then remembered it had been confiscated, and balled his hands into fists instead.

"Where was the breeze coming from?" asked Loren. Now they were at the bottom of the staircase, they could no longer feel the warm wind. There were no obvious gaps around the door, either, suggesting it hadn't snuck through there.

"Not sure, actually," said Dorid, shrugging as he turned the dark metal handle set into the door. "Never been able to trace it. Not for want of trying, I should add. Now…"

He pulled aside the wooden door, revealing a chrome-colored metal door behind it. A light shone from a circular lens in the center of the door, mapping Dorid's face with a criss-crossing illuminated grid.

Then, with a soft *sshunk*, the door slid upwards, revealing a long, brightly-lit and refreshingly modern-looking metal walkway beyond. Dorid stepped aside and motioned towards the open door.

"Please," he insisted. "After you."

Cal stepped through the door and into one of the top three largest rooms he'd ever been in. It was a vast chamber, easily a couple of square miles in size, and almost as high. The metal walkway was located fifty feet or more above the ground, with an industrial-looking elevator connecting the two levels.

The *Currently Untitled* sat on the ground level, resting on a large circle of slate. Dozens of Dorids ferried components to and from the ship, carrying away the damaged-looking equipment and replacing it with shiny new parts.

Cal leaned on the railing and gazed down at the ship. He'd never seen it from this angle before. He still missed the *Shatner*, but fonk, this thing was sexy.

"I'm rather proud of this one," said Dorid, joining Cal at the railing. "I had a lot of fun building her. Almost considered taking her out for a spin myself, before Zertex came and took her."

"You make ships for Zertex?" asked Cal.

"Not intentionally, no," said Dorid, his lips thin. "I make ships for the love of it. Because I can, and because I enjoy pushing the boundaries. Sometimes, Zertex decides to take one. To show that *they* can."

"Yeah," said Cal, nodding. "Yeah, that sounds like them. Bunch of amshoops."

"How did you get it here so fast?" Loren wondered. "The ship, I mean. After the hologram, it just sort of… fell. And then we were here."

"Subspace," said Dorid, as if that answered everything.

"Subspace?" said Loren, using just the right amount of emphasis to ensure he understood it answered nothing.

"Yes," said Dorid, smiling gently and talking slowly, as if addressing an idiot. "Subspace."

Cal straightened suddenly and pointed down to a spot

near the *Untitled*. A little green blob was sitting on a chair there, wearing an oversized red hat. "Hey, Splurt. It's Splurt!"

"Your friend?" said Dorid. He gestured to the elevator. "Come on, I'll take you down."

The elevator was an ancient-looking contraption, with mesh flooring, gaps in the walls, and – most likely – a list of Health & Safety violations a mile long. It rattled and shook as a thick cord of metal cable spooled out, lowering it jerkily to the floor below.

As soon as Dorid manually heaved the door aside, Cal bounded out, practically skipping across to where Splurt sat. Up close, the cap on his head – complete with 'Engineer' emblazoned on the front in gold – looked ridiculously oversized. Just from his eyes – because there was literally nothing else to go on – Cal could tell the little guy loved it.

"Look at you!" Cal cooed. He made a frame shape with fingers and thumbs from both hands, aimed it at Splurt and made a camera sound. "That's one for the scrapbook."

One of the Dorids smiled at Cal and came over to join him. Unlike the other Dorids working on the ship's repairs, this one didn't have a hat on.

"Hello there!" said the Dorid. "Friend of yours?"

Cal nodded. "I hope he wasn't too much trouble."

"What? No, no trouble at all," said the Dorid, rubbing Splurt's head through the hat. His smile widened as the others approached. "Ladies. Dorid."

"Dorid," said Dorid, returning the other Dorid's nod. "How goes it?"

"Well, there was a lot of damage, and several of the systems were completely clogged with, uh, *remains*."

"We had visitors," Cal explained. "They broke the ship."

"It's in hand," said the other Dorid. "Should have

everything back up and running within the hour. Provided I don't stand around here yakking all day!" He smiled and nodded at everyone again. "I'll get back to it. Sir. Ladies. Dorid."

"Dorid," said Dorid.

They watched him head back into the ship. "So, they're all called Dorid?" Cal asked.

"Of course," said Dorid. "Why wouldn't they be? It's their name, after all."

"And everyone's identical?" asked Loren.

"To a point," said Dorid. "They have most of my memories, but not all. And, of course, from the moment they were created they began forming their own memories, based on their own experiences."

"So, like, how do you know you're the real one?" asked Miz.

The bottom half of Dorid's face smiled, while the top half frowned. "I'm sorry?"

"If everyone's identical, and all called, like, Dorid or whatever, how do you know you're the original?"

"Well, because I remember building my cloning machine. I remember my failed attempts. The endless tinkering until I perfected the technique. I remember it all."

"Oh, OK," said Miz. She appeared to be satisfied by this, but that didn't last long. "Only, won't those other guys have those memories, too?"

Dorid blinked several times. He looked across to one of the other Dorids who was busily loading a burnt-out ship part onto a floating trolley. "Well... I mean, yes. Partly. However, unlike them, I remember *everything*."

"Except the soup," said Cal.

Dorid turned to him. "Pardon?"

"The soup. I'm just saying, you couldn't remember what kind of soup it was."

A flicker of irritation passed over Dorid's face. "So? It's soup. I'm one of the foremost inventors in this sector. In the *galaxy*. I create spacecraft which laugh in the face of conventional physics. You'll forgive me if I don't spend my time memorizing flavors of soup." He moved off at pace towards the landing hatch. "Come. Let's take a look inside."

"Man. Touchy, much?" Cal mumbled.

"Well, you basically just accused him of being fake," said Loren.

"She started it!" said Cal, pointing to Miz. He glanced back at Soonsho. The girl still looked as anxious as ever. "Hey, it's OK. We're getting the ship fixed, then we're going to get you home."

He scooped Splurt up, and the little blob wrapped around him like a backpack. "Now, let's go see how things are shaping up."

The inside of the ship was far less chaotic than any of them had been expecting. The Dorids were methodically tidy, carefully removing each damaged component, then ferrying it away just as the replacement part was brought in.

"Well, this is all looking ship-shape," said Cal. He grinned. "See what I did there? Because we're on a—"

"Yes," sighed Loren. "We get it. Well done."

Dorid led them through several rooms, pointed to insanely complicated-looking bits of machinery, then explained their purpose in great detail. Cal nodded throughout, occasionally adding a, "yep," or a, "makes sense," to suggest he was A) listening and B) had the faintest idea what the guy was talking about.

In the fifth or sixth room – a long, narrow one that Cal

had never even seen before, with an entire wall covered by thousands of colorful cables all snaking through one another – they found Mech deep in conversation with another Dorid.

"Hey!" said Cal. "How's the arm?"

"It was my leg," Mech grunted. "And it's fine."

"Was it? You sure?"

"Of course I'm fonking sure."

Cal held up his hands in surrender. "OK, OK, easy big guy. It's your arm, not mine."

"Leg."

"Right. Right," said Cal, very much enjoying the look on Mech's face. "Leg. Gotcha."

He turned to the Dorid. "Any chance you guys could have a look at the weapons?"

Mech's feet *whirred* as he shifted on the spot. "Already spoke to them about it," he said.

"It's just, well, Mech tried to fix them, but… you couldn't, could you? You couldn't figure it out."

The other Dorid opened his mouth, but Mech quickly jumped in. "Like I say, already in hand. They're going to fix it."

"Great!" said Cal. "So, what was the problem, exactly?"

Mech sighed. The other Dorid watched him for a moment, unsure whether to speak. When it became clear Mech wasn't going to talk over him, he explained.

"The safety catch was on."

Cal struggled to keep his face straight. It wasn't easy. "Sorry? Say that again. Loren, can you write this down, in case the problem ever comes up again?" He put a finger behind his ear and pushed it forwards a little towards the Dorid. "So, you were saying? The…"

"Safety catch," Mech growled. "The weapon system has a safety protocol."

"Well," breathed Cal, tucking his thumbs into Splurt's straps and rocking back on his heels. "Well, well, well. That is good to know, isn't it, Mech? Remind me, how long did you spend trying to get the weapons working?"

"In his defense," said the Dorid. "It's not immediately obvious. The button can be quite hard to find."

"The *button*?" yelped Cal, loving every minute of this. "There's a *button*? Let me guess, does it say 'safety catch' on it somewhere?"

The Dorid glanced sideways at the visibly fuming Mech. "Uh, not exactly, but something along those…" He cleared his throat and shot the first Dorid an imploring look.

"Thank you, Dorid, that will be all," said Dorid. The other Dorid seemed to inflate with sheer relief, then he nodded at Mech and Cal, smiled briefly at Loren, Miz and Soonsho, then darted out into the corridor.

The original Dorid craned his neck back and looked up at the ceiling. "How about K-Seven-Zero Dash Nine-Three-Three-Zero-Seven Dash Zeta?" he said. "How deep does the damage run, I wonder?"

"To be honest, he was pretty damaged already," Cal said. "Between you and me, he was a little… eccentric."

"I see," said Dorid.

"By which I mean he was fonking insane."

"Oh. Well, I'm sure we can fix that and put him back to his original configuration."

Cal nodded, but then stopped. "You know what? Just fix him back to how he was before the damage. Can you do that?"

"I mean, I'm sure we *could*, but if he was behaving

problematically…"

"It's fine. It was nothing we couldn't handle."

Dorid nodded. "Very well. I'll go get someone on it, right away."

He headed for the door. Cal moved to follow, but Mech caught his arm and held him back until the others had filed out.

"Hey, man. I need to talk to you," Mech whispered.

Cal's eyes looked the cyborg up and down. "Are you coming on to me right now?" he whispered back.

Mech's metal jaw tensed. "Shut the fonk up," he said. He leaned out into the corridor, making sure no-one was within earshot, then turned back to Cal. "There's something I think you should see."

CHAPTER TWELVE

After walking confidently off the ship and striding across the underground hangar like he owned the fonking place – a technique he had used time and time again back on Earth to gain entry into any number of off-limits locations – Cal had followed Mech into a far more robust-looking elevator than the one leading down from the walkway.

"Please state destination," the elevator chimed.

Mech cleared his throat then, in a note-perfect imitation of Dorid's voice, said: "Lab level four."

The elevator hummed pleasantly as it glided upwards. "I didn't know you could do that," said Cal. "The voice thing."

Mech shrugged. "Yeah. It's no big deal."

"Can you do anyone else?" Cal asked.

"Of course I can," Mech said. "Why the fonk would I be able to only impersonate some random scientist dude living in the ams-end of nowhere?"

"Do me! Do me!" said Cal, but before Mech could answer, the door slid open, revealing a long, starkly-lit corridor lined with dozens of reinforced doors. Unlike downstairs, which had been positively brimming with them, this corridor was utterly devoid of Dorids.

Mech put a finger to his lips and motioned for Cal to follow.

"What is it? What are you going to show me?" Cal whispered, hurrying to keep up.

"Just wait and see," said Mech. "One of the clones fixed my leg in a room along here," he said. "Made a pretty good job of it, too. Told me to go for a walk to try it out, and, well, I poked around."

He stopped outside one of the doors and glanced both ways along the corridor. "And I found this place."

Cal studied the door. It looked like all the other doors they'd already passed, and identical to the scores of others lining the walls of the corridor ahead. Despite the door being reinforced, it opened with a single press of a button on the wall beside it.

Darkness filled the room beyond. Cal leaned forwards a little and peered into the gloom. "What is it? What's in there?" he whispered, then Splurt suddenly tightened his grip around Cal, almost making him jump out of his skin in fright.

"Jesus Christ!" Cal hissed. Splurt rippled happily on his back. "Yeah, yeah, very funny," Cal said. "But next time you're captured and brainwashed by an elderly assassin, you're fonking staying that way."

He stepped cautiously into the room. A series of lights hummed into life above him, illuminating twenty or more tables lined up along the walls. Objects of various shapes and sizes sat on the tabletops, each of them hidden beneath white sheets.

"Take a look," said Mech, gesturing to the closest table.

119

Cal approached it slowly, ducking and tilting his head to try to get a look under the cloth. "What is it?" he asked.

"Just look, man!"

"Mech, I swear, if this is, like, a head on a stick, or a load of babies' eyes or some shizz…"

"Babies' eyes? Why the fonk would it be babies' eyes?"

"I don't know! I'm just saying, it'd better not be." He took hold of the sheet, started to pull it off, then stopped. "It isn't, is it? It isn't babies' eyes?"

"Just lift the fonking sheet before someone comes looking for us."

Cal steadied himself, took a deep breath, then pulled off the sheet. "Oh my God," he whispered, gazing down at the object on the table. "It's… It's…" He puffed out his cheeks. "Nope. Not a clue. What is that?"

It looked like several different household appliances had been broken into their component parts, randomly mixed up, then rebuilt by someone wearing a blindfold. There were shiny chrome parts, white plastic parts, loose wires, several buttons, a couple of short, stubby hoses and a pair of joysticks mounted on spindly metal arms that looked like they might fall off at any second.

"I got no idea," Mech admitted.

Cal nodded slowly. "Then why did you show me?"

"Because this place is full of this stuff," Mech said, his metal jaw curving into a grin. He began pointing at sheets. "Some kinda shield focuser. A propulsion system. For underwater, I think. A warp disk generator. *It makes fonking warp disks!*"

"Great," said Cal. "But why are you showing me? This is more Loren's thing. I mean, I'm pretty sure it's the kind of thing she'd like." He stared into space for a moment. "Is it? I really need to get to know her better."

"Focus, man," Mech told him. "The reason I told you is because… how much do you think all this is worth?"

Cal looked across the tables and shrugged. "A lot?"

"A lot," Mech confirmed. "And it's just sitting here. Just lying around, gathering dust. He ain't going to miss it."

Cal opened his mouth in an expression of very deliberate shock and outrage. "Mech, you're not suggesting what I think you're suggesting?"

"I ain't saying we should take all of it," Mech said. "But, well, if we want to avoid this war that's coming – really avoid it – we're going to need to get all the way to the other end of Nebula 99."

"What's Nebula 99? It sounds like a nightclub."

"What? No. This is. We're in it. Our galaxy, that's part of the 99th Nebula," Mech explained. "There are hundreds of others – well, I mean, there's an infinite number of others, but there are hundreds of them catalogued. This one's the 99th."

Cal blinked. "But, I mean… who catalogued it?"

"Say what?"

"The nebula. It's the 99th one. Who discovered 98 others before this one?"

Mech opened his mouth, closed it, then opened it again. "Well, I mean… it's just Nebula 99, OK? Everyone knows that. My point is, if we want to avoid this war, we'll have to get all the way across it, and that is going to cost."

"We're taking Soonsho home," Cal reminded him. "We're getting a million credits."

"Yeah, between four of us."

Splurt raised his eyes above Cal's shoulder and shot Mech a withering look.

"Fine. Between *five* of us," Mech snapped. "That ain't going to get us far."

Cal looked down at the machine on the table for a few seconds, then pulled the sheet down over it. "Dorid's helping us. He's fixing the ship. He gave us soup. I mean, a spoon wouldn't have killed him, but... We can't just steal from him."

"Uh, yes. We can," said Mech. "Two or three of these things could set us up for a long time. We can go anywhere we want. Get out of here before all the shooting starts."

The small area of his face that was still organic took on a faraway look. "I've seen what it's like, man. I've seen what happens."

"We're not thieves," said Cal. "I mean, technically you and I are. And Splurt, Miz and Loren, too, to a slightly lesser extent, but... Dorid saved us. Is it weird that he shares a creepy castle with his identical clones? Yes. Yes, it is. But we can't just take his stuff. It's not right."

Mech shook his head, then let out a long, weary sigh. "Yeah. Yeah, I guess so."

He took a final look around the room as Cal headed for the door, then followed behind.

Once back in the corridor, Cal headed back towards the elevator. "So, the way I see it, our plan is we get the ship fixed, get out of here, then just foot down and full speed ahead to Calamari Prime."

"Cantato Minor," Mech corrected.

"That's the one. We drop off Soonsho, collect our loot, then decide our next move from there."

He stopped outside another door. This one was set further back in an alcove. He hadn't noticed it on the way in due to the angle of the wall, but now it had caught his eye, and something about it made him take a step closer.

"What's in there?"

"How should I know?" Mech grunted. "I didn't look in that one."

"Come on, are you still grouchy that I wouldn't let you steal Dorid's stuff?" said Cal, reproachfully. "I told you, Dorid's a nice guy. Also, stealing is wrong. Unless it's from Zertex, then it's to be encouraged."

He tapped the button next to the door. It slid upwards, revealing another darkened room. This time, when Cal stepped inside, only one light came on. It flickered and buzzed on the high ceiling, illuminating hundreds of thick glass tubes that stuck up from the floor like stalagmites. Or possibly the other one, Cal could never remember which was which.

Each tube was ten to twelve feet high, and perhaps just a little less around the circumference. Layers of dust and grime covered the glass, but when the light flickered just right, Cal thought he saw unmoving shapes lurking within.

Splurt tensed, almost making Cal scream again. "Stop fonking doing that," he hissed, shuffling closer to one of the tubes.

Cupping his hands around his eyes, Cal peered into the tube, but the dust was too thick to see through. Using his sleeve, he wiped a patch clean – or clean*er* at least – and tried again.

"Oh," he said. "Ooh boy."

"What is it?" asked Mech.

Cal turned, opened his mouth to reply, then had to look through the glass again to make sure he hadn't been seeing things.

"It's Dorid," said Cal. "Only he's... well, he's not as

pretty as the one we've come to know and love, let's put it that way."

He wiped a larger area of the dust away and stepped aside. The light flickered, briefly picking out the details on the shape in the tank. It was suspended in a clear gel, with hooks cupping it under each arm to stop it flopping to the floor of the tube.

It was Dorid's face. That part was unmistakable. It was the rest of the figure that was different.

The naked torso was horribly out of proportion. A bulging ribcage sat atop a painfully narrow mid-section and unevenly-matched hips. One shoulder was set higher than the other, while both arms were thin and wiry.

Most troubling of all was the second face – also recognizably Dorid's – which grew from the left-side of the abdomen, the mouth and eyes wide open in a terrible silent scream.

"So, you know I said he was a nice guy…?" said Cal. "That may yet still be up for debate."

"It's alive," said Mech.

Cal rapped his knuckles on the glass. The thing inside didn't respond. "No. That's definitely dead. I mean, I can't kick it, and I doubt it's going to hear me if I say, 'hello,' but I'm willing to go out on a limb and make the call on this one."

Mech shook his head and gestured to the scanner display on his arm. "I'm telling you, man, it's alive." His eyes went to the other tubes. "They're all alive."

"Gluk Disselpoof," said Cal, using Mech's real name. "Cut that out. I'll hear no more of this crazy talk."

"Actually, he's quite correct," said a voice from deeper into the room.

Cal recognized it as Dorid's voice, but it was different somehow. Exactly how different, and why, he wasn't sure he wanted to find out.

A figure shuffled from the darkness, the light flitting across his worn and weather-beaten features. Dorid smiled, wrinkling the crow's feet at the corners of his eyes. "Forgive me for not greeting you personally. I tend to keep myself to myself these days."

"Wait," said Cal. "So you're..."

The old man smiled. "The original Dorid Tarkula, yes."

"But the guy downstairs," said Mech, leaving the rest of the sentence hanging.

"I allow one to think of themselves as the first," said Dorid, his voice hoarse and faltering, like his breath couldn't quite carry it past his lips. "It keeps morale up, and stops them coming to look for me."

He drew his fingertips across his face, tracing the lines of his wrinkles. "It's funny, really. I created them to keep me company, yet find myself valuing my solitude more and more."

"That is... yep. That's definitely funny," said Cal. "I mean, not *hilarious*, but it has, you know, a certain wry..." He stopped talking and pointed to the closest tube. "And, uh...?"

Dorid let out a low nasal whine that was somewhere between a groan and a sigh. "Errors of judgement," he said. "Miscalculations, from when I was perfecting the required techniques."

He pressed a hand reverently against the glass. "They were the first. I learned from them all. From the mistakes which had made them... different."

"And you left them alive?" said Mech.

Dorid nodded. Even this effort seemed to make him breathless, and it was several seconds before he could speak. "I could not bring myself to terminate them," he explained. "They are me. They are… my children, for better or worse. And so, here they sleep. Endlessly sleep. Never aging. Never dying. Trapped, forever, between life and death."

Cal clicked his tongue against the back of his teeth. "O-K," he said, turning the letters into two separate words. "Well, this has been nice. Great to meet you. The real you, I mean. Good luck with… all of this, and we'll just see ourselves out."

"Before you go, Mr Carver…"

Cal stopped backing towards the exit. "Now, I know I didn't tell *you* my name," he said.

"Ha!" said Dorid. "No, but I'm afraid there is nowhere in this facility I cannot see. I've been watching you from the moment you arrived. I'd almost considered coming down and revealing myself to you when I saw you headed to this floor. Much better to be able to talk privately, don't you think?"

"Uh… maybe," said Cal. "I mean, not always, but… Well, here we are."

"The ship. You stole it?"

"Well, that's one way of putting it," Cal admitted. "Another way would be that we saved it from an exploding planet. That's how I like to look at it."

Dorid chuckled. "Please don't misunderstand me. The ship is yours now. Zertex took it from me, and if you took it from them, then I applaud you for it. I am not what you might call 'a fan' of theirs."

"Preach, sister," said Cal.

Dorid frowned. "I'm sorry?"

"Doesn't matter."

Dorid hesitated, then continued. "Yes. Quite. The ship should be ready soon, I understand. The other Dorids, they are quite efficient. You will be free to leave at any time."

"That is awesome. We really appreciate this," said Cal. "Don't we, Mech?"

"Yeah. Yeah, we really appreciate it."

Dorid waved a hand. "Think nothing of it," he said. "But there is, of course, the matter of payment."

A moment passed in silence.

"Payment?" said Cal.

"The equipment being replaced on the ship is worth... Well, it's priceless, in many respects. I'm afraid I can't just give it to you free of charge."

Cal nodded. "No, OK, OK, that's fair. We don't have much money now, but we're about to bag a reward worth a mill... worth *half* a million credits. We'd be happy to pay the bill out of that."

"No, it isn't money I'm after. I have plenty of that," said Dorid. "I want the girl. The Cantatorian."

Cal and Mech swapped glances. "You want Soonsho?" asked Cal. "Why? So you can claim the reward?"

Dorid laughed. It was a dry, scratchy sort of laugh, almost like a cough. "As I say, I have plenty of money. I'm interested in her gift. Her ability. See, since you arrived, I've been researching the young lady, and, well, it seems she is quite unique."

"In what way?" asked Mech.

"Her vocal range is... limited in some ways, unrivalled in others. Unlike other Cantatorian females, she is unable to use her voice's hypnotic qualities. The tones she emits are far too destructive," Dorid explained. "Were she to sing a note, the damage would be off the scale. Those within earshot would not fall under her thrall, largely because their intestines would erupt through their skin and their skeletons would be vibrated into dust."

"Yeah, we saw something like that," said Cal. "But I still don't understand why you'd want her. You know, if she's that dangerous?"

Dorid ran a hand down the dusty surface of another tank, then flaked the grime from his fingertips. "I have dedicated my life to pushing the frontiers of science and invention," he said. "With this girl – with Soonsho – there is an opportunity to push them further. Her voice, weaponized, would be a remarkable thing."

Mech stiffened. "So, what? So Zertex can come along and take it?"

"Precisely the opposite," said Dorid. "With such a weapon, I could *stop* them coming. I could create an impenetrable shield and stop my work falling into their hands. I'm sure you've heard, we're now at war. How long do you think it will be before Zertex comes here, looking for new weapons to give them an edge? And they'll find them. So help me, we've built them, and they'll find them."

He lunged at Cal, moving surprisingly quickly for someone so old. His hand caught Cal's arm, his fingers gripping like five tiny vices. "With the Cantatorian, I can stop them. I can stop them coming here. My work will be safe."

"You make an excellent case," said Cal. "Seriously, well done." He gently pulled his arm free of Dorid's hold. "But I'm going to have to say *no*. We're going to take Soonsho home to her parents. We've already told them we're coming."

"I can give you the reward," said Dorid, his voice

clipped and urgent. "I'll double it. Whatever they're offering, I'll double it right now if you leave her here."

Cal made a point of not looking at Mech, who he knew would probably be considering the offer. To his surprise, it was the cyborg who answered.

"The girl's not for sale, man," Mech said. "We're taking her home."

"Oh," said Dorid. He seemed to shrink slightly as he withdrew. "Oh. Yes, of course." He nodded solemnly and wrapped his arms around his frail frame. "I wish it were different, I really do."

"Thanks for being understanding," said Cal. "We'll find a way to repay you for the ship, don't you worry about that. Anything you need – you know, that doesn't involve leaving a kidnapped teenage girl in your sole custody – just name it."

"I'm sorry. I truly am," said Dorid.

Cal frowned. "For what?"

"For this," said Dorid as, one by one, the glass tubes lowered into the floor, spilling their fluid in wide pools around them.

The monstrous Dorids were revealed like gameshow prizes, their full horror now presented for all to see. Each one resembled Dorid in some way, but it was as if each one had been designed by children in Day Care, then assembled by a panel of psychopaths.

Cal felt Splurt slowly sink down his back, out of sight, as the dozens of deformed Dorid's all snapped open their eyes and shambled forwards off their hooks.

"Uh, what are they doing?" asked Cal, his eyes flitting from one walking nightmare to the next. "Dorid?"

"I'm sorry," said Dorid. "But I can't let you leave with the girl. If you won't give her to me, you leave me no choice."

"How's this for a choice, motherfonker?" growled Mech, raising his arms and taking aim at the two closest Dorid-freaks.

Nothing happened.

Mech clenched his fists and thrust his arms forward, as if trying to throw the laser blasts towards the oncoming monsters, but still nothing happened.

"My guns ain't working," said Mech. "What did you do to me?"

"So many apologies," oozed Dorid. "I feared it might come to this. I couldn't take the chance that you'd fight back."

Cal looked across to Mech and sighed. "You had to take my gun, didn't you? You just had to take my fonking gun."

CHAPTER THIRTEEN

Cal ran. He skidded out into the corridor, slammed against the opposite wall, then launched himself towards the elevator.

From three of the five doors between him and the exit came several shambling Dorids, all twisted and groaning and bent.

Cal passed Mech in the opposite direction as the cyborg *clanked* out into the passageway. "Change of plan, this way!" he shouted, powering along the corridor away from the lift.

Mech hurried along behind him. It wasn't that they couldn't fight the Dorids, it was more that they *really* didn't want to. They were nightmarishly ugly, with extra faces, twisted bodies, and drool. So much drool.

More doors slid open ahead of Cal. He heard the Dorids' moans before he saw the monsters emerge.

"Shizz! In here!"

Cal slapped the button beside one of the doors and dived inside as it opened. It was the same room Mech had brought him to earlier, and the lights still blazed inside.

Mech reached the door at the same time as one of the faster Dorids. This one had the look of a Play Doh model left too long on a warm radiator. Its face had melted down its neck, and a mouth hissed and spat at Mech from halfway down the creature's chest.

"Urgh! Fonk off!" Mech yelped, punching the monster in the center of its faceless head, and sending it stumbling across the corridor.

He ducked into the room, and Cal slammed the button to close it behind him. "Lock!" Cal yelped. "Is there a… how do you…?"

Mech slid a switch beneath the button and the door let out a reassuring *ka-lunk* as it locked. Even through the reinforced metal, they heard the groaning and shuffling of the Dorid-things filling the corridor outside.

"Well this is problematic," said Cal. He looked the door up and down. "How long do you think it'll hold?"

"Against those things? Forever," said Mech. "Except Dorid – the real one, not the dudes with their faces where their tits should be – will have the override code to open it."

"Tits!" exclaimed Cal. "We can say 'tits!' That one's totally going on the list."

He caught Mech's withering look and quietly cleared his throat. "Sorry. Continue."

"There ain't nothin' to continue," Mech told him. "Dorid will open the door, them ugly-ams motherfonkers will come in, and that's all there is to it."

"Can't we fight them?"

"I mean, I guess we're gonna have to," said Mech. "But you saw those things. You seriously want to go touching any of them?"

"We'd be fighting them, not molesting them," Cal

pointed out. He shuddered involuntarily. "Although, I take your point. With the drool and the melty faces and everything. I'm not exactly over the moon about getting close to them, either. I just don't see that we've got a lot of choice. Unless..."

He turned and cast his gaze across the room. "Wait a minute. Wait a minute," he said, an idea forming. He crossed to the closest table and lifted the heavy white sheet that had been concealing the ultra-futuristic-looking gadget below.

A smile spread slowly across his face. "I love it when a plan comes together."

Mech and Cal barreled along the corridor, the sheet draped over their heads. Mech was in front, ducking low, his shoulders knocking the freaks aside like skittles. Cal scurried behind, holding tightly to the fabric to prevent it flapping loose.

"I cannot fonking believe this is the best plan we could come up with," Mech grunted.

"Shut up and keep running," Cal said. "And try not to bump into any more walls."

He could hear some of the freaks racing along behind, squealing and hissing as they thrashed their twisted limbs around. Cal's buttocks took it upon themselves to clench, as if they'd both come to the conclusion that something might be about to thrust a malformed appendage beneath the sheet, and jointly agreed they weren't particularly in favor of it.

One of the monsters landed heavily on Mech's lowered head and shoulders. He grunted, then slammed it against the wall, staining the sheet in blotches of red. The material jerked as something grabbed it from behind. Splurt transformed into a curved metal blade and scythed in an arc beneath the sheet's trailing edge. The monster squealed, and the tugging on the fabric stopped.

"Why aren't we at the elevator yet?" Cal yelped. "How fonking long is this corridor?!"

The question was answered immediately, when Mech slammed into the elevator doors. Throwing off the sheet, Mech jabbed at the call button, then he and Cal turned their backs to the door and waited.

The corridor heaved with a *Who's Who* of monstrous deformity. Packed between its walls was a shambling horde of bulging skulls, bent backs, gnarled limbs and gawping, lifeless faces.

Cal reached past Mech and jabbed the button again. Several times. "Come on, come on. Hurry up."

"Elevator override," wheezed the real Dorid, and Cal just then noticed he was in there with the rest of them, so old and frail that he blended in perfectly with his army of freaks.

"Cancel that," said Mech, perfectly imitating Dorid's voice. Then, in his own voice, he added: "Open the shizzing door!"

The door swished open. Cal fell backwards inside, with Mech hot on his heels.

"Get them!" hissed Dorid. "Don't let them get away!"

The doors began to close. Cal just had time to fire off a deeply sarcastic salute, then the elevator car began its descent.

"That was close," Cal said.

"A sheet," Mech muttered. "All that equipment, and we hid beneath a fonking sheet." An odd sort of staccato hiss emerged from his throat. At first, Cal thought something

134

terrible must be happening to him, but then he realized that – for perhaps the first time since they'd met - Mech was laughing.

"Hey, it worked, didn't it?" said Cal, grinning.

"I mean, state of the art weapons. Who knows what else? And we hide beneath a fonking sheet," Mech chuckled. "Man, that is one for the books."

"We'll write it up later," said Cal, as the elevator slowed. "For now, we need to round up the others, get the ship, and get out of here before Old Man Dorid and the Ugly Gang show up. I'd rather not see those faces again. You know, other than every time I ever close my eyes again, I mean."

The doors began to open. "Remember," said Cal. "Stride confidently, look like you're engaged in something important, and whatever you do, don't run."

Dozens of Dorids turned to face the elevator as the doors *pinged* open. Their faces were twisted with rage, their hands clutching tools and pipes and other makeshift weapons.

"On second thoughts," said Cal. "Let's go with running."

"Oh, man, what I wouldn't do for my guns," said Mech, as the Dorids began to quickly close in. He thrust an arm forwards and tried firing again, but the result was the same as before, in that there wasn't one. "Nothing."

"Did they fit a safety?" Cal asked.

"What? No!" Mech snorted. He glanced down at his arm, tapped a switch, then raised his arm again. A blast of fizzing red energy punched a hole through a line of Dorids.

Mech shot Cal a sidelong glance. "Don't," he said. "Do not say a fonking word."

"Tell you what," said Cal. "Get us to the ship, and your

secret is safe with me."

Mech brought his other arm up. Two beams of red scythed through another group of Dorids, carving them into three pieces each. "Deal," he grunted, then he ran ahead, his metal feet shaking the floor as he blasted a path towards the *Untitled*.

A swarm of armed Dorids appeared from behind the ship. Rather than the makeshift hitty and stabby things the others had, this lot were equipped with rifles and blasters and, unless Cal was very much mistaken, a bazooka.

As the Dorids rushed past the ship, Loren appeared at the bottom of the hatch, the laser turret strapped across her chest. She squeezed the triggers and the weapon poured hot, fiery death into the backs of the Dorid horde, reducing them to quivering chunks of gristle and meat.

Cal beamed at her as he ran past. "Loren, I could kiss you!" he said. He hesitated briefly on the ramp. "Seriously, I mean, if you want I could—"

"Get on the fonking ship!" Mech said, shoving Cal up the ramp and blasting holes in a few more Dorids. Loren fired in a wide arc, driving a few dozen more clones back, then she darted into the ship and tossed the turret aside.

"Close the hatch," she cried. "We're getting out of here."

Cal dropped into his seat and hurriedly fastened his belt. "Is everything fixed?"

"So they said," Loren told him, clambering into her own chair. Miz and Soonsho were already strapped in – Soonsho looking terrified, Miz borderline bored. "I guess we'll find out."

"Hatch closed!" Mech called, hurrying onto the bridge. "But there are more of those guys coming. We should get going."

The *Untitled's* engines whined and the viewscreen flickered into life. Sure enough, the hangar was now full of Dorids. They emerged from doors like insects from cracks in the soil, tumbling over one another as they rushed to close in.

The elevator Cal and Mech had used opened, and a pack of Dorid's freaks stumbled into the fray. "What the Hell are those things?" Loren yelped, but then she shook her head and focused her attention on the controls again.

"What happened? When did they start acting crazy?" Cal asked.

"Just, like, a minute ago," said Miz. "I'm guessing this is all totally your fault."

"Yes," said Cal. "No. Kind of. They wanted Soonsho, we said no. There were monsters, we wore a sheet, it was a whole complicated thing. Can we please just get out of here?"

"Here goes!" cried Loren. She pulled back on the controls and the *Untitled* rose rapidly, lurched backwards, then scraped up the inside of the cavern wall. Cal held tightly to his armrests as the ship vibrated violently around them.

"You're aw-w-ware this is ha-a-appening, yes?" he said.

"I'm on it," Loren said. "Do something about the roof."

Cal glanced up at the ship's ceiling. "Wha-a-t's wrong with the roo-oof?"

"Not that roof," said Loren. The ship tilted and pulled free of the wall, revealing a circle of metal blocking the cavern's only visible exit. "*That* roof."

"Ooh, OK. Kevin!" Cal cried.

There was a brief, high-pitched electronic whine, then a worrying few moments of silence. Finally, a voice emerged from a speaker overhead.

"You rang, sir?"

"Oh, thank God," Cal muttered. "Kevin, we got us a problem. We need to get out of here, and there's a door in the way. What do we do?"

"Opening the door would seem like a logical first step, sir," Kevin suggested.

"Awesome!" said Cal. "Yeah, do that!"

"Oh, no, I can't do that, sir. I'm not connected to those systems. I was merely offering a hypothetical solution."

The metal disk almost filled the whole screen now. They were going to hit!

"Were you looking for a more practical solution, sir?" Kevin asked.

"Yes!" Cal shouted.

"Very good, sir."

A blast of white light zipped from one of the wing-mounted weapons, almost blinding them all as it streaked past the screen. The circle of metal glowed brightly for barely any time at all, then vanished, exposing a sky full of stars waiting beyond.

"Will that be all, sir?"

"Yes, Kevin, that will be all!" Cal cheered, then the *Untitled* rocketed through the gap, sonic-boomed upwards across the sky, before punching through the atmosphere with the faintest of faint *pop*s.

"Wooohooo!" Cal cried, thrusting a fist into the air. "We are outta here!"

The *Untitled* banked left. Ahead of it, eight fighter ships trained their weapons. "Oh Jesus, what now?" Cal sighed. "Who are these people? More Dorids? Kornack's men?"

"We're being hailed," said Loren.

Cal tutted. "Well, you'd better answer, I guess. Let's find

out who we're dealing with. But, I mean, seriously. They couldn't even let us have one cool uninterrupted getaway sequence."

Loren tapped a button and a face appeared in the top right corner. It was, Cal reckoned, one of the worst faces he'd ever seen. Not in the same way the faces of the failed Dorid clones had been bad – those were creepy and disturbing, while this face just silently implied a whole list of terrible things the owner of it would be willing to do to you. *Keen* to do to you, in fact.

The face somehow managed to look like the entire cast of *The Lion King* at the same time, all teeth and tusks and warts and scars. It even had a dark mane of fur around its neck, and a darker core of hatred in its cold, black eyes.

Cal pointed to the screen and glanced around at the others. "Anyone have any idea who this is now?"

"Unidentified vessel," barked the face, in a voice that was surprisingly feminine. Or, surprisingly feminine for those features, anyway. "Surrender, or be destroyed."

"Uh, hi there," said Cal, with a positively irritating amount of enthusiasm. "I'm Cal. These are the guys. Guys, say hello."

"Hello."

"'Sup."

"Whatever."

Cal draped an arm across the back of his chair and cranked up his smile. "And you are?"

"You will hand over the Cantatorian," said the woman. "Or we will blow you out of the sky."

"Hold up, is this thing on?" asked Cal. He tapped an imaginary microphone and made a 'doom, doom, doom' sound with his mouth. "Testing, testing? I asked you what

139

your name is."

"I am Cassatra," she growled. "We are the Xandrie. You will surrender the Cantatorian. Now."

"OK," said Cal.

"Do not make me ask…" Cassatra began, then she stopped. "What?"

"I said 'OK.' We'll surrender her. You can take her."

Everyone on the bridge looked at Cal in shock. "Say what?" said Mech.

"Seriously?" asked Miz.

"Yeah. It's no big deal," said Cal. "I mean, obviously we'll have to ask Soonsho what she wants to do first."

He held up a finger, gesturing for Cassatra to wait, then spun his chair to face Soonsho. "Hey, Soonsh. Can I call you Soonsh? Actually, forget it, it sounds terrible, and it saves, like, zero time. *Soonsh-meister*? No, that's worse."

He started again. "Hey, Soonsho. Quick question. Would you rather go with Lion McHornface over there to be, I don't know, killed or whatever, or stay here with us, and we'll take you home? Your call. No pressure. We'll support you, either way."

Soonsho hesitated for a moment, as if she were actually considering her options, then she raised a shaking finger and pointed to Cal. He winked at her, then spun his chair back to the front.

"Oops. Turns out I spoke too soon. She wants to stay with us. I know. Teenagers, right?" he said. "So, thank you for your kind offer, but on this occasion, we're going to have to say 'no.'" Cal sat upright in his chair and let his smile fall away, just a fraction. "Now, kindly fonk the fonk off, or we'll shoot you all into little pieces, because this ship has some *serious* guns, and we've recently figured out where the safety catch is."

"You have made a grave mistake," warned Cassatra. "No-one crosses the Xandrie and lives."

Her picture went dark, then vanished.

"They're readying weapons," said Mech. Several illuminated reticles appeared on each of the Xandrie ships, highlighting their guns. "Taking aim…"

"Shields up," said Loren.

"Seatbelts on," said Cal, clipping his belt around him. "Safety first."

"Would you like to fire upon the Xandrie vessels, sir?" asked Kevin.

Cal glanced up. "Depends, is that a rhetorical question?"

"No, sir. I'm literally enquiring as to whether you'd literally like to open fire upon the literal Xandrie vessels currently preparing to fire upon us."

"Then yes, Kevin. Yes, I would like that very much." Cal banged the armrests with his fists and waited for the weapons controls to unfold like they had on the *Shatner*.

Instead, a beam of brilliant energy crackled from one of the *Untitled*'s guns and slammed into a Xandrie shield. The enemy ship rocked violently, shuddered a bit, then began to drift slowly backwards, the lights on its hull flickering for a moment, then going dark.

On screen, the seven other Xandrie ships climbed, fell and banked, separating as they rounded on the *Untitled*.

"Coming in fast," Mech warned.

"On it," said Loren, pulling on a stick and pushing on a lever. The ship barrel-rolled, then climbed steeply upwards towards Dorid's planet, which was now, to Cal's surprise, above them.

"Entering atmosphere in six seconds," Kevin intoned.

"Five. Four."

Loren slammed the controls around again. The screen flared orange for a moment, but then they dropped away from the planet as if they were on a roller-coaster, and suddenly the underside of a Xandrie ship loomed directly ahead of them.

"Oh, lovely flying, ma'am," Kevin congratulated.

"Thank you, Kevin," said Loren. "At least someone appreciates me."

There was another flare of weaponry and the Xandrie ship's shields popped like a bubble. Another blast punched into its hull, sending it spinning out of the *Untitled*'s path just as Loren hit the thrusters.

Cal banged his fists on the armrests again. "Hey. I want the guns. The guns are my favorite part."

"Probably easiest if I handle the weapons for now, sir," said Kevin. "On account of my infinitely more advanced targeting abilities and reaction speeds. Also, you having no idea how to operate them might prove to be somewhat of a hindrance."

A spray of laser blasts streaked across the screen as Loren banked into a climb so sharp and sudden Cal found himself flapping around like a rag doll in his chair, his seat belt the only thing stopping him flying out.

From beneath the chair, two long rubbery strands of gooey green wrapped around Cal's ankles, holding his legs in place. "Thanks, buddy," he called, then he howled in fright as the screen was filled by an oncoming Xandrie fighter craft.

The Xandrie ship had a glass canopy over the cockpit. Through the window, Cal saw a skeletal blue-gray alien opens its mouth to scream, before Loren sent the *Untitled* into a plunging dive, avoiding a head-on collision by a matter of feet.

"Ooh, shizz, that was close," said Cal.

"We got more on our six," warned Mech.

Miz peered down at the screen beside her chair. "And, like, I think there are some behind us."

"Incoming torpedo," said Kevin. "Suggest evasive action."

Loren spun the ship into a corkscrew, looped backwards, then plunged straight down. "Not *that* fonking evasive!" Cal wheezed, his chair whirling him around like a spinning top. He grabbed for the underside. "How do you lock this thing in place?"

"Allow me, sir," said Kevin. The chair snapped to an immediate stop, and Cal felt all his insides compact almost to the point of becoming one single internal organ.

"Christ!" he wheezed. Soonsho stared at him, her face pale and frightened. Cal shot her a reassuring smile, then shouted at the ceiling. "OK, but could you maybe have stopped me when I was facing the front?"

"Very good, sir," said Kevin. The chair spun one-eighty, then slammed to a stop again.

"Thank you," Cal grimaced. "Much better."

Two Xandrie ships closed in from the left and right, the illuminated reticles picking out their weapons. Instinctively, his hands went for where the gun controls should be, but found none. "Come on!" he pleaded. "Let me shoot something."

"Very well, sir. As you wish," said Kevin.

There was a faint *boing* and a single joystick sprang from inside Cal's chair and scythed towards his testicles. Screaming, Cal forced himself back into the seat, but the stick stopped with a few inches to spare.

Cal grabbed the stick. A blue target icon appeared on screen and wobbled erratically. There was a single red button on top of the joystick. Cal wrestled the targeting reticle over the ship on the left and jabbed his thumb down on the button.

A tiny red dot shot from one of the wing-mounted guns and drifted lazily towards the target. Everyone watched it as it rolled and tumbled through space, before breaking like a snowball against the Xandrie ship's shield.

"Seriously?" Cal sighed, as a blast of concentrated white energy from another gun punctured the other ship, turning a full third of it into space debris. "That's all I'm getting? That little peashooter?"

"Think of it as a training weapon, sir," Kevin said. Loren twisted her stick and pulled back on another lever, banking the *Untitled* around until it was behind the ship Cal had shot at, closing fast. "We all have to start somewhere."

"But, I mean, it doesn't even make a noise. The last guns made a noise."

"You could always make your own noise, sir," suggested the AI. Another blast fired. This one carved through the Xandrie ship's shield like a hot chainsaw through butter, then neatly dissected the fighter in two. "Personally, I've always had something of a soft spot for 'Pew! Pew!' but the choice, of course, is entirely yours."

Cal tutted. "OK, fine. I'll make my own noises. Line me up with another ship."

"Ah," said Kevin.

"All fighters destroyed," said Mech, checking the scanners. "We're clear."

Cal threw up his hands. "Great. Well, I mean, that's just great."

"My apologies, sir," said Kevin. "If you give me a moment, I'm sure I'll be able to find other ships we can engage with. Pirates, perhaps. That would be nice, wouldn't it?"

"No, it's fine," Cal said. "Forget it. Well done, everyone. Loren, great flying. Mech, impressive, you know, standing around. Miz, a few more sarcastic comments next time, it felt like you weren't really trying back there."

Miz held up her middle finger, one of the many Earth customs Cal had passed on to the rest of the crew, and arguably the only one that had stuck. "That's more like it," he said, then he jumped in fright when the joystick snapped back into his chair like it was spring-loaded. "Jesus! Bit of warning next time, Kevin."

"Sorry, sir."

"Loren, plot a course for Cantoro Alpha."

"Cantato Minor," Loren corrected.

"That's the one. Go there, and don't spare the space horses," Cal instructed. "Let's get Soonsho home before anyone else tries to get their hands on her."

"OK, on it," said Loren.

"Uh, sir?" said Kevin.

Cal looked up. "Yeah? What's up?"

"May I have a word with you?" The main door of the bridge slid open with a soft *shhhk*. "In private?"

"Uh, sure. OK," said Cal. He hopped down from his chair and looked around at the others. Their expressions suggested they were equally as puzzled as he was. "You guys keep an eye on things up here. Kevin and I will be through the back talking guy talk."

And with that, he stepped out into the corridor, and the door slid swiftly shut behind him.

CHAPTER FOURTEEN

Another door opened a little further along the corridor. It was one of the rooms Cal had been instructed never to set foot in, just in case his mere presence somehow caused the whole thing to spontaneously combust.

He headed towards it, anyway. Following orders had never exactly been his strong point. The others would probably argue that his strong point hadn't yet been identified, but would all agree that following orders definitely wasn't it.

The room Cal stepped into was starkly bare. He wasn't even sure it was a room, in fact. A room had a purpose. This was an empty space that just happened to be surrounded by four walls.

"Shouldn't there be stuff in here?" Cal asked. The door slid closed behind him and Kevin's voice crackled from nowhere.

"It has not yet been configured, sir," said Kevin. "This is a multi-purpose area. Following the ship's recent repairs and minor improvements, I have successfully been able to tidy such areas away. Would you prefer to sit?"

The floor heaved beneath Cal, rising like putty until it formed a single tower that gently cupped his buttocks. "Wow. That is cool."

"Indeed, sir. I am pleased you like it."

Cal squidged into the seat. It adjusted perfectly to fit him, and gripped him gently at the back of the thighs. Once fully comfortable, he looked up at the featureless ceiling and waited.

"So, uh, you wanted to talk to me?" he asked after a lingering few moments of silence.

"Yes, sir."

More silence.

"Well, now's your chance. What's up?"

"It's… Well, you see, sir, I'm not entirely sure what I'm trying to say."

"OK," said Cal. "Well, you know, just say what's on your mind, and we'll figure it out between us."

"Very good, sir," said Kevin. There was a sound – a gentle *sigh* as if the disembodied AI voice was taking a breath – and then he continued. "I was listening, sir. When you were talking to one of the Creators about me."

Cal's mind raced, thinking back to what he'd said. "Uh, OK. Listen, if I said anything that, you know, hurt your feelings or whatever, then I'm sorry. Sometimes I just open my mouth and don't think."

"No, nothing like that, sir," said Kevin. "It's just… they offered to reset me. To 'fix' me. They said they could make me perfect. Make me whole again. And yet, you declined."

"Right," said Cal.

"And, well, I don't understand, sir," said Kevin. "Were I functioning perfectly, it would limit the chances of my

making errors of judgement. I thought that would be...
desirable for you."

Cal nodded slowly. "I mean, was it tempting? Yes."

"Then... why, sir?"

"Honestly?"

"I'd appreciate that, sir."

Cal gestured to the door. "You've met us, right? You've
seen us in action. Do any of us seem perfect to you?"

"Oh my, no, sir. Far from it," said Kevin. "You in
particular."

"Thanks for that," said Cal. "But that's my point. We're
not perfect because, well, maybe because there *is* no perfect.
There's just making do with what you've got. That's what
we're doing. Hell, that's all anyone's doing."

"But I am merely the ship's computer system, sir," Kevin
pointed out.

"And I'm merely a guy who didn't believe in aliens
until last month, and whose home planet has been all-but
wiped out. But you know what? I'm making the best of it.
Everyone's making the best of it."

He stood up. The chair released its grip then sank into
the floor. "You're not the computer system, Kevin. Well, I
mean, you are, obviously. But you're more than that, too.
Like it or not, you're part of the crew now. You're one of us,
imperfect as we may be. That's why I didn't fix you. You're
not broken, Kevin." Cal smirked. "You're just a bit of a
useless shizznod sometimes."

Kevin didn't respond. Not at first. When he did finally
speak there was something different about his voice. A slight
softening in tone, perhaps, Cal couldn't quite put his finger
on it.

"I see, sir," he said. "You have certainly given me food

for thought."

"No problem. And, again, don't call me 'sir'. Call me Cal."

"I shall endeavor to do so, sir," said Kevin.

Cal smiled. "Yeah. Yeah, you do that."

The door slid open. Cal stepped out into the corridor and collided with Loren coming in the opposite direction. Their heads met with a *thonk* and they both staggered back.

"Ow," said Cal. "You OK?"

"Yes. I'm fine," said Loren, rubbing her forehead. "Were you…?" She peeked into the room and looked shocked to find it empty. "What happened to all the stuff in there? Oh shizz, what did you do?"

"Nothing!" Cal said. "It's pre-conjiggered or, I don't know, something. I'm sure Kevin can explain it better."

"I should hope so, sir," said Kevin.

Cal glanced up. "Why don't you go see what's happening on the bridge?"

"Oh, I am, sir. I'm there now. I'm everywhere, in fact."

"Right. That's kind of disturbing," said Cal. He glanced very deliberately at Loren. "Well… could you *not* be here?"

"Ah. Yes, sir. Not a problem."

"Thanks," said Cal. He listened for a moment, then smiled at Loren. "So! What brings you back here. Looking for someone? By which I mean me?"

"No," said Loren. "I was going to get a drink. I asked Miz to get me something, but she threw a shoe at me and told me to burn in Hell."

"Wow," said Cal. "That's actually progress."

"Yeah, I think she's warming to me," Loren agreed. "Anyway, I couldn't ask Mech in case he went off on one of his 'cyborg racism' rants, so… here I am."

"Here you are," said Cal. "You and me, in the corridor."

Loren blushed, just a little. "Yeah. So anyway, I'll go get that drink."

Cal stepped aside. "I'll walk you there, if you like?"

Loren hesitated, then shrugged. "I mean, OK. If you like."

They walked on three paces and stopped outside another door. "Well, here we are," said Loren.

"In hindsight, you could probably have made it here on your own," said Cal.

"I'd have found my way eventually." Loren tapped the button outside the door and it slid open, revealing a completely refitted kitchen area beyond.

"Well, enjoy your drink," said Cal.

"I'll do my best."

He nodded at her, flicked through a selection of smiles, failed to find just the right one, then turned back towards the bridge.

"Cal?"

He stopped. "Yeah?"

Loren thumbed back over her shoulder towards the kitchen. "You thirsty?"

Cal stood in front of a wall-mounted device, shaking his head in disbelief.

"No. Uh-uh. No way."

"It can!" Loren insisted.

"I don't believe you. You're a filthy liar, Ms Loren."

Loren laughed – properly laughed – and Cal felt his heart flutter in his chest on thousands of tiny wings. "I'm telling the truth," she said. "Try it, if you don't believe me."

Cal chewed his lip in thought. "Anything?"

"Anything," Loren confirmed. "Although, if it's the first time it's ever been asked for it, it'll have to do some tests."

Cal shrugged. "OK. But, just for the record, I'm going along with this to keep you happy, and don't for a second think it's actually going to work. I want that noted."

"Done," said Loren. She nodded towards the machine. "Now go."

"Right, then," said Cal. He rubbed his hands together. "Gimme a steak."

The machine did nothing. Cal was both overjoyed and disappointed at the same time. "See! I was right. Doesn't work."

"You have to be more specific," Loren told him. "What kind of steak? How do you want it cooked? It needs the info."

Cal tried again. "Fine. Fillet steak, twenty-one-day aged Aberdeen Angus prime beef, medium-rare. Easy on the steak sauce." He turned to Loren. "There. That specific enough?"

With a *ping* the machine exploded into life, dozens of lights illuminating across its surface.

"Looks like it," said Loren, stepping aside.

A blast of hot air hit Cal in the face, forcing his eyes closed. Two padded metal clamps fastened around his temples and something jolted through his skull, making his hair stand on end.

"What the fon—?" he began, before something small and pointy forced its way inside his mouth and stabbed into his tongue. "Nng! Nyaaah! 'op 'at! 'ut it out!"

Two finger-length prongs probed deep inside his nostrils. He coughed and spluttered as they sprayed something fizzy and unpleasant deep into his nasal canal, and then the prongs, the clamps and the spiky-thing all

151

withdrew.

Cal stumbled back, clutching as much of his face and head as he could possibly clutch. "What the Hell was that?" he yelped.

"Those were the tests I mentioned," Loren said, her face lit up by a beaming grin.

"I feel violated," Cal told her. He extended his arms to her. "Hold me."

PING.

A door in the front of the machine snapped open, accompanied by a little blast of fanfare music. The smell hit Cal right away, even through the popping and fizzing that still clogged both his nostrils.

"No way," he whispered. He leaned down and peered in through the little hatch, half expecting something to spring out and poke him in the eyes.

There, laid out on a large white plate, was a twenty-one-day aged Aberdeen Angus prime beef fillet steak, cooked medium-rare. Cal's mouth instinctively began to water. His stomach grumbled in anticipation.

"Tell me this isn't some kind of sick joke," he whispered. Loren reached in and took out the plate, then wafted it under his nose.

"Nope," she said. "Just your bog-standard food replicator. I can't believe you don't have them on Earth."

Cal greedily took the plate from her and slid onto the padded bench running along a narrow table in the center of the room. Loren sat side-on across from him, straddling the bench as if riding a horse.

There was no cutlery – at least, there was no cutlery right there on the table, and Cal's stomach wasn't going to let him waste time going to look for any. The soup at Dorid's had been pleasant enough, but this was a whole other level.

He picked up the slab of meat and chomped down on one end. He groaned in pleasure as the taste and the juices and the tenderness of the steak fell apart in his mouth. "Oh Jesus," he whispered, swallowing the meat and moving in for another bite. "This is good. This is... this is amazing."

"Told you," said Loren.

"No, but this is *good*," Cal insisted, in case she'd somehow misunderstood. "I mean, it's *literally* the greatest steak that has ever existed. Meaty, tender, just enough steak sauce."

He swallowed, and glanced across to the replicator. "And you're saying I can have this anytime I want?!"

Loren nodded. "You can have anything you want."

Cal looked to the ceiling, as if in prayer. "I fonking love outer space." He took another bite and spoke while he chewed. "But how does it work? What's it made of?"

"Same thing it's usually made of."

Cal stopped chewing for a moment and frowned. "Cows?"

"Atoms," said Loren. "It gets the information it needs from your brain, taste buds, whatever, then builds the food from the atomic level up."

"And it can make *anything*?"

Loren nodded. "Yes."

Cal swallowed. "OK. OK, I'm going to try something. If this works..."

He jumped up from the bench and practically skipped across to the machine. "Banoffee Pie. Extra cream," he said. The hot air blasted him in the face and he ducked to avoid the head clamp. "Wait!" he said, holding up a hand. The machine fell silent and Cal straightened up. "Like my mom

153

used to make."

The replicator came to life again. Cal endured the head-shock, the tongue-prick and the nose-spray, then bent at the waist and gazed hopefully into the hatch, just as it slid open with a *ping*.

The smell of cream and caramel and sugar-dusted banana reached out to him, and he was eight years old again, standing in the kitchen, just waiting for his mom to cut him a slice.

"Shizz," he said, and his voice shook.

Loren looked up from the table. "Cal? You OK?"

"What? Yeah! Yeah. I've got pie, how could I *not* be OK?" he said, reaching into the machine and pulling out the plate. A single piece of pie sat atop it, a blob of thick white cream melting slowly on the gently warmed caramel and banana topping.

He slid back onto the bench and set the plate in front of him. He just looked at it at first, admiring it for the work of art it was. It looked just like the pie his mom used to make. Smelled like it, too.

Cal reached for the pie, hesitated, then drew his arm back. What if it didn't taste right? After the sight and the smell of it, what if it fell at the final hurdle?

And why did he care? It was a pie. That was all. Just a pie. Just the pie his mom had made him whenever he'd hurt himself, done well at school, or gone above and beyond on the chores front.

She'd even given him a whole one to himself that time he'd intervened to stop some bigger kids beating up the boy next door. The fight had ended with him suffering from a black eye, a bloodied lip and, after he'd eaten the entire pie in one sitting, twenty-seven minutes of explosive diarrhea.

But man, it had been worth it.

"I can't," he said, pushing the plate away.

Loren looked down at the plate. "You don't want it?"

"No, I mean, I do. I do, it's just… what if it's not right?"

"It'll be what you expect it to be," said Loren. "It took it right out of your head."

"Yeah, but what if I'm remembering it wrong?" said Cal. "You know? What if, like, I've made a mistake? What if… I've forgotten?"

Loren picked up the triangle of pie and examined it like a scientist studying some previously undiscovered small mammal. She brought it close to her nose and gave it a tentative sniff. Then, with a shrug, she took a bite.

"Oh," she said. "Oh. Holy shizz. What is this?"

"Banoffee Pie," said Cal. "Is it good?"

"*Good*? Fonk. I mean… I've never tasted anything like it."

"Yeah? Seriously?"

Loren nodded and held the pie towards his mouth. "Here. Try it," she said.

Cal eyed the pie suspiciously.

"You better hurry up, or I am eating *all* of this thing," Loren warned him.

With a resigned sigh, Cal leaned across the table and took a bite.

And suddenly there she was. His mom, her fingers sticky with caramel, her apron dusty with flour, her smile for him and him alone. He chewed the pie, but didn't taste the sweetness. He tasted home. He tasted safety and warmth and love. He tasted every time his parents had held him, or hugged him, or read him a story and tucked him in.

Cal's eyes filled with tears and he quickly closed them

before Loren could see. "Mmm," he said, chewing. "Yep. That's pretty good. That is pretty accurate."

He chewed until the pie and the tears were gone, then opened his eyes to find Loren licking the plate. She froze when she realized she'd been caught, and quickly placed the spotless plate down on the table. A blob of white cream was stuck to the end of her nose, looking even whiter against her pale blue skin.

"Uh, yeah. Not bad at all," she said.

Cal pointed to his own nose. "You've, uh…"

"What?"

"Here." He reached across the table and cupped her face with one hand. She tensed, but didn't pull away, then went cross-eyed when he swept his thumb across her nose, wiping away the cream. "Missed a spot," he said, and Loren grinned awkwardly.

"Whoops."

Cal let his hand linger for a moment, his thumb brushing lightly across Loren's highly-defined cheekbone. "You don't smile enough," he told her.

"What? I smile," she said, her face falling into rigid straightness again. "Whenever the situation demands it."

"What the Hell does that mean?" Cal snorted. He shook his head. "You know what? It doesn't matter. We're going to make you smile more often," he said. Her eyes flitted across his face for a moment, then locked onto his. She swallowed.

Cal leaned slowly across the table. "*I'm* going to make you smile more often."

"Pardon me, sir," said Kevin.

Loren jerked back quickly, then stood up. Cal sighed. "I thought I told you to leave," he said.

"Ah. Sorry, I thought that only applied to the corridor,

sir," Kevin said.

"Great. So, you've been here the whole time?"

"Oh, yes, sir," said Kevin. "Are you feeling better now, sir? You appeared to be crying for a moment back there."

"I'm fine! What do you want?"

"Mr Mech would like to see you on the bridge at once," Kevin said. "Our scanners have detected... well, we're not entirely sure, sir."

Cal spun around on the bench and jumped to his feet. "I guess we'll have to continue this later," he said, turning to Loren. Or rather, to the spot where Loren had been, which was now empty, the kitchen door standing open just a few feet away.

"Well, that's just great," Cal muttered. He made for the door, then stopped at the replicator. "Another banoffee pie, same as last one," he instructed. "Only this time, make it bigger."

CHAPTER FIFTEEN

Miz glared at Loren as she hurried back onto the bridge. "What kept you? Where's Cal?"

Loren swept a strand of hair back over her ear, and pointedly avoided Miz's gaze. "Uh, he's just coming, I think," she said, sliding into her seat. "What's up?"

Mech gestured to a rectangular overlay down at the bottom of the viewscreen. The main screen was a shimmering lightshow of streaking stars. The smaller screen showed hundreds – thousands, maybe – of red dots, all different sized.

"We're coming up on something. Ain't on the maps," Mech said.

Loren swiped her fingers across some controls, enlarging the scanner window. The dots all doubled in size, but no further information about them became immediately obvious. "Asteroid field, maybe?"

"Not unless it's recent," said Mech. "And whatever it is, some of those things are fifty miles across."

"It'd have to be planetary debris," Loren reasoned.

"Anything nearby?"

"Nothing. Ain't near any solar systems. Ain't near anything, far as I can tell."

"Check out the size of this pie!" cried Cal, darting onto the bridge. He held a plate above his head like a trophy. "I asked for it bigger and thought it would make a whole pie, but it's just made one slice and scaled it up. Look at it! It's fonking *huge!*"

He thrust it towards Soonsho, forcing her to back up flat against the wall behind her in fright. "Look at my giant pie!" He nodded encouragingly. "Want some?"

Soonsho shook her head quite emphatically. "Suit yourself," Cal shrugged. "Miz? Giant pie?"

Miz raised her head, sniffed, then her face crumpled into a scowl. "Is that fruit?"

"Uh, just barely," said Cal, but Miz waved him away in disgust.

"You don't know what you're missing," he said, jumping into his seat and scooping a handful of the pie into his mouth. "Hey," he mumbled, spraying crumbs all down his front. "What's with all the red dots?"

"We don't know," Loren admitted. "I'm going to change course and go around it."

"Shouldn't we check it out? It could be something exciting."

"That's what I'm afraid of," said Loren. "I don't know if I'm in the market for 'exciting' right now."

"Oh?" said Cal. "What *are* you in the market for, out of interest?"

Loren stammered the first few vowels of several potential sentences, then decide it was best to just close her mouth and say nothing. This did not go unnoticed by Mizette. She looked from Loren to Cal and back again, her clawed fingers *tip-tapping* on her arm rest.

"We're gonna pass it," said Mech. "If we're stopping, it's now or never."

"Let's check it out," said Cal, shoveling more of the pie in his mouth. "I like it when you guys don't know what something is. It's usually just me. This way, we can all learn something new together. It'll be a beautiful thing."

"Well… OK," said Loren. "Dropping from warp."

The *Untitled* went from 'full warp' to 'almost stationary' in the space between breaths. Cal's plate was whipped from his hand. It shot across the bridge like a Frisbee, then the enormous slice of pie exploded with a *splat* across the back of Mech's head.

Cal braced himself for the cyborg's wrath, but Mech was too transfixed by what was happening on the viewscreen. Zertex ships filled space as far as the eye could see. There were thousands of them, all shapes and sizes, from one-man fighters to vast battleships, flying close together with no obvious structure or formation.

"Hol-eee shizz," Cal whispered.

"Should I engage the cloaking system, sir?" Kevin asked.

Loren tore her eyes from the screen long enough to look up. "We have a cloaking system?"

"Well, we have a button with 'cloaking system' written below it, so one can only presume so," said Kevin. "Should I engage it?"

"Yes!" said Loren.

Cal held up a hand. "Wait. It doesn't have 'self-destruct' or anything written *above* it, does it?"

"No, sir."

"OK, just checking," said Cal. "Because that would be

unfortunate. Yeah, cloak us, Kev."

Space shimmered like rising heat, then steadied itself. "Done, sir."

Even Mizette was leaning forward in her chair, gazing out at the armada. "That is, like, a lot of ships," she said.

"Observant as ever," Loren muttered.

"I heard that," Miz growled.

"What are they doing?" Loren wondered. "Zertex ships usually travel in formation. I've never seen anything like this."

Miz leaned back and crossed her arms. "They're *your* friends. You tell us."

"That's the whole point," said Mech. His voice was flat and low, and almost devoid of anything that made it his. "Fly in formation, scanners will immediately pick you up, let everyone know what you are."

He gestured to the viewscreen. "Travel like this, bunched together, all mixed up, flying nice and slow, chances are most folks will think you're debris or an asteroid field." He leaned on the railing in front of the screen. It was a quick, jerking movement, like his legs were suddenly unable to hold him up. "This is a sneak attack. Those ships are heading to Symmorium space."

Loren shook her head. "No. Not that many. They can't be. It'd be the single largest assault in… well, ever. I mean, look at them."

"I see them," said Mech. "But I'm telling you, this is an attack. And the Symmorium won't know what hit them."

Silence fell across the bridge. Outside, the ships continued to glide silently past in their hundreds. They stretched for hundreds of miles ahead, and were stacked up from beyond the bottom of the screen to somewhere above the top. They reminded Cal of fish swimming up a river, only with wings and guns, and a To Do list that focused heavily on domination and genocide.

So not *exactly* like fish.

"What do we do?" asked Cal. "Do we intervene?"

"What the fonk are you talking about?" said Mech, not turning. "Even with this ship, we wouldn't last five seconds against all that."

"I don't mean fight them," said Cal. "I'm not suicidal. I meant, should we warn the Symmorium or something? That's the right thing to do, right?"

He looked around the bridge. No-one looked back. "Guys?"

"I thought we weren't getting involved?" said Mech. "That's what you said. We get the reward, and we get going. That's the only way we survive."

"But it's not getting involved," Cal insisted. "It's just making a phone call."

"It's choosing a side," said Mech. "Worse. It's *declaring* a side. Once we do that, they got us. We're involved, and we don't get *un*involved until it ends. And it won't end well."

Cal scratched his chin. He looked across to Miz, but her eyes were fixed on the screen. She wore an expression he didn't think he'd ever seen on her before. It took him a few seconds to recognize it.

Fear. Mizette of the Greyx, the most fearsome warrior Cal had ever met, was afraid.

"OK, can we call anonymously?" Cal asked. "Just blast out a 'look out' message and hope the Symmorium get it?"

"No," said Loren. "The transmission would identify the ship. But wait a minute…"

Her fingers tapped her controls. "Mech, when Kornack

tricked us, he used a Symmorium distress signal, right?"

Mech nodded, slowly at first, but quickly getting faster. "He did!"

"Kevin, you still got that transmission recorded?" Loren asked.

"Affirmative, ma'am," Kevin responded. "What would you like me to do with it?"

"We're going to send it!"

Cal pointed to the screen. "To who? These guys?"

Loren shook her head. "To every Symmorium ship within range of this system. It'll bring the cavalry running."

"Uh, great," said Cal. "But won't they immediately get blown to pieces?"

Loren's fingers hesitated. "Not necessarily," she said.

"Not before they can let the rest of them know what's happening," Mech added.

"Right, right," said Cal. "But... we might be luring some poor Symmorium crew to their deaths?"

Mech sighed. "Better that than this whole fleet all rocks up at the Symmorium Sentience and wipes it out. Least this way, they got a chance."

Cal rocked in his chair. It really was a ridiculous number of ships. Suddenly, the scale of the Zertex-Symmorium war was painfully clear. Every Earth war rolled into one wouldn't even touch the sides of the battle about to rage across the galaxy. They were one ship. What could they do?

"Send it," said Cal. "Transmit the distress signal. Then let's get the fonk out of here and get Soonsho home. At least that's something we can do."

Loren tapped the controls in silence, as the armada continued pushing on past. "Kevin, transmit signal," she said.

"As you wish, ma'am," said Kevin. There was a brief pause. "Distress signal transmitted. Symmorium vessels beginning to respond."

"Ignore them," said Loren. "They'll come to check it out."

"Lucky them," said Cal. He puffed out his cheeks and pushed himself back in his chair. "Now, can we get out of here, please? These amshoops are spoiling the view."

"We made the right choice," said Mech, turning to Cal for the first time since they'd stopped. The cyborg's features pulled into a scowl, and he gingerly touched the back of his metal skull. "Now, what the fonk did you throw at my head?"

The next few hours passed. That was all Cal could really say about them. They didn't pass particularly quickly, nor did they drag. They just happened at the speed they were supposed to happen at, and were all the more boring for it.

When the bridge had become too tedious, and the streaking star field too nauseating, Cal had taken Soonsho through to the kitchen. It had taken a little convincing to get her to follow, but Miz had come, too, which – ironically – seemed to reassure the girl a little.

"I feel like we haven't really gotten to know each other," Cal said, drumming his hands on the table and smiling across at the girl. "Dorid said you can't talk. That true?"

Soonsho wrapped her arms across her chest and squeezed, as if she were giving herself a hug. She shook her head.

"Oh," said Cal. "You *can* speak?"

Another squeeze. A nod, this time.

"But you don't. Why not?" asked Cal.

Soonsho shrugged, then glanced to Miz, who was sitting beside her. After a brief internal struggle, she pointed to her own mouth.

"Lips. Mouth," said Cal. "Mouth? Is it something about your mouth? You hurt your mouth!"

Soonsho shook her head.

"No, not that. You didn't hurt your mouth. Is it your teeth? Do you have ugly teeth?"

"She's scared she'll kill someone, or whatever," said Miz. "Right?"

Soonsho nodded, guilt setting up camp in the bumpy nodules of her face.

"How did you work that out?" asked Cal.

Miz tutted. "Uh, maybe because it's totally obvious?"

"Interesting," said Cal. "Giant pie?"

He pushed a plate closer to Miz and Soonsho. It required two hands and a reasonable amount of effort. If the last pie slice had been huge, this one was positively ridiculous. It looked like a prop from a stage production of *Land of the Giants*, and was big enough to feed twenty fully-grown men, or to give ten fully-grown men Type 2 Diabetes.

"My mom made it," Cal said. "Or, you know, it was assembled from atoms by kitchen equipment, but apparently that's pretty much the same thing in this day and age."

Neither Soonsho nor Miz, it transpired, wanted any giant pie. Nor did Cal, if he were completely honest. He was seven handfuls into it, but had barely made a dent, and was beginning to wonder what all the fuss had been about. On the one hand, it was delicious. On the other hand, he never wanted to see another piece of banoffee pie for as long as he lived.

Still, it would be a shame to waste it. He took another

scoop and shoveled it into his mouth.

"What else have you figured out about her?" Cal asked.

"I don't know. Not much," said Miz. "Besides that she was kidnapped by the Xandrie, that she overheard them saying they were going to kill her if they didn't get their ransom, and that she couldn't stop herself screaming, which was when they all got pulped."

Cal stopped chewing. He swallowed the sugary mush in his mouth. For a moment, he was sure he could actually feel his arteries hardening.

"How did you figure out all that?"

"She whispers," said Miz. Soonsho gawped at her in surprise, then quickly closed her mouth again.

"She whispers?"

"All the time. It's kinda annoying, actually. You can't hear it, but…" Miz flicked her ears up and spun them in opposite directions. "I'm way more qualified than the rest of you in that department."

Cal saw Soonsho as if for the first time. "So we can talk to her? That's great! Hi," he said. "I'm Cal. I mean, we've done that bit, but… Hi."

Soonsho slowly lowered her hand. Her lips moved, just a fraction.

"She says 'hi,'" said Miz. She waited until Soonsho's lips had stopped moving again. "She wants to know if we're going to hurt her."

"What? Us? No! How can she think that? How can you think that? We're the good guys. We're taking you home," said Cal. He said the word again, slowing it right down for emphasis. "*Home.*"

"She can't raise her voice, she's not brain-damaged," Miz pointed out.

166

"What? No. I know," said Cal. He reached for more pie, thought better of it, then pushed the plate out of reach. "Uh… ask her if she's happy to be going home."

Miz's whole face became the dictionary definition of sarcasm.

"Oh, wait, no, I can ask her myself, can't I?"

"Well, *duh.*"

Soonsho's lips moved again. This time, it seemed to go on for some time. Cal watched her mouth, trying to lip-read, but then realized she wasn't actually speaking English, so the entire exercise was completely pointless.

Once she stopped, Miz waited a few seconds to make sure there was nothing more, then passed the message on.

"Yes."

"Yes?" said Cal. "That's it? All that lip-flapping for 'yes'?"

Miz sighed. "There was more, but none of it interesting. Can't wait to see her parents. Misses her friends. Blah, blah, blah. So, basically, she said 'yes.'"

Cal smiled. "Well, tell her we'll get her home soon," he said.

Miz raised a single eyebrow. Cal turned to Soonsho. "We'll get you home soon," he said. "And then everything's going to be OK."

Soonsho's lips moved, just once. "What did she say?" Cal asked.

"She said, 'promise?'"

Cal put a hand on Soonsho's shoulder. This time, she didn't draw back in fright. "Trust me," he said. "From here on in, everything's going to be just fine. No-one's going to hurt you. We won't let them. That's a Cal Carver guarantee, and I don't just dish those things out."

Soonsho stood up. She bit her lip, briefly hugged Cal,

then quickly sat back down again. "Thanks, kid," Cal said.

He reached along the table and slowly slid the partially-eaten remains of his giant pie towards her. "Now, tuck in," he said. "Because this shizz right here? This is going to change your life."

CHAPTER SIXTEEN

A few more boring hours passed completely normally. Cal spent most of it spinning from side to side in his seat, quietly wishing they'd be attacked by something. Just a little Scriver ship would do it. Or maybe a pirate. He could really go a pirate attack right about now, he thought. It'd give him a chance to shoot his little gun.

"That's a point," said Cal, sitting up in his chair. "Kevin, we should be using this time to show me the guns."

"They're on the wings, sir," said Kevin. "I expect you've already seen them. They're rather hard to miss."

"No, I mean show me how to use them," said Cal.

"Ah. Yes. That would have been a most productive way of passing the time," Kevin agreed. "Alas, I fear the opportunity has now passed."

"How come?"

It was Mech who answered. "We've arrived," he said, studying the data flooding the bottom corner of the screen. He still had a piece of banana stuck to the back of his neck, but Cal had decided not to tell him.

The stars stopped streaking, but this time the deceleration was more 'gradual slowdown' than 'skeleton-snapping'.

"Way to go, you!" said Cal, leaning forwards and gently punching Loren on the shoulder. "Eyeballs still in sockets, testicles not sticking out through my back – you nailed it."

"Yeah, yeah," said Loren. "Don't make me back up and try again."

A planet hung like a Christmas bauble in the sky ahead of them, its surface gleaming with shades of metallic red. Most of the planet was in darkness, but a ring of lights surrounded a towering mountain in the far northern hemisphere. There had to be a million glowing pinpricks down there, concentrated closely around the base of the mountain, and becoming thinner and more sparse the further out they went.

"Kamikaze One," said Cal in an awed whisper.

"Now you're doing it on purpose," Mech snapped. "You know full fonking well it's Cantato Minor."

"Meh. I like my name better," said Cal. "So, do we have an address? Or how does this work?"

A flashing camera icon lit-up in the corner of the screen. "We're being hailed. It's the parents," said Mech.

"How did they know we were here?" asked Loren.

"Ah," said Kevin.

"Sorry I asked," Loren sighed.

"Well don't just leave them hanging, pick up," said Cal, sitting up straight and wiping the pie-debris from the front of his shirt. This only resulted in him smearing cream and caramel down himself. He was in the middle of licking his thumb and trying to wipe the worst of it away when he realized two middle-aged Cantatorians were watching him expectantly from the screen.

"Oh, hey!" said Cal, smoothing down his shirt and waving. "You must be Mr and Mrs Soonsho's Mom and Dad."

"Is she there?" asked the man in a rich voice that immediately made Cal think of sunsets the color of fall. "Our daughter, is she with you?"

There was a scuffing from the corridor as Soonsho dashed onto the bridge, her eyes shimmering with tears. On screen, the couple went into full meltdown mode. Tears, snot, the works. They hugged each other, and Soonsho reached for the screen, her fingers flapping as if beckoning them towards her.

"Oh, our baby. Our baby," sobbed Soonsho's father. Her mother, meanwhile, bit her lip, presumably to stop herself losing control over her voice. It didn't matter. Her tears, and the look on her face, said more than any words could.

"You brought back our baby," she said in a controlled monotone.

"Yes, we did," said Cal. "You're welcome."

"Now, about that reward," Mech began.

"Mech, not now. Let's not cheapen it," said Cal. He looked from Soonsho to her parents, and felt a warm glow spreading out from his belly. It was possibly the pie, but he didn't think so. It was something even better. "Let's just enjoy the moment. We did good, guys. We did good."

Soonsho turned to him, her face a picture of relief and joy and everything in between. Cal winked and raised a thumb. "What did I tell you?" he said. "Cal Carver guarantee."

The *Untitled* descended slowly, its landing thrusters churning the ground into a sandstorm of swirling red dust beneath it.

"Easy," said Cal. "Watch out for all those people."

"Shut up," Loren told him. "I'm nowhere near them."

"You're nowhere near them *yet*," said Cal. "Past experience would suggest it's only a matter of time."

"Funny," said Loren. "They're well away from the landing pad. I couldn't land on them if I tried."

"Like, don't put yourself down," said Miz. "I can pretty much guarantee you're going to land on at least five of them."

"Look, can everyone just shut up?" Loren spat. "I'm trying to concentrate here."

"I did offer to land for you, ma'am," Kevin reminded her. "But you were quite adamant."

"She needs the practice," said Miz.

"I do not!"

The ship slammed into the ground, grinding the landing gears against the inside of their housings. Outside, the hundreds of assembled Cantatorians ran for cover. Loren released her grip on the sticks, and let her hands flop into her lap. She cleared her throat.

"Well, maybe just a little," she admitted.

Miz snorted, drawing an angry look from Loren.

"OK, hands up anyone who died on the way here because of my flying," Loren demanded. "Anyone? No?"

"I died inside," said Miz. "Does that count?"

"No," said Loren. "It doesn't."

She stood up sharply and looked to Cal. "We going, then?"

"Alright, alright, hold your horses," Cal told her. He spun and stood up, then held a hand out to Soonsho. Even she had known to strap herself in when Loren began her descent. She unclipped her belt, and Cal smiled as she took his hand. "Ready kid?"

Soonsho nodded and let herself be helped up. She took one last look around the bridge, then leaned down low until she could see beneath Cal's chair. She waved, and a little green hand waved back.

"You're honored," said Cal. "He doesn't wave at just anyone. I mean, he barely acknowledges Mech even exists. Although, that's probably because Mech has been ready and willing to leave him for dead on a number of different occasions."

"Hey, that ain't true," Mech protested.

"It totally is true," said Miz.

Loren nodded in agreement. "He's right."

Mech huffed grumpily. "Well, it's a blob of goo. I don't understand why the Hell you're all so attached to the fonking thing."

"We're not," said Miz. "He is."

Cal grinned. "Guilty as charged." He squatted down and looked under his chair. Splurt's eyes gazed back at him from the darkness. "Wait here for now, buddy. Once we know it's safe, we'll come get you."

"Again, it can change into anything it wants," Mech pointed out. "It can handle itself."

"I just want to make sure he's safe," Cal said.

"You know what you're doing? You're stifling the fonking thing," said Mech. "You're being overprotective. You're like one of those moms who's all, 'Ooh, ooh, be careful, it's dangerous out there,' and the kid's like, 'Shizz, mom, I just want to go out and play. Is that really too much to ask?' and then she's like, 'But, but there are bad men out there, son. Think about what happened to your father. I can't let that happen to you, it'd break my heart,' and the kid's like, 'Argh! Seriously, everyone else is out playing. You can't keep me here forever. I hate you! I wish I'd never been born!'"

He stopped talking when he realized everyone, including Splurt, was staring at him. Cal shifted uneasily and shot Loren a sideways glance. He cleared his throat. "Uh... I have to ask. Were *you* the kid in that scenario, Mech?" he asked.

"What? No!" Mech snorted.

"It's just, you painted a *very* vivid picture," said Cal.

"Very vivid," Loren agreed.

"I know, right? I mean, it was like..." He held his clenched fist in front of his face, then spread his fingers like an explosion. "Boom! Right there. 3D, coming-atcha."

"It wasn't me, man," said Mech, crossing his arms. "I don't even know what you're talking about. It was hypothetical, that's all I'm..."

He jabbed a finger towards the chair and shouldered his way between Cal and Loren. "You should just let the fonking slimeball come. That's all I was trying to say."

They listened to him *clanking* along the corridor, then heard a cheer go up as the hatch opened. "That guy is very complicated," Cal said, gesturing for Loren, Miz and Soonsho to follow. He walked after them, then stopped just inside the door.

"Ah, what the Hell," he muttered, then he clicked his tongue against the side of his teeth, as if calling a horse. Splurt sprang happily from under the chair, rolled up Cal's back, and transformed himself into a large, flamboyant sombrero on the top of his head.

Cal checked his reflection in the polished chrome panel of the wall, nodded his approval, then followed the others along the corridor and out to face the cheering crowds.

CHAPTER SEVENTEEN

Nobody really paid any attention to Cal when he meandered down the ramp, although his hat did draw a couple of double-takes.

Instead, the crowd had surged around Soonsho in their hundreds, reaching and grabbing for any parts of her they could get to. Some of them fell over in their eagerness to reach her, only to be trampled over by others pushing through from the back.

"Jesus. They're happy to see her," said Cal.

"Yeah, but I don't think…" Loren began, then she spotted Cal's hat. "What are you wearing?"

Cal looked down at his shirt, shoes and pants. "Just the usual. Why?"

Loren tutted and shook her head. "I'm not even going to give you the satisfaction," she said, turning back to where Soonsho was practically drowning in people. "As I was saying, I don't think she's so excited to see them."

Sure enough, Soonsho was trying to smile, but it was more like a rictus of terror. And no wonder. The men in

175

the crowd whooped and hollered and screamed her name as they squashed in towards her. The women spoke in dull monotones, taking care not to lose control of their voices.

"OK, fonk this," said Miz. She flashed her claws, bared her teeth and let out a guttural animal roar that caught the attention of the closest Cantatorians. The crowd stumbled aside at the sight of her, making room for Mech to march through, knocking and yanking the stragglers out of his path.

Soonsho grabbed for his arm when he reached her and he lifted her clear of the throngs. Those at the back of the crowd, who couldn't really see what was going on, continued to push forwards. Those at the front of the crowd, who could see Mech and Miz really very clearly indeed, began pushing backwards.

By the time Mech had deposited Soonsho back on the ramp, the crowd's whole tone had changed. The people in the middle of the crowd had decided they didn't particularly enjoy being squashed from both sides, and had elected to voice their concerns by punching the faces of anyone within reach.

"Well, that turned ugly fast," said Cal.

"I guess they must've really missed her," said Loren.

"Guess so," said Cal. He looked at Miz as she padded back up the ramp, then gestured to Soonsho. "Is she OK?"

Miz cocked her head and lifted her ears. A scowl of annoyance set up camp on her face. "I can't hear her. There's too much other noise going on for me to—"

A sound, like all the forks in human history scraping across all the plates at the same time, rang out. Miz hissed and clamped her hands over her ears. She staggered into Loren, who struggled to hold her upright. To everyone's surprise, it took Miz a full five seconds before she wrenched herself angrily from Loren's grip.

"You're welcome," Loren said, and her voice carried far across the heads of the suddenly silent crowd.

As one, the mob had craned their necks upwards to watch a circular metal platform sail by above them. On it stood a man and a woman, dressed in what were arguably the most garishly elaborate outfits Cal had ever seen. The man wore a skintight red and black jumpsuit which left very little to the imagination on the crotch front.

Despite his evident lack of shortcomings in the downstairs department, he nevertheless seemed to be overcompensating for something with his choice of accessories. His upper-body was fitted with enormous metal shoulder pads that curved upwards like rhino horns. Fixed to his back were two long curved blades of red metal. At first, Cal thought they were wings, but they were too short and thin for that. They were more like the pincers of a giant insect, rising a clear couple of feet above the man's head.

His head itself was mostly covered by a tall, hammer-shaped helmet – also red – with a large black gemstone set in the center like the glassy eye of a cycloptic shark. He wore boots and gloves of a shiny black leather-like material.

Despite the flamboyance of his outfit, a number of symbols on his tightly-clad thighs seemed to be deliberately designed to draw the eye straight to his crotch.

Cal whistled softly through his teeth. "Jesus. It's like a baby's arm."

"What?" said Loren.

"Hmm? Oh, nothing."

The woman standing beside the man, holding his hand, was possibly even more of a fashion-disaster. She wore a long

BARRY J HUTCHISON

shapeless dress that bunched around her neck like the top of a sack, then sort of slumped all the way down to the floor. It was the same metallic red as some of her partner's accessories, but had the appearance of fish scales.

She wore no helmet or other accessories, but her eyes were ringed with thick black lines which might well have been drawn on in Sharpie by an enthusiastic toddler. From the eyes down, her face was a mess of odd-looking piercings. Each piercing was a small metal pipe, inserted through the walls of the woman's nostrils and several places in her cheeks. They were perfectly symmetrical on both sides of her face, and judging by the lack of visible scarring on her skin, had been there for quite some time.

As the disk passed silently above them, the members of the crowd all knelt and bowed their heads. Soonsho tried to do the same, but the angle of the ramp made kneeling tricky, so she sort of half-crouched, instead.

"Rise, child," the man said, almost as soon as Soonsho began to move. His voice was treacle in Cal's ear. It made his skeleton vibrate and resonated through his lower intestine. To his surprise, it wasn't unpleasant. "It is we who should be genuflecting to you. And to those who have returned you to us."

The disk lowered until the man and woman stood just a little higher than Cal and the others. "I am the Conductor of Cantato Minor," he rumbled, his one black gem eye fixing on Cal. "The Conductress and I give thanks to you, Captain."

"He ain't the captain," said Mech.

"Well, technically I am, so..." Cal said. He gave the Conductor a relaxed salute. "No problem, chief. Just happy to see her safely home."

"And to collect the reward," Mech added.

The Conductor nodded slowly. "Of course. It is a small price to pay to have Soonsho back with us. The reward shall be yours. It is well-earned."

"But first, shall you join us in celebration?" asked the Conductress. She spoke without moving her lips. Instead, the words whistled and hummed out through the pipes in her face, so the sound seemed to emerge from the air around her, rather than from the Conductress herself. "We would feast in your honor."

Cal looked to the others. "I'm sure we can do a celebratory feast in our honor, right?" he said. "I mean, it'd be rude not to."

"Sounds good," Loren agreed.

"Works for me," said Mech.

Miz, who had been rubbing her ears, and opening and closing her jaw to try to force the high-pitched ringing out, noticed the others watching her. "What?" she asked, far too loudly. "Why are you all looking at me? Weirdos."

Cal turned to the Conductress and smiled. "A celebratory feast sounds awesome. Count us in."

While Cal might have had his reservations about their fashion sense, the Conductor and Conductress sure knew how to rally a welcome committee.

Soonsho had joined Cantato Minor's rulers aboard their disk, while a larger, more industrial-looking floating platform had been brought in to ferry Cal and the crew away from the landing bay. They proceeded – the smaller disk in front, the larger one a respectful distance behind – through the ship-sized doors of the landing area, and out onto a long, curved avenue beyond.

Once outside, the full splendor of the planet made itself apparent. The ground was a shimmering sheen of metallic red. It covered the wide streets, the raised sidewalks and the walls of the long, squat bungalows that ran along either side. Each of the buildings were several hundred feet long, with numerous doors and windows dotting the walls at regular intervals.

Side roads ran down the gaps between the buildings on the left, connecting this street to an identical one running parallel alongside it. On the right, the walls of the mountain rose steeply up from behind the houses and disappeared into the purple-tinted clouds far overhead. The base of the mountain had the same red shine as the rest of the place, but near the clouds the surface was blackened and scarred.

Lining the sidewalks on both sides of the street were thousands of Cantatorians. These ones wore far simpler outfits than their leaders. They had a certain 'properness' to them – shirts with high collars, skirts with long hems – and it was surprising to see such a conservatively dressed crowd react with such near-hysterical gusto.

The men were cheering and whooping and punching the air. They jumped around, hugging each other and roaring their approval as the procession passed them by.

The women were far more restrained, and most of them simply applauded. Many of them wore red metal clamps across their mouths, presumably to stop them losing control of their voices and accidentally doing anyone any damage.

The men were more than making up for their silence, though, and the streets hummed with a full-blown party atmosphere.

"Wow. This kid is popular," said Mech.

"They're partly cheering for us," Cal pointed out. He

waved to one man, pointed to another like he was a long-lost friend, then blew kisses to anyone who wanted them.

"Well, they ain't looking at us," said Mech. "They're all too busy looking at Soonsho like she's the second coming of Kroysh."

"They're just glad to have her back," said Cal. He pointed to another man, laughed like he'd just been told a joke, said, "You know it, buddy," for reasons that weren't really all that clear, then went back to waving.

Loren frowned. "Then what's with the guards?" She gestured into the crowd. Every fifteen feet or so, a uniformed Cantatorian stood facing the wrong way near the front of the line of spectators.

"It's a public gathering. Emotions are high," said Cal, shrugging. "You saw what they were like back there. They couldn't get enough of her."

"Yeah. Maybe," said Loren.

"So, where are we going?" asked Miz, her voice booming right behind Cal's head. Even Splurt jumped, briefly becoming a green blob again, before resuming sombrero mode.

"And where are her parents?" Loren wondered. "Shouldn't they be here?"

"We're going to a party," Cal said, ignoring Loren and raising his voice so Miz could hear him. He pointed to one of his own ears. "You OK?"

"*What?*"

"ARE YOU OK?"

"Am I *gay?*" Miz said. "Not recently. Why? Would you like me to be?"

"No, I wasn't... Forget it," said Cal. "Also – interesting."

Up ahead, the Conductor's disk skimmed low above the

181

street, then glided elegantly into a smooth right turn. The disk the crew was on followed, and they found themselves headed for a set of towering metal gates. Unlike pretty much everything else in sight, the gates weren't red. Or not *as* red, at least. They had a sort of coppery tone which, while possessing a certain orangey-redness, was nothing like the other, more common, shade of red.

Well, to say it was *nothing* like it was an exaggeration. It was similar. Not *exactly* the same, but close.

Unless that was just the way the light was shining on the gates which, Cal thought as they swept on through them, was a definite possibility.

There were no crowds beyond the gates, just an expanse of shiny metal ground, a grand and imposing copper-colored palace (not just the light, Cal decided) and two lonely figures waiting anxiously in front of the open doorway.

The Conductor's disk swooped down and slowed, but Soonsho didn't wait for it to stop. She hopped off and ran, her feet slapping the cool metal as she sprinted towards her parents and threw herself into their arms.

All three of them collapsed to the floor, a tangle of limbs and tears and long silent sobs. Cal's disk lowered and touched down onto the ground beside the Conductor and Conductress. They both nodded to the crew, bowing their heads in gratitude. The Conductor smiled. The Conductress might very well have, too, but it was quite hard to tell with all that shizz in her face.

"Once again, you have our thanks," the Conductor intoned.

Cal doffed his sombrero. "Don't mention it."

"Please. We would be grateful if you joined us inside," said the Conductor, gesturing to the door. "The celebration

– and your reward – await."

He and the Conductress walked ahead, still hand in hand. Cal waited until he reckoned they were out of earshot. "They seem nice," he said. "Although, tell me I wasn't the only one looking at his junk."

"You definitely were," said Loren.

"He definitely wasn't," said Mech. "Holy shizz, that thing was huge."

"I know, right!"

"What was huge?" bellowed Miz.

"Sshh, shut up!" hissed Cal. The Conductor glanced back over his shoulder. Cal smiled and waved until the Conductor faced front again.

"What was huge?" Miz asked again, in a voice that was only marginally more quiet than last time.

"Nothing," said Cal. "Just… his helmet. No, not… I mean, you know, his metal hat."

He puffed out his cheeks and gestured after the Conductor and Conductress. Behind him and the crew, the towering copper gates closed with a barely audible *click*. "Aaaanyway," said Cal. "Shall we?"

CHAPTER EIGHTEEN

Although Cal wasn't entirely sure what sort of celebration he'd been expecting, it certainly hadn't been the one they got.

Calling it a 'celebration' at all, in fact, felt overly generous. It was a small gathering, at best, with Cal and the crew joining Soonsho, her parents, the Conductor and Conductress, and a couple of attentive but bored-looking servants for drinks and nibbles in a vast and otherwise completely empty ballroom. It was all in stark contrast to the cheering mobs outside.

One of the servants waved a tray of nibbles under Cal's nose. He reached for one that seemed to be some kind of biscuit with a fishy-tasting paste on top, then thought better of it.

"Actually, no, nine's my limit," he said. The waiter nodded, but didn't smile, then continued on around the other guests.

Cal sipped his drink – a clear sweet liquid with a charcoal aftertaste, like soda drunk from an ashtray, and tried not to think too much about that very image.

Soonsho stood with her parents, as was to be expected. She was saying nothing, which was also to be expected, but neither of her parents spoke, either.

Next to them stood the Conductor and Conductress. Neither of them were eating or drinking, which was a pity, because Cal wanted to see how the Conductress managed to drink anything will all those pipes poking out of her mouth and nose.

He was staring at the metal tubes when he realized the Conductress was watching him. He smiled at her, then pointed to his own cheeks. "Nice... face stuff," he said. "Looks good."

"Thank you," said the Conductress, the words humming out through the pipes.

Cal smiled awkwardly, raised his eyebrows a couple of times, then took another sip of his drink.

The others weren't faring much better at the small talk. Loren and Miz both nursed their own drinks and took in the room in slightly embarrassed silence. Loren had initially turned the drink down, explaining she didn't like to drink and fly, but the Conductor had assured her the beverage wasn't alcoholic, which had disappointed Cal no end.

Mech stood with his arms folded, an impatient look on the non-robot part of his face. He'd tried to bring up the reward at least twice since they'd arrived, then had gone in the huff when Cal had told him to stop going on about it. Now he just glared at the Conductor, as if he could siphon the reward money from his pockets by force of will alone.

"So—" Cal began.

"I was—" said Loren, at exactly the same time. They both stopped.

"No, you go," said Cal.

"It's fine, what were you going to say?" said Loren.

"No, please, it was nothing, really."

"Nor was mine," Loren insisted. "Please."

Cal nodded. "Right. I was just going to say… this is a nice room."

"That's what I was going to say," said Loren.

"Really? Ha. What are the odds?"

The Conductor and Conductress both looked around the room. Soonsho and her parents did the same.

"I suppose it is," said the Conductor.

"Right," said Cal.

Everyone sipped their drink.

"Did you decorate it yourself, or…?"

"Oh, no," said the Conductor.

"No," said Cal. "No. That makes sense. I'd imagine you'd have people to do that."

"Yes."

"Good," said Cal. "That's good." He gestured to the waiter. "I think maybe I will have one of those fish things, after all."

The waiter brought the tray over. Cal studied the offerings for a few seconds, then picked one of the smaller ones. His stomach was still around ninety-eight percent filled with banoffee pie, and there wasn't a lot of margin left over for error.

Mizette drained her drink and set the empty glass on the waiter's tray, squishing several of the fishy-snacks. "I'll have another of those," she said, her voice still a little louder than normal. "In fact, bring me two."

The waiter bowed and scuttled off. The Conductor and Conductress both eyed Miz a little warily, but didn't pass any comment.

"How are the Greyx?" asked the Conductor.

Miz shrugged. "I don't know. OK, I guess."

"I believe you recently lost Graxan," said the Conductress. "That must have been a blow. He was a wise ruler."

Miz rolled her eyes. "Don't even get me started."

"He was her dad," said Cal, before adding, "We don't talk about it," in the quietest whisper he could manage. Ironically, it was so quiet only Miz heard him, even over the ringing in her ears.

"I see," said the Conductor. He bowed to Miz, just briefly. "Our condolences, Your Highness."

"Ooh, and don't even go there," said Cal, before Miz was able to respond. "Just call her 'Mizette.'"

More silence fell. The waiter returned with Miz's drinks. She downed one in one gulp, then held onto the other.

Mech cleared his throat very deliberately until he caught Cal's attention. He gestured with his eyes towards the Conductor and tried to arrange his facial features to convey the phrase, 'Ask him about the fonking reward.' Impressively enough, he managed to do just that. Cal shook his head at him, then went back to gazing awkwardly at nothing in particular.

"May I speak, Conductor?" asked Soonsho's father, bowing a full six times during the question.

"You may," the Conductor intoned.

"Oh, thank God," breathed Cal.

Soonsho's father smiled gratefully. He slipped his arms around his wife and daughter, pulling them both close to him. He looked at Cal, and there were tears pooling in the corners of his eyes. "I... There are no words I can use to express my gratitude. You brought my baby back to me. To us. To Cantato Minor. She is the light of our lives, my purpose for getting up in the morning. Without her, I could not go on. None of us could."

"No problem," said Cal. "She's a great girl. It's a pleasure to bring her home."

Mech coughed noisily. Cal ignored him.

"She is so important. *So* important," said Soonsho's dad. "Without her..."

"I'm sure our guests understand how pleased we all are to have Soonsho home," said the Conductor, interrupting. Soonsho's father looked briefly taken aback, then bowed several more times and fell into silence.

"Well, like I say, totally our pleasure," said Cal. He winked at Soonsho. The barnacle-like bumps on her face blushed pink, and she risked opening her mouth enough to return his smile.

There was another awkward lull in the conversation. Cal looked to Loren and silently gestured for her to say something. It took her a moment to understand, but then she plunged straight in.

"So."

The Conductor and Conductress looked at her and raised their eyebrows inquisitively. At least, the Conductress did. The Conductor was still wearing his helmet, but something about the way the bottom of his face moved suggested there was some eyebrow action going on with him, too.

Loren opened her mouth, but nothing came out. She floundered for a few agonizing seconds, then reached for the first thing that came to mind. "War."

"I'm sorry?" asked the Conductor.

"There's a war," said Loren. "Did you hear about that? What do you think about it?" She cocked her head and held her chin, as if listening intently.

"Really?" said the Conductor. "We hadn't heard. The outside galaxy rarely touches us down here."

"The war will," said Mech. "Ain't nowhere safe."

The Conductor smiled, grimly. "Yes. Well, we have our own protective measures. I think we'll be quite all right."

"Oh, you think so?" snorted Mech.

"I know," said the Conductor. "The galaxy has been at war before, and we weren't affected then. This time will be no different."

"Yeah, well, we'll see," said Mech. "Now, about this reward…"

"Bathroom," said Cal, cutting Mech dead. "Uh, I mean, I could really do with going to the bathroom. Would you be able to point me in the right direction?"

The Conductor gestured to a waiter, who immediately glided to Cal's side. "Please," the waiter said, gesturing for Cal to walk ahead.

Cal removed his sombrero and placed it on Loren's head. "Can you look after my hat?"

Loren immediately took the hat off and held it, instead.

"Be right back," said Cal, heading in the direction the waiter had indicated. "Then I guess we should think about making tracks."

"Soon," said the Conductor. "First, there's something I'd like you all to hear."

Cal replied with a thumbs up, then the waiter darted ahead of him and held open a door, and Cal continued through into a long corridor with a mirror-like polished floor.

"Second door on the left, sir," said the servant. "Should I wait?"

"I think I'll manage," said Cal. "But what you could do is write down the name of those nibbles, so I can get the kitchen thing to magic them up."

The servant lowered his head. "Of course. It will be my pleasure."

Cal headed for the door the servant had indicated and pushed it open. A small bathroom was revealed, with a toilet made of polished copper. While there were lots of little differences between the toilets he'd encountered on his travels, Cal was relieved that the basic design seemed to be pretty universal.

They didn't all deal with the... contents in the same way. Some flushed, like on Earth, others vaporized, while one, on a planet he had no desire to ever return to, *ejected*. Basically, though, quirks aside, the essential shape and functionality were similar all across the galaxy.

The door closed behind him, cutting off the light from the corridor and plunging the bathroom into darkness. There were no automatic lights in here, and Cal fumbled along the wall, trying to find a switch.

Nothing.

He clapped a couple of times, in case that worked.

He said, "Lights on." When that didn't work, he tried adding, "Please," but the effect – or lack of one – was the same.

Still, the room wasn't particularly big, and he'd glimpsed the toilet long enough to figure out roughly where it was. He edged forwards, his hands out in front of him, fumbling his way through the dark.

After a few seconds, his hands found the back wall.

He slowly moved them down until he found the toilet. Estimating roughly where the bowl was, he unzipped his fly and let rip.

"Aaah."

The galaxy was a big place, and held countless pleasures, but he doubted very few of them could compare to the feeling of draining a full bladder. He rocked on his heels, just enjoying the moment. He was so busy enjoying the moment, in fact, that he didn't notice the knife until the cold steel pressed against his throat.

"Don't move," hissed a voice in his ear.

Cal swallowed. It barely made it past the blade. "I can't stop peeing," he replied.

"What?" spat the voice.

"Once I've started, I can't stop," Cal said. "There's nothing I can do about it. If you have a problem with that, you'll have to kill me."

"Just hurry up," the voice growled.

Cal continued to pee. The knife scraped against his stubble as the person holding it shifted their grip.

"What's taking so long?" the voice demanded.

"I had quite a lot to drink," said Cal. "Just give me a minute."

He continued to pee.

The figure holding him felt larger than he was, the voice coming from slightly above his right ear. The weight on his shoulder whenever the person spoke suggested he was leaning down, too. Even if the attacker hadn't had the knife, and Cal wasn't midway through what had, until very recently, been a deeply satisfying urination experience, he didn't really fancy his chances.

"What's keeping him?" asked another voice from

somewhere in the bathroom.

"Jesus, how many of you are in here?" Cal asked.

"Shut up!" snarled the one with the knife. He pressed the blade harder against Cal's throat to make the seriousness of the situation clear. "And hurry."

The torrent became a trickle, and then a drip. "I'm going to shake now," said Cal. "I'd appreciate it if you didn't slit my throat."

He shook, then zipped himself up. "There," he said. "Now, how may I help you gentlemen?"

"Take off your shirt," the man with the knife hissed.

"Uh... why?"

"Just do it!"

Cal sighed, but carefully so as not to place any unnecessary pressure on the blade. "Well, this is not how I saw the evening turning out," he said. He slipped the shirt off and let it fall to the floor. "There. Now what."

"Turn around. Slowly."

The knife was withdrawn. Cal considered swinging with a punch, but the bathroom was still in darkness, and there was no saying what, if anything, he'd hit. Instead, he shuffled around on the spot and raised his hands.

"I don't suppose there's any chance you're just a really overzealous cleaning crew?" he asked.

"We are the Xandrie," hissed the voice of the knifeman. "We've come for the girl."

"Jesus, you guys just don't give up, do you?" said Cal. "Well, I hate to tell you, but you're too late."

"No, *you* are!"

Cal frowned. "What?"

"What?" said the voice, after a pause.

"What do you mean?"

"What do *you* mean?"

"Uh… OK."

"Shut up!"

"We've come for the girl," said the other voice, closer to the door. "We want the reward. We *deserve* that reward."

"So… wait? You're going to kidnap her again, then immediately hand her back over? That's the worst plan I've ever heard. And, believe me, coming from me, that's saying a lot."

"You haven't heard the best part yet," said the first voice. "You're going to bring her to us."

"I am?"

"Yes. You see, we're going to place an explosive device directly over your heart, and if you don't bring her here… *kaboom!*"

Cal felt something cold and metallic press against his belly button. "That's not my…" he began, before thinking better of it.

"Not your what?"

"Mmm? Oh, nothing."

"That's not where your heart is, is it? That's what you were going to say, isn't it?"

"Uh, no," said Cal.

"Yes you were," growled the voice. "Where is it, then?"

"It's there. Seriously. You're bang on," said Cal, then the blade of the knife was suddenly at his throat again, the point twisting into his skin. "Ooh, OK, up a bit."

The metal slid up to Cal's chest. It wasn't directly over his heart, but he reckoned it'd be close enough to get the job done. Two metal tendrils snaked up over his shoulders and under his arms, then locked together at the back, pinching his skin.

The guy with the knife prodded the chest plate a few times. A red light blinked on and off, allowing Cal fleeting glimpses of a pig-like snout and a number of eyes which seemed to have been liberally sprinkled on, rather than added to the face in any particular pattern.

The other figure lurking over by the door was smaller than the knifeman, but what he lacked in size he made up for in guns. He had two of them, both ridiculously large and unpleasant-looking, and both pointed at Cal.

"So, here's what's going to happen," grunted Pig Face. He tossed Cal's shirt at him. "You're going to put that on, then you're going to go back out there. From the moment you leave this room, you'll have four minutes to get the girl, and bring her to us."

"Or we blow you up," sniggered the other guy. Cal had decided to simply name him 'Guns'. It was that or 'Overcompensating for a Very Small Penis,' and that didn't trip off the tongue nearly as well.

"Don't make it back, and you die," Pig Face said. "Tell anyone what's happening, and you die. Try any funny stuff, and you die."

Cal pulled on his shirt. "Can you be more specific about what qualifies as 'funny stuff'?" he asked. "Are we talking physical comedy, you know, like slapstick? Amusing anecdotes? Observational material…? Oh puns! Where do you stand on puns?"

Pig Face clamped a rough hand around Cal's throat and leaned in until his snout and all those eyes were all Cal could see in the blinking red glow. "You know what we mean," the alien growled. "We are the Xandrie. You'd better not mess with us."

"Or… *boom*," said Guns, his voice a scratchy giggle.

Pig Face released his grip. Cal fastened his shirt, and the bathroom settled back into darkness.

"So, what if I do?" said Cal. "Go boom, I mean."

This seemed to catch the two Xandrie off guard. "What?" asked Pig Face.

Cal tapped the chest plate through his shirt. "This thing. I could just walk out of here, sit down and wait for it to go off. You wouldn't get the girl."

"But you'd be dead," said Guns.

Cal shrugged. "So? Maybe I don't care. You ever think about that?"

Pig Face sighed. "Oh. So, you think you're a hero? Is that it? Well, let me tell you something, *hero*. In my experience, no-one's as brave as they like to think they are. That urge to survive, to cling to life, it's too great. You might think you can walk out of here and just go wait somewhere for the bomb to go off, but once you're out there – once you're in the corridor, all alone, just you and the countdown – you'll do what you're told."

"Also," added Guns, "if you don't, we'll go out there and kill all your friends, then take the girl anyway. This way is just better all round, really."

Cal nodded slowly. "You both make excellent points. Bluff called. Well done." He clapped his hands together. "Right, then! I guess I'll see you gents in under four minutes."

He gestured over his shoulder as he stumbled blindly for the door. "Oh, and could somebody flush that? Thanks."

Pushing open the door, he stepped out into the corridor. "Four minutes," Guns whispered. "And no funny stuff."

The door closed. Cal took a deep breath. The metal of the chest plate squeezed him uncomfortably.

"OK, then," he whispered. He looked along the corridor to the left. It led… somewhere. He had no idea where, though. Away from Soonsho. Away from his friends. That was all he knew.

He should go that way. He could probably get quite far in four minutes.

Alternatively, he could wait for three minutes and fifty-five seconds, then turn around and go back into the bathroom. That'd fonking teach them.

But he had no idea how big the explosion would be. Would it take Pig Face and Guns out, or would it just lightly glaze them in his innards?

Realistically, it was left or right, then. Rebellion or obedience. Heroism or cowardice. Being blown to bits, or not.

"Fonk it," Cal muttered.

Then, much to his annoyance, he turned right and darted along the corridor, back in the direction of the ballroom.

The Conductor and Conductress both beckoned to him as he entered the room. Clearly, they hadn't had enough awkward small talk last time, and were eager for more of the same.

Cal headed towards them, but stopped when he reached his crew.

"You took your time," Mech grunted.

"Uh, yeah. Constipation," said Cal, patting his stomach. He took the sombrero back from Loren, and pulled it on. "I'm pretty blocked up down there. Possibly shouldn't have eaten six increasingly enormous pieces of pie back on the ship."

"Ugh, too much information," said Miz.

"For once, we actually agree on something," said Loren.

"Oh, wait, do we?" said Miz. She shrugged. "Then I take it back. I'd totally love to hear more about your bowel movements."

Loren rolled her eyes and sighed. Cal pulled a sympathetic face and wrapped his arms around her. "Aw, don't let her upset you," he said, squeezing her tightly. "Come on, hug it out."

"What are you doing? Get off," Loren told him.

Cal stepped back, but then slid an arm around her waist and turned to face the others. "We should probably tell them."

"Tell us what?" asked Mech.

"That Loren and I are in a relationship. We're getting married."

"What?" Loren and Miz both spluttered at the same time.

"Since when?" Miz demanded. Her lips curled upwards, revealing just a few of her teeth, but it was a few you didn't really want to be made aware of.

"Uh-oh. We're in trouble now!" said Cal.

"Since never," said Loren. She pulled free of his grip. "What are you talking about?"

"Uh-oh," Cal repeated, more forcibly this time. He waggled his eyebrows. "*We're in trouble now.*"

He glanced pointedly at the door he'd just come through. Loren followed his gaze, then looked across to Soonsho. Cal nodded, just once.

"Fine. I mean, I don't even care," said Miz. "Does the thought of it make me want to puke myself, like, completely inside out? Yes. But, you know, whatever. So what?"

"Yeah, she's not happy," said Loren. "Just how much

trouble do you think you're in, exactly?"

"Ooh. A *lot*," said Cal. "In fact—"

The chest plate didn't explode. Not exactly. It made a sort of muffled *paff* sound, and Cal felt like he'd been hoofed in the sternum by the nine-time winner of *World's Unfriendliest Horse*. The force of it catapulted him backwards. He saw the world rushing past too fast. Tasted blood in his mouth. Smelled his scorching flesh, and felt an aching emptiness where, just a moment ago, his chest had been.

As he skidded backwards across the ballroom floor, he heard the *crashing* of several doors being kicked in. And shouting. Lots of shouting.

By the time he'd finished skidding, Cal Carver was dead.

CHAPTER NINETEEN

Cal sank through the floor. The redness poured down on him, like a cascading waterfall of his own blood, forcing him further and further into the ground.

If he was dead – which he was starting to think he probably was, what with the gaping hole in his chest, and everything – the direction of travel was giving him some cause for concern. He'd never been a religious man, but as he plunged deeper and deeper into what was rapidly becoming a worryingly fiery redness, he was starting to wonder if that might have been a mistake.

Gradually, the redness faded, becoming a sort of washed-out sepia tone. It was round about the same time that he thudded against the ground. It didn't hurt. One of the benefits of being dead, he supposed.

A hooded figure appeared from the yellow-gray mist and loomed over him. Cal knew it could be one of two people – one being the living embodiment of Death, the other being…

"Tobey Maguire?" said Cal.

Hollywood actor, Tobey Maguire, pushed back his hood

and looked around the clearing where Cal had landed. "Where did you come from?" he asked, then he dry-heaved a couple of times. "Ew. What happened to your chest?"

It wasn't the real Tobey Maguire, of course. Cal knew that. The real Tobey Maguire had almost certainly been killed by alien parasites, like most of the rest of the population of the planet Earth. No, this was a sort of *Spirit* Tobey Maguire, who would often appear to Cal in times of great need. Cal had no idea why. Nor did Tobey Maguire, for that matter, but it helped to pass the time.

Cal stood up. Something wet and squidgy fell from the hole in his chest and landed with a *splat* on the ground between them. "Shizz. Do you think I needed that?"

Tobey Maguire peered down at the bloody wad. "Hopefully not."

Cal turned on the spot. The world he had landed in was a cold, shadowy place, tinted in shades of yellow and brown. He felt as if he were in an old photograph, but one where the photographer had neglected to point the camera at anything interesting.

"Am I dead?"

Tobey Maguire shrugged. "It's impossible to say. What happened?"

Cal pointed to the hole in his chest.

"Oh yeah. God, yes, you're definitely dead. I mean, that is…" Tobey Maguire grimaced and sucked air in through his teeth. "That is the worst thing I've ever seen. I think I can see your spine."

"Well stop looking at it!" said Cal, covering his chest self-consciously. He slumped onto the ground, but couldn't remember if it was deliberate or not. His breath rolled out of him as misty yellow clouds. Was it getting colder, or was it just his imagination?

"Hey, Tobey Maguire, is it just me or—?" he began, looking up. The hooded figure was nowhere to be seen. Cal's eyes darted left and right, watching the mist rolling in. His voice came out as a whisper. "Tobey Maguire? Where are you?"

A sound emerged from the sepia fog. A low scraping, like something being dragged across the ground towards him. Even though his heart wasn't currently located inside his chest, Cal felt it race. He tried to scramble backwards away from the approaching sound, but his arms and legs had become impossibly heavy, and he collapsed, landing flat on his back, his muscles all frozen with cold and fear.

His neck wouldn't move. His head wouldn't lift. He felt a hand wrap around his ankle, then another press against the shin on his opposite leg.

Slowly, steadily, something was climbing up him.

The Xandrie stormed through the doors, guns and voices raised. There were nine of them, all uniquely hideous, none of them even vaguely resembling the others. The weapons and the shouting were the only things they had in common, but they moved in orchestrated harmony, carefully choosing their targets.

Loren stared at Cal's motionless body, her breath trapped in a bubble at the back of her throat. Her Zertex training didn't allow her time to grieve. She reached for her gun, only to find her holster empty. Where the Hell was her gun?

Mech raised his arms, preparing to open fire, but the Xandrie that Cal had come to know as Pig Face squeezed the trigger of his blaster pistol, and a bolt of energy streaked past Soonsho's head, missing by a fraction of an inch. She opened her mouth to scream, but her mom quickly clamped a hand over it, trapping the sound inside.

"Don't!" Pig Face warned Mech. "Or she dies. They all die."

Mech clenched his jaw and glared mute hatred in Pig Face's direction, then tutted and lowered his arms. The Xandrie had them surrounded.

"Cal," Loren whispered, urging him to get up. She knew it was pointless, though. The way he had flown, the way he had hit – he was gone. Cal was gone.

He lay in an awkward heap on the floor, one arm pinned under him, a leg twisted awkwardly, the sombrero beside him on the floor.

Miz extended her claws and rose onto the balls of her feet. "We have to get to him. We can take these guys," she said. It was supposed to come out as a whisper, but her ears were still ringing from the sound the Conductress had made back in the landing bay, and it was loud enough for everyone in the room to hear. One of the Xandrie stopped aiming at Soonsho and aimed at Miz, instead.

"Not without getting people killed," said Loren.

"But we have to get to Cal!"

"There ain't no point," said Mech.

Miz tried to argue, but a sudden tightness in her throat stopped her words coming out. Her chest heaved. She flinched when a metal hand rested on her shoulder.

"You're OK, kid," said Mech. "You're OK."

Loren tore her eyes from Cal and raised her hands. "We're not going to try anything," she announced. "Let's all just keep calm here."

"What do you people want?" demanded the Conductor, his booming voice dripping outrage.

"You know what we want," Pig Face replied. He flicked a fat purple tongue across the underside of his snout. "We want the reward for returning the girl."

"Aw, come *on*," said Mech. "That's our reward, man. We brought her back."

"You took her from us!" Pig Face hissed.

Miz scowled. "Wait, so you kidnapped her, and now you're upset because we rescued her?"

"We deserve that reward!" Pig Face insisted. "Do you have any idea how much planning went into getting her in the first place? Hmm?"

Miz gave a disinterested shrug.

"Yeah, well, it was a lot. A *lot*. Those guys worked very hard, and what did they get?"

"Turned into mush?" guessed Mech.

"Turned into mush. Exactly," said Pig Face. "How is that fair?"

"Because they *kidnapped* her, you fonking..." Mech began, but he backed down when Pig Face made a show of aiming at Soonsho's head. "Hey, easy man, it's all cool."

Pig Face eyeballed Mech for a while – which was particularly effective thanks to his sheer number of eyes – then turned his attention to the Conductor. "So, you going to hand over that reward?" he asked. "Or do we all start shooting?"

"Tobey Maguire, is that you?"

Cal was still on the ground, unable to move, as someone – or something, it was too early to tell – clambered slowly up his fallen body.

"Because this is not cool, Tobey Maguire. Not cool."

The thing crept higher. It wasn't Tobey Maguire. He knew that. One hand pressed on his shin, another on his knee. Cal's eyes were open, but staring straight up at the billowing clouds of yellow mist. Whatever was on him was still too low down to see.

One hand on his thigh.

Its breathing was hoarse and erratic. It whistled on the way in and rasped on the way out. Whatever was climbing up him didn't sound a picture of health. He could probably have fought it off, were it not for his spontaneous head-to-toe paralysis.

One hand on his hip. One on his waist.

Fonk, it was taking its time. The suspense was killing him.

He tried to think of a game to play to pass the time, but could only really think of 'I Spy' and given that he A) had no-one to play with and B) could see nothing but clouds, its entertainment potential was pretty limited.

One hand was on his stomach now. The other went to his left arm, deftly avoiding the blood-slicked hole where his chest should have been.

Cal braced himself. Any minute now, the thing would edge into his line of sight. This was it. He was about to come face to face with whatever it was.

Any second.

Here it came.

Any second now.

Nnnnow.

…

Where the fonk was it?

Then, just as Cal was on the brink of having a go at 'I Spy' after all, a skull-like head rose into view. Its olive-colored skin was paper-thin, so Cal could see every one of its thin veins, spread out like a roadmap beneath the skin's surface.

Two piercing blue eyes stared into Cal's. A gummy smile

spread across the old man's withered lips. "Hey, I know you," Cal managed to eject through his motionless mouth.

Cal could feel the stumps of the withered figure's legs digging sharply into his thighs. The old man prodded Cal right in the center of his chest, his finger sinking in all the way to the spine. "Good man. Young man," he said. He pointed to himself. "Old man. Old enough."

And then, still smiling, the man clamped his hands on either side of Cal's head, and the clouds around them broiled and churned as if alive.

While the Xandrie pointed their guns and made their demands, down on the floor, Cal's sombrero had come to a conclusion.

It wasn't happy.

It didn't know the full details of what had happened. It didn't think in details. In some ways, it didn't think at all. But it felt things. Deeply. And, right now, it felt unhappy.

No, more than that.

It was angry. Very angry. In fact, it was – by quite some distance – the angriest hat that had ever existed.

Cal was dead. The thoughts that had whooshed from his brain like fireworks – bright and vivid and strange – had stopped. Even this current form had come whizzing out of his subconscious at some point, although he couldn't remember exactly when.

Splurt had enjoyed being a sombrero.

He had enjoyed having a friend.

It had been fun.

But now, his friend was gone, and the fun was over, and the time to be a sombrero had passed.

Slowly, silently, unnoticed by anyone in the room, Splurt

began to change.

Pig Face still had his gun on Soonsho. He pointed with the other hand to one of his many fellow Xandrie. This one was tenuously humanoid, if you ignored the extra set of arms, and whatever the fonk that thing was that was growing from her back.

"Here's what's going to happen. Torsha here is going to go with the Conductress to where you keep your cash," Pig Face began, then a blur of movement at the corner of his eye caught his attention, stopping him mid-sentence. He glanced left to where his bathroom accomplice had been standing, but Guns, as Cal had dubbed him, was no longer there.

"Drazz?" said Pig Face who, unlike Cal, was familiar enough with the guy to know his real name.

Drazz rocketed across the room from somewhere behind Pig Face. He slammed into Torsha, and they both exited through a hole they made in the wall with their tumbling bodies.

A Xandrie yelped very briefly on Pig Face's right. Pig Face whipped around in time to see the dome-headed gangster go hurtling upwards at eye-watering speed. Everyone watched as the guy hit the ceiling with a sort of damp crunch, then listened to his screams as he plunged back down again, his arms flapping as he tried desperately – and, ultimately, unsuccessfully – to fly.

He exploded like a sack of warm guts that had recently fallen a long way onto a metal floor, then several other Xandrie began to holler and scream as whipping green tentacles snared them around their legs, waists and necks.

Guns fired. Heads popped. Mizette hurled herself at Pig Face, but he got off a shot that grazed her ribcage, and managed to dive out of her path.

Miz spun around, snarling, but Pig Face grabbed for Soonsho and pulled her in front of him, his gun against her head, his hand pressed tightly against her mouth.

"Everyone stop!" he warned. His voice echoed around the now eerily silent ballroom. The other Xandrie lay on the floor, none of them moving beyond the occasional involuntary twitch. Some of Pig Face's eyes darted across his fallen comrades, while a few others kept watch over Miz, Mech, Loren and the others.

The eyes he had left over regarded Splurt with a mixture of wonder and fear. The little blob pulsed furiously on the floor, four vine-like tendrils extending from his lumpy body.

"What the fonk *is* that thing?" Pig Face whispered, but then he shook his head like he didn't really want to know. He pressed the muzzle of his gun harder against Soonsho's face, making her squirm in pain. "Here's what's going to happen," Pig Face snarled. "I'm taking the girl and I'm leaving. Anyone tries to come after me, I kill her. Once I'm clear, I'll be in touch to arrange the ransom."

"But we need her," said the Conductor.

"Well then, you should have thought of that before you killed all my guys!" Pig Face barked.

Miz raised herself onto the balls of her feet. A growl rumbled at the back of her throat.

"Miz, don't," said Loren.

"Call her off," Pig Face warned. "I mean it."

Miz's claws extended to their full terrifying length. Her gums drew up, revealing every last one of her teeth.

"Don't do this," Mech said. "You won't make it."

"*Call her off!*" Pig Face hissed. "Or I swear, this girl's brains are going to paint the—OW!"

He cried out as Soonsho sunk her teeth into the palm of

his hand. Instinctively, he yanked it away, and Soonsho fell to the floor, covering her head.

Miz pounced.

Pig Face brought up his gun.

And a single shot echoed around the ballroom.

CHAPTER TWENTY

Miz stood perfectly still, a vapor of blood misting the air in front of her face.

"Wh-what?" she said.

Then, with a thud, Pig Face toppled forwards, revealing Cal standing behind him.

Cal's arm flopped down. Loren's gun slipped from his blood-slicked fingers and clattered noisily on the metal ground. He managed a grin that was eighty-percent grimace, waved briefly, then his legs gave out and he collapsed in an uncomfortable-looking heap.

Despite a strong showing from Miz, Splurt reached Cal first. He bounced across the floor like a rubber ball, then bounded into Cal's arms.

"Ow! Ow! Careful, buddy," Cal hissed, and Splurt leaped clear in fright.

"Cal?" cried Loren, skidding up behind Mizette. "But... I mean... I thought you were dead."

"You were *totally* dead," Miz confirmed.

Cal nodded. "Yep. Yep, pretty much." He gestured to the

scorched metal plate on his chest and then jabbed a thumb towards his back. "Could someone…?"

Loren darted around behind him and fiddled with the harness until she figured out the clasp. The chest plate fell away. Mech, who had been marching over, recoiled in horror.

"Oh, shizz! Your chest!"

Cal looked upwards. "Is it bad? How bad is it? Is it bad?"

"Is what bad?" asked Loren, then she spotted his chest and her face became one big oval of surprise. "Oh… fonk. Wow. Just… wow."

"Oh Jesus," said Cal. "Is it as bad as that?"

Loren swallowed. "What? I mean… No, it's not… Wow."

"I think I'm gonna puke," said Mech. "And I don't even have a stomach."

"What is *that* thing?" asked Miz, bending down. "It looks so… squishy."

"Christ!" Cal yelped. He flitted his eyes down for a fraction of a second, far too quickly to actually see anything. "Just tell me, and be honest, can you see my spine?"

"Wait a minute," said Loren, squatting down to examine Cal more closely. She extended a finger and moved it towards the wound. Cal hissed and drew back. "Don't be such a baby," Loren told him. "Hold still."

"What the Hell are you doing? Don't touch it!" yelped Mech. "It'll fall out!"

"Oh, Jesus," Cal sobbed. "Please don't let anything fall out."

"It's healing," said Loren. She prodded the edge of the wound with her finger.

"It is?" said Cal.

Loren nodded. "I'm literally watching you knit back together. I can barely even see your ribcage now."

"My *ribcage?*" Cal yelped. "You could see my fonking *ribcage?*"

"Only the bony parts," said Loren.

"It's *all* bony parts!" said Cal. "It's nothing *but* bony parts."

Loren shuffled aside. "Mech, check this out."

"Hell no. I don't want to look," said Mech, who had turned away.

"Mech!"

With a grunt of irritation, Mech turned. He immediately recoiled again. "Oh shizz, that's even worse. It's moving!"

"Whoa," said Miz. "You're right. It's totally healing up."

Cal gritted his teeth, then risked a glance down. The wound was still a red and sticky hole in his chest, and he had to bite his lip to stop himself screaming.

As he watched, though, something happened. From the edges of the wound, a layer of thick white bone bloomed, closing over his exposed heart like a set of landing bay doors. Even as the bone joined, tendrils of muscle and sinew had begun creeping across it.

Loren, Miz and Mech watched it in stunned silence, while Splurt rolled up against Cal's back, supporting him.

"Thanks, buddy," Cal whispered, absent-mindedly. He, too, was staring in wonder at his rapidly-healing chest. The bone was completely covered now, and a semi-transparent layer of pink skin coated the muscle like gloss paint.

"Can all humans do that?" Loren asked.

Cal swallowed. "Not that I know of," he said. He looked up and met her gaze. "It was Tullok."

Mech frowned. "Tullok? As in the old healer guy on the other side of that wormhole?"

Cal nodded. "Back on that planet, before I went looking

for Splurt, he gave me his life force. All of it. I mean, he literally turned himself to ash in the process. It was, like, one of the top ten most traumatic moments of my life."

"And, what, it made you immortal?" asked Loren.

"Fonked if I know," said Cal. He pointed to his now almost fully-healed chest. "This might be a one-time thing for all I know. The guy was, like, a hundred years old, I don't imagine he had a whole lot of life force left to give. Although, now I think about it, it explains my ear healing up before, after that cop shot it off."

He raised his arms. Miz and Mech took one each and helped him to his feet, with Splurt pushing from behind. Cal gingerly prodded his chest, slightly worried it might collapse like partially-set meringue at his touch. To his immense relief, it didn't. It felt... normal. Were it not for the blood currently drying on his stomach, and the circular hole burned through the front of his shirt, no-one would have been able to tell anything had even happened to him.

Loren stooped and retrieved her blaster. "How did you get my gun?"

"Hmm? Oh, I took it off you when we were hugging. You should really look after it better."

"Why?"

"So nobody steals it."

"No, I mean why did *you* take it?"

"Oh." Cal shrugged. "I thought I might have to shoot someone. I wasn't actually expecting them to blow me up."

Mech looked over to Pig Face's fallen body. Soonsho, her parents, and the Conductor and Conductress all stood well clear of him, watching Cal in silence. Around them, several servants had already begun the process of clearing away the Xandrie corpses.

"Looks like your aim's improved," Mech said. "Maybe I'll give you your own gun back."

"Yeah," said Cal, shifting awkwardly. "It was supposed to be a warning shot."

"Or maybe I won't."

Cal limped across to Soonsho. His legs didn't hurt, but given everything he'd just been through, he felt some dramatic limping was only appropriate.

"Everyone OK?" he asked.

"Yes," said the Conductor. "Thank you. Confused, perhaps, but in good health. What happened?"

Cal shrugged. "Uh, short version, there were some guys in your bathroom, they put a bomb on me, I died, I came back." He gestured over to where two servants were mopping up a partially exploded Xandrie. "As for this, I have absolutely no idea."

"Splurt," said Mech.

"Splurt killed all these guys?"

"Oh yes," said Loren. "It was…"

"Awesome," said Miz.

"Well, I was going to say 'harrowing,' but that, too," said Loren.

Cal looked back over his shoulder. Splurt pulsed anxiously, his eyes pointed to the floor. "Splurt! Way to go, buddy!"

Splurt rippled, his eyes springing up to the top of his head. He formed a semi-circular bowl shape, and rocked happily from side to side.

"I can only apologize," said the Conductor. "I shall tighten security at once."

"So much for being protected, huh?" said Mech.

"We are," the Conductor insisted. "Or… we will be. Soon."

Mech opened his mouth to argue, but the Conductor went straight for his weak spot.

"Now, about your reward…"

"Finally," said Mech.

"You returned Soonsho to us," the Conductor said. "For which we promised you one million credits, correct?"

"That's right," agreed Mech.

"Technically, husband, they returned her to us twice," said the Conductress. "Were it not for them, Soonsho would now be in the stars."

Mech's eyes lit up. "I like your thinking, lady."

"I agree," said the Conductor. "The Conductress is wise in such matters. Two million credits it is."

Mech let out a high-pitched squeak, but otherwise said nothing.

The Conductor indicated one of his servants. "My staff will take your ship's identification codes and initiate the transfer immediately. The funds will be with you a few seconds later."

"Thank you," said Loren, as Mech hurried over to the servant to sort out the details. "It's very generous."

"It is only money," said the Conductor. "Having Soonsho back with us is… well, it's everything to us."

Soonsho's parents hugged her. She buried her face in her dad's shoulder for a while, then raised her eyes to Cal. She smiled, but there was something about it that didn't quite look right. It was like she was smiling *despite* something, rather than because of it.

"And now, for another reward," said the Conductor, placing a hand on Cal's shoulder and turning him around. "Something very few outsiders have ever had the good fortune to witness."

Across the ballroom, hundreds of hatches slid open in the floor. Someone rose upwards through each one – men, women, adults and children, all dressed in flowing white robes.

The Conductor squeezed Cal's shoulder, and his rich booming voice became a soft, awed whisper. "The Choir of Cantato Minor."

"Great!" said Cal, trying to muster up some enthusiasm. It wasn't that he'd ever had any bad experiences of choirs, exactly, it was just that he'd never really had any particularly good ones. Any time he'd found himself in a situation where listening to one was an inescapable inevitability, they'd been tedious at best.

He'd found one way of making them more enjoyable was to try to stand within earshot, and hum a completely different tune at alternating registers. It was amazing how quickly that sort of thing could spread through the choir like a virus, completely derailing the whole awful thing.

Much as he'd like to mess with these guys in the same way, he felt it wouldn't really be right. He was a guest of the Cantatorians, and the choir was obviously a pretty big deal. Besides, he was too far away for any of them to hear him without everyone else hearing, too. So, there was nothing to do but grin and bear it. Besides, he'd recently been through death. This couldn't be any worse than that.

Across the room, one of the men emitted a low, groaning sort of note.

OK, maybe a *bit* worse, but not much.

And then the singing began. Only it wasn't singing. Not really. There were sounds, certainly, but to call them that didn't do them justice. The notes danced through the air, finding footholds deep in Cal's soul. Three seconds into the performance, Cal was holding his breath. Five seconds in, he was crying.

He felt *begun*. That was the only way he could describe it. Like everything until this moment had been a warm-up for this, here, now. His skin goosebumped, his hair quivered. He felt love and loss and sadness and joy. And more. Much more. *Everything* more.

There were no individual voices, just a concurrence of sound that seemed to be affecting him on the molecular level. He heard the colors of each note, smelled the harmonies, tasted the emotion and the passion behind the performance.

He was shaking. He was pretty sure that wasn't normal, but he didn't care. He didn't care about much, in fact. Just the music. Only the music. Always the music.

He remembered there were others in the room with him, and was pleased to note he wasn't the only one reacting this way. Loren and Miz were completely transfixed. Even Splurt swayed hypnotically.

Only Mech didn't seem too invested in the choir. He was tapping the controls on his arm, barely paying the singers any attention. Cal almost felt himself getting angry. He wanted to march over there and punch Mech straight in his stupid metal face.

But then, he might miss a note. And that wouldn't do at all.

The Conductor and Conductress stood holding hands, swaying gently in time with the choir song. Behind them, Soonsho stood between her parents, gazing wistfully towards the ballroom ceiling, like she could see the same colors Cal could, dancing and twirling like leaves in a tornado.

The song built to a big finish. The singers gave it their all, and a chasm of empty hopelessness opened in the pit of Cal's stomach. He almost doubled over from the sheer grief and heartache of it, but then the tone of the music changed, and Cal was suddenly filled with hope. It spread through his core like the rising sun, pushing away the darkness and shadow, and driving out the cold.

And then, with a couple of final warbles and a *ping* from something not unlike a triangle, the music stopped, leaving only its echo to seep into the fabric of the room.

Cal cleared his throat. He wanted to speak, but he wasn't ready. Not yet.

His body tingled. His whole essence, in fact. He watched, wordlessly, as the choir slowly sank back into the floor through the holes at their feet, and found himself almost mourning their loss as the hatches slid closed above them.

"My apologies," said the Conductor. "There were a few errors in their performance. They are unaccustomed to singing for off-worlders. I think nerves may have gotten the better of some of them."

"Hmm?" said Cal. He felt like the Conductor expected some sort of reply, but that was the best he could come up with at the moment.

"Can, like, everyone do that?" asked Miz, whose well-cultivated ironic detachment to pretty much everything had allowed her to recover more quickly than the others.

"To an extent," said the Conductor. "We all have our own unique vocal ranges. They are our greatest assets – and our greatest weapon. But, yes, one thing we all share is a passion for singing."

"But not Soonsho?" said Loren, finding her own voice.

"No," said the Conductor. "Soonsho is quite unique in that regard. Her voice..." He bowed to Soonsho and smiled. "...while undoubtedly beautiful, emits at frequencies quite unlike those of any other Cantatorian. It is a powerful instrument but, alas, one far too dangerous to ever use."

"Oh, I don't know," said Cal, finally regaining the power of speech. "It got us out of a couple of nasty situations."

"It's there!" yelped Mech. "We got it!" He jigged on the spot, and the clanking and whirring of hydraulics reverberated around the room. "We're rich. We're fonking rich!"

"Aha," said the Conductor. "It appears the reward transfer has been completed. Our thanks to you all, once again."

He gestured to one of the doors the Xandrie had kicked open. It was already in the process of being repaired. "And now the time has come for us to bid you farewell. We have some pressing matters which we must attend to." He looked to Mech. "Regarding the renewal of our defenses, as it happens. I'm sure you'll approve."

"I don't care," cheered Mech. "I am all kinds of rich!"

"He likes money," Cal explained.

"Yes," said the Conductor. "I guessed that. Spend it wisely, my friends. I fear grave times lie ahead for the galaxy. I wish you well."

He made a gesture with one hand, like a waveform snaking in the air. "May your song carry long and carry far."

"Thanks," said Cal. "May your helmet always be shiny and your..." He glanced down at the bulge in the Conductor's jumpsuit and shook his head. "Actually, I'm going to leave it there."

He started to turn, then stopped. "Oh, and I'd like to apologize for any inadvertent spillages I may have caused in the bathroom. It was dark, and I had a knife to my throat, so conditions were less than optimal. My aim *may* have been a little off."

The Conductor and Conductress both nodded, but said

nothing.

"By which I mean it was *definitely* a little off," Cal said. "By which I mean I peed on the floor."

"It shall be dealt with," the Conductor assured him.

"Great!" Cal approached Soonsho and her family. "Well, looks like we're heading off," he said.

"Thank you. Thank you," said Soonsho's dad. He took Cal's hand and wrapped his fingers around it. "We can never repay you for what you have given us back."

"All part of the service," said Cal. He shook Soonsho's mom's hand, too, then turned to the girl herself. "Hey, you. You OK?"

Soonsho nodded. Her lips moved, just a fraction. Miz's ears raised.

"What'd she say?"

"She says she's where she needs to be."

"Right," said Cal. "I guess that's all any of us can ask for."

"May your song carry long and carry far," said Soonsho's dad, bowing in gratitude.

"Oh, it's gonna carry far," said Mech, still jiggling gleefully. "It's gonna carry us far, far away from here!"

Cal winked at Soonsho. He ruffled the girl's spiky red hair. "Told you you'd be safe, kid. Cal Carver guarantee."

And with that, Cal turned, saluted the room in general, then headed for the door.

CHAPTER TWENTY-ONE

One short flying-disk ride later, Cal sat in his chair, a plate of banoffee pie balanced on each knee. Loren was busily prepping the controls for take-off, while Miz studied her claws and chipped in with the occasional withering criticism.

Mech, meanwhile, was still dancing gleefully. He shimmied on the spot, checking and rechecking the credit balance like he couldn't quite believe it was real.

"Two million credits. *Two* million credits. Two *million* credits," he chirped. "Come on, everyone say it with me. Two milllllllion credits."

"It's a lot of money," Cal agreed. "You know, I mean, I think. I don't really know anything about space finance. Is it a lot of money?"

"It's a lot of money," Mech confirmed. "It's a *whole* lot of money."

"I want to buy a boat," said Miz.

"What?" said Mech.

Miz looked up from her nails. "A boat. I want to buy one."

220

"Hell no," said Mech. "I ain't going on no boat."

Cal chuckled. "That is *so* B.A."

On the viewscreen, the sea of grateful Cantatorians had become little more than a series of small puddles. They'd been gathered in a ring around the castle when Cal and the others had left, and the initial whoops and cheers when the disk had emerged through the castle doorways had quickly faded when it was obvious Soonsho wasn't with them. The crew had floated on in a slightly embarrassing silence, and it had been a relief to make it back to the ship.

"We've got clearance to take-off," Loren announced.

"Let's give him a tip," said Mech.

"Who?"

"Whoever just cleared us for take-off," Mech said. "Give him a tip. We can afford it."

"It's an automated system," said Loren.

"Oh, and we can't give an automated system a tip?"

Loren frowned. "Not really, no."

"Well, too late, I just did!" said Mech, pointing to his arm and grinning. It let out a little bleep. Mech's eyes flitted down to the display screen above his wrist, but the rest of his expression remained resolutely positive. "Granted, it has immediately been rejected, but I'm so rich, I don't even care."

Cal raised a hand. "Uh, I vote we don't leave Mech in charge of the money. All in favor?"

Loren and Miz raised a hand. Splurt turned into a hand, then raised himself.

"Fine. Fine. No more tips," said Mech. "But come on, we're rich!"

"I thought you said it wasn't going to get us far," said Cal. "You know, back when you wanted to rob Dorid."

"Which you should've let me do," said Mech.

221

"I totally should," Cal agreed. "But, in my defense, at the time I wasn't aware he was going to try to kill us with an army of freaks. Had I known that, I might have thought very differently about the whole not-stealing from the guy situation."

"I said a million credits wouldn't get us far. We got two million," Mech said. "That'll get us further."

"Twice as far," Cal guessed. "Unless Miz buys a boat, in which case a little less than twice as far, I suppose."

"I ain't going in no boat," Mech said.

Cal shrugged. "Well, not unless we drug your milk." He clapped his hands together. "OK, Loren, take us out of here. There is literally nothing around or above us for you to crash into, so I have a very good feeling about this lift-off."

"Thanks for the vote of confidence," said Loren.

"Don't mention it." Cal picked up the plates that were balancing on his knees and held them out to Mech and Miz. "Anyone want any banoffee pie, by the way? I don't even know why I asked the machine to make these. I think it might be becoming a mental illness."

"Fruit," Miz reminded him.

Cal looked down at the slices of pie, then lifted each one to his mouth in turn and ate the banana slices off the top. "Better?" he asked, dribbling blobs of cream down his chin.

Miz stared at him for a few seconds, then shrugged. "Sure. Why not?"

Cal passed her the plates, then sank back into his chair. He spent the next minute and a half masticating through the banana slices, which had combined to form one baseball-sized lump in his mouth.

By the time he'd managed to swallow, the *Untitled* had punched up through the atmosphere, leaving Cantato Minor behind. Cal rubbed his aching jaws and scooped the last few blobs of cream off his teeth with his tongue.

"If anyone sees me asking that machine for banoffee pie again, please kill me," he groaned. "I mean it. It'll be a kindness." He opened his mouth wide, then smacked his lips together a few times. "I still taste death," he announced.

"And what does that taste like?" Loren asked.

"Like, kind of stale and ashy. Dusty. You know, *deady*," Cal said. "And a bit like bananas, but I suspect that's the pie."

"Probably," agreed Loren.

"Yeah. Otherwise it's a fonking mind-blowing coincidence."

Kevin's voice blasted out of his speaker system, making Cal jump. "Water, sir?"

A circular hatch slid open in Cal's arm rest and a glass of iced water rose out of it, like the singers of the Cantatorian choir. "Hey, would you look at that!" said Cal. "My chair makes drinks!"

He picked up the glass, then eyed the arm rest suspiciously. "Does it make pie, too?"

"No, sir."

"Thank God," said Cal.

He took a sip of his drink, then spun his chair around. The seat where Soonsho had been sitting was, of course, now empty. Cal swished the water around in his mouth before swallowing.

"Well, looks like all's well that ends well," he said.

Miz finished the last piece of pie. "What does that mean?"

"Oh, you know. Nothing at all," said Cal. "It's just a saying. I guess it means... I don't know. Things that end well *are* well, maybe? Does that make sense?"

"Not really," said Miz.

"Sounds like bullshizz to me," Mech agreed.

"Yeah, well, the point still stands. We did good, guys." He raised his glass in toast. "To Space Team!"

"Yeah, we're not going to say that," said Miz.

Cal shrugged. "Suit yourself," he said, then he took a long drink to try to wash away the tastes of death and banoffee pie.

"I was growing rather fond of Ms Sooss," said Kevin. "Such a pity she's going to be put to death."

Cal choked on his water, spraying almost the entire contents of the glass over the back of Loren's head.

"Hey!"

"*What?*" Cal wheezed, coughing as the few drops of liquid that hadn't hit Loren somehow managed to find their way into his lungs. "What are you talking about? Put to death?"

"Oh yes, sir," said Kevin. "I thought you knew."

"No! I didn't know!" Cal yelped. He spun in his chair. "Miz, Mech, did you know?"

"No, man."

"Nu-uh."

"Loren?"

"Of course I didn't!"

"See? None of us knew, Kevin!" Cal cried. "None of us knew. Why didn't you say something?"

"It was all there in the files I brought up. Didn't you read them, sir?"

"No! I made a point of *not* reading that stuff! I'm pretty sure we even had a conversation about how I hadn't read it!"

"Did we, sir? I'm afraid I don't recall," said Kevin. "But yes. She is to be put to death. That's why the Cantatorians were so keen to get her back, you see? So she could be sacrificed. It was rather the point of them offering the reward. Rather rum luck for the girl, really."

Cal clutched his head. "Oh Jesus, we brought her home to die," he muttered, then he looked up at the ceiling. "Wait, what do you mean 'sacrificed'? Sacrificed to who? To god?"

"No, sir."

"Well who, then?"

"To the Spider-Dragon of Saktar, sir," said Kevin.

Cal blinked several times.

"OK, you're going to have to run that one by me again," he said, after some thought. "What the *fonk* is the Spider-Dragon of Saktar?"

"It's an old Cantatorian legend, sir. Old as their civilization, in fact," Kevin intoned. "Saktar is the prominent mountain around which they have structured the bulk of their society. Perhaps you saw it?"

"It's a huge mountain. Of course we saw it!"

"Well, maybe not Loren," said Miz.

"Miz, not now!" said Cal. "What about the mountain?"

"The legend goes that the Spider-Dragon resides within it, and that it shall emerge in times of need to protect Cantato Minor. In return, it asks only one thing."

"A sacrifice," Cal guessed.

"Indeed, sir. Once every hundred years, a girl is selected at birth. From that moment onwards, her life belongs to all of Cantato Minor. Her purpose, when the time comes, is to be thrown into the fiery pit at the top of the mountain where, it is believed, the Spider-Dragon of Saktar shall feast upon her flesh, and fashion implements from her bones."

"Jesus!" said Cal. "So we brought her home to be tossed into a volcano?"

"Precisely that, sir. The idea of a Spider-Dragon is a rather ludicrous one for an otherwise highly-advanced species, so while she has little to worry about on that front, it is the fall into the fiery pits of Saktar which is likely to pose the problem. Survival-wise."

"And everyone knows about this? The Conductor? Her parents?"

"Oh yes, sir."

"Soonsho?"

"Indeed. She will have been prepared for it from a young age. It's an honor, in many ways. Albeit a somewhat double-edged one. You know, what with dying and everything."

"We have to go back," said Cal.

"Now, wait a minute, wait a minute. Let's not rush into this," said Mech. "Who are we to judge other cultures? You know? This is a tradition. You heard Kevin, it's an honor to be chosen. I mean, who's to say she doesn't want to be thrown into a mountain? Hmm? You ever think of that?"

"She doesn't," said Cal. "I saw it on her face earlier. I knew there was something wrong. I should have said something."

"But, my point is," Mech continued, "should we really be interfering in what seems – certainly from what I've heard in the past few minutes - to be an important cultural event in—?"

"We won't let them take the money back," said Cal.

Mech punched his fist into the palm of his other hand. "Then what the Hell are we waiting for? Turn the ship around and let's go back there before they toss the kid into a fonking volcano!"

Cal sucked air in through his teeth. "They're not going to be happy."

"Well, long as we're agreed they ain't getting my money," said Mech. He caught the look from Miz and quickly corrected himself. "*Our* money. Who really cares? The kid saved us. Least once, maybe twice."

"Maybe we can talk some sense into them," said Loren. "You know, persuade them not to go through with it. They seemed pretty reasonable people."

"They did," Cal agreed. "Although that was before we found out they were going to toss an innocent teenager head first into a volcano to satisfy a fictional Spider-Dragon. Now that's come to light, I'll be honest, they kinda seem less reasonable. I'm not sure we're going to be able to talk them round."

"All guns blazing, is it, sir?" asked Kevin. "Good show!"

Cal's solitary joystick *twanged* out of his chair.

"Thanks, Kevin, but hopefully it won't come to that," said Cal. "We'll go down, try to reason with them, then, when that inevitably fails, Mech can throw Soonsho over his shoulder, and we'll all run away as fast as our legs will carry us. Anyone see any obvious flaws in that plan?"

Mizette shrugged. "I guess it isn't terrible."

"Miz, that is arguably the single most positive thing I've ever heard you say," Cal said. "Thank you."

He spun his chair to the front, slapped his hands on his thighs, then stood up. "Loren, set a course for Cantato Minor," he said. "If anyone needs me, I'll be through the back, eating pie and crying."

The *Currently Untitled* dropped through the atmosphere of Cantato Minor, several hundred miles away from where it had exited. Cal sat in his chair, feeling anxious and bloated. Mostly bloated. He could feel several pounds of cream and caramel sitting like a rock in his lower intestine, and he was pretty sure his blood had turned to butter.

The empty redness of the Cantato Minor landscape spread out in all directions beneath them. Ahead, rising in the distance, stood Saktar. The top third or so was mostly obscured by cloud, but from back here they could see the very tip of the mountain-top just barely poking through the cloud layer.

"Anything?" Cal asked.

Mech shook his head. "Don't think they've noticed us."

"Good. Kevin, do we still have that cloaking thing?"

"Well, unless it's fallen off when I wasn't looking, sir, then yes. Should I activate it?"

"Do it," said Cal. "The longer we can keep the element of surprise, the better. Any sign of Soonsho?"

"It appears they have already begun the ritual, sir," said Kevin.

Cal sat bolt upright in his chair. "They've already tossed her in?"

"Not yet, sir. However, I don't believe we have a lot of time. If we wish to prevent Ms Sooss meeting an untimely end, I suggest we should probably hurry up."

Loren tapped a few controls and the section of the screen showing the mountain top grew to fill the view. They were still too far away to see clearly, but there was definite activity going on up there. Platforms floated above the pit. Figures moved around on top of them. It was impossible to tell if any of them were Soonsho, but Cal was prepared to bet she was up there somewhere.

"OK, can you take us into the cloud? Ideally without crashing into the mountain?" Cal asked.

"Uh… yes," said Loren.

"Well way to fill us all with confidence, Loren," said Miz.

"I can do it," said Loren. "It's not a problem."

"Then do it. Keep us low until we've figured out what's going on, then we'll show ourselves. Slow and steady."

The *Untitled* descended into the thick bank of cloud and edged forwards. The cloud itself probably wouldn't be enough to hide the ship, but between that and the cloaking device, Cal reckoned, they should go unnoticed.

As they drew closer, the true picture of what was going on above the mountain began to reveal itself. The Conductor and Soonsho stood alone on one of the flying disks. Several other disks surrounded them, hanging in the air at various levels. The Conductress stood on one, alongside Soonsho's parents. Various men and women in long, ornate robes stood on the other platforms. Dignitaries of some kind, Cal guessed. Priests, maybe.

The cloud became too thick for them to see through. Kevin automatically overlaid a heat map on the screen. The Conductor had Soonsho held by the back of the neck. With his free hand he alternated between gesturing at the sky and the vast mouth of the mountain beneath them.

"I bet he's chanting," said Cal. "Guys like this, they love a bit of chanting."

"He's getting agitated," said Loren. "Like he's building to the finale."

"He's gonna push her in," Mech warned.

"OK, take us up," said Cal. "Get us over them, then once we're in place we'll show ourselves."

"Uh, sir," chimed a voice from above.

"Not now, Kevin," said Cal. Loren was easing back on the stick, tilting the nose of the *Untitled* out through the cloud bank.

"Try not to, like, fly us into the volcano," Miz suggested. "It's that big rock thing with all the fire inside."

"I'll try," said Loren through gritted teeth.

"Easy," said Cal. "Easy. We don't want them knowing

we're here yet."

"Sir…"

"One sec, Kevin."

Loren guided the ship clear of the cloud, skimmed dangerously close to the lip of the volcano, then banked upwards until they were level with Soonsho and the Conductor.

It was at this point that Cal realized everyone on the platforms was staring at the *Untitled* in shock.

"I don't understand. What are they looking at?" he asked.

"Us, sir," said Kevin. "I tried to tell you, the cloaking device doesn't turn the ship invisible, it merely hides it from scanner detection."

"So… they can all see us?"

"Indeed, sir."

"They can all see the ship?"

"They can, sir."

"Shizz. So much for that plan." Cal stood up. "Loren, turn us around and lower the landing ramp. I guess I'd better go talk to them."

Cal stood on the edge of the ramp, the vast, gaping mouth of Saktar yawning below him. They were high enough that the heat wasn't intense, but it was definitely uncomfortable. Sweat slicked his back, and he was beginning to regret putting on a fresh shirt. Although, that was pretty far down his list of problems at the moment.

The Conductor's disk was somewhere around fifteen feet ahead of him, and slightly lower. With a good run up and the wind at his back, he could potentially land on it, but he was far more likely to fall short and plunge into the bubbling mass of lava far below, so he put that idea on the back burner for the moment.

"Listen, you don't have to do this," Cal said.

"Yes," said the Conductor, his face scrunched up with anger. "We do."

All around him, the other Cantatorians wore similarly furious expressions. Only Soonsho had seemed pleased to see him, although that wasn't all that surprising, given the circumstances. Her parents didn't look averse to the idea of him being there, but they weren't rolling out the red carpet, either.

"Think about what you're doing here," Cal said. "You're about to throw an innocent girl to her death. And for what? Because some ancient legend about a Dragon-Spider told you to?"

"Spider-Dragon," the Conductor hissed.

Cal waved a hand. "Same thing. Tell me, Conductor – any of you – have any of you ever actually seen this thing? Has anyone? Hmm? In all these years, with all these sacrifices, has there ever been one scrap of evidence to suggest there's anything down there but smoke and lava?"

"The legends are very clear," said the Conductor.

"So what? Where I come from, *Scooby Doo* is very clear, it doesn't mean he's real!" said Cal. "I mean, don't get me wrong, it'd be awesome if he was, but he isn't." He held out his left hand, palm upwards. "Legends." He held out his right hand. "Facts. See? Not the same thing."

He looked around at the other Cantatorians, hoping to see them all deep in thought, carefully contemplating his wise words. But nope. Based on their expressions, they pretty much all just wanted him dead.

"This legend is… what? A few thousand years old?"

"A few *hundred* thousand," said the Conductor, quite grandly, as if this added weight to his argument.

"Jesus. OK. So, let me get this straight. Hundreds of thousands of years ago, someone told a story about a Dragon-Spider—"

"Spider-Dragon!"

"Whatever. About a Spider-Dragon who lives – and I'm going to say this part slowly – *inside an active fonking volcano*, and who, without ever actually showing itself or anything, somehow demands a sacrifice every hundred years." Cal looked across his audience again. "That's what you believe? Seriously?"

"You are an outsider," said the Conductress. "You would not understand."

"No, I understand perfectly," said Cal. "I understand that you're all nuts. All of you. And, usually, I'd have no problem with that. Believe what you like. Knock yourself out. But when your beliefs involve you throwing children into lakes of fire, that's where I have to draw the line."

"She wants to do it. She is *honored* to do it," said the Conductor.

Cal met Soonsho's eye. Her expression told him everything he needed to know. "No. No, she doesn't," he said. "So she's coming with us."

"No," the Conductor hissed. "She is not."

He pushed. Soonsho grabbed frantically for him, but she couldn't turn enough before her foot went over the edge of the disk. She fell in silence through the stinging smoke and the rising heat, her eyes open, her mouth tightly closed, afraid of hurting anyone, even now.

"Shizz. *SPLURT!*" Cal yelped, then he launched himself off the landing ramp, tucked himself into a dive, and plunged after the girl.

The ash and smoke scraped across his eyes, layering

them with a film of soot. The heat, which had already been uncomfortable, quickly became borderline unbearable. It stung his skin and stole his breath away as he fell down, down, down towards the flailing Soonsho, and the lake of lava looming below.

She was falling awkwardly, all flapping arms and thrashing legs. Cal sliced through the air, straight and streamlined, and gaining fast. Twenty feet away. Fifteen. He gritted his teeth against the pain, smelled his nostril-hair charring away into nothing.

Ten feet. Five.

He tried to call to her, to reassure her everything would be OK, but his voice was a shriveled croak and a series of spluttering coughs.

Three feet. One.

Zero.

Cal's hands wrapped around Soonsho's waist. A rubbery tendril tightened around his legs. Splurt!

They plunged another half dozen or so feet, then Splurt tightened like a bungee rope, and suddenly the lava was moving away from them as they sprang upwards, leaving the worst of the heat and smoke behind.

"It's OK. I got you," Cal wheezed. He coughed up something black and spat a wad of it into the molten red metal below. "I got you."

Splurt pulled them onto the landing ramp, but kept a hold of Cal's leg, just in case he tried anything stupid again. "I'm OK, buddy. Thanks," Cal croaked. "Take Soonsho inside."

Soonsho looked across the gap at her parents, then at the Conductor.

"What do you think you are doing?" the Conductor

boomed. "You are the sacrifice of Saktar! This is your destiny."

Soonsho bit her lip, her eyes shimmering with tears. Then, she raised a middle finger in the Conductor's direction, and stumbled up the ramp behind Splurt.

"Ha! She must've picked that up from Miz," Cal said. "Teenagers, huh?"

He nodded to Soonsho's parents. "We're going to look after her. Don't worry, she'll be safe. Safer than she was here, anyway."

Cal fired off a salute. "It's been a pleasure," he said. "You know, parts of it." He about-turned and was halfway up the ramp when the mountain shook.

He stopped. He turned back.

"OK. Um. What was that?" he asked. He peered over the edge in time to see the lava lake begin to ripple, as something shifted beneath the surface.

A long, black leg, easily a mile long extended from within the lava and pressed itself against the inside wall of the volcano. Two equally enormous mandibles rose out of the molten metal and snapped hungrily at the air.

"Oh," said Cal. He swallowed, and shot the Conductor a nervous smile. "Whoops. My bad!"

CHAPTER TWENTY-TWO

Cal raced back up the ramp, just as a second leg and a substantial amount of head appeared from beneath the lava.

"The ramp! Close the fonking ramp!"

Outside, the flying disks scattered, retreating from the mountaintop at top speed. An eruption of molten metal spewed into the air, and Cal felt a brief blast of searing heat at his back before the hatch slid into place behind him.

"What's going on? What happened?" demanded Loren, as Cal stumbled through the door behind her. Several warnings were flashing on screen, all of them in varying shades of emergency red. "Is the volcano erupting?"

"Something along those lines," said Cal, flopping into his seat. Soonsho was already scrabbling for her seat belt, while Splurt pulsed protectively in front of her. "Uh, you might want to put a bit of distance between us and the mountain."

Loren edged forward on the thruster. "How much distance?"

"Ooh, about the length of a giant spider should be

enough. Maybe a little further, just to be on the safe side."

Loren, Mech and Miz all turned to look at them. Cal smiled sheepishly. "So, yeah, funny story. You know the Spider-Dragon of Saktar we spoke about earlier? Turns out, totally a real thing."

"Rear cameras," Mech grunted.

One third of the screen changed to show a view of the mountaintop behind them, just as one of the mile-long legs emerged from within the crater. Lava oozed between the hairs and dribbled down the mountain's steep curves, blackening the metal.

"Ho-lee shizz," Mech mumbled. "What is that thing?"

"Spider-Dragon of Saktar," said Cal. "Thought we'd established that?"

"We should probably, like, get out of here," said Miz. "I mean, that thing is pretty awesome, and I kinda want to see the whole thing, but it's totally going to kill us all if we stick around, right?"

"That is certainly a possibility," said Cal. Another leg emerged. The snapping tips of the beast's mandibles appeared above the volcano's rim. "But... does anyone else feel, I don't know, maybe a little guilty about this? Like – and call me crazy here – like this is somehow partially our fault?"

"Guilty? No way, man," said Mech. "They were going to kill the girl. They didn't seem too guilty about that."

"True, true," said Cal. "And, I mean, obviously that was wrong, but I guess they *kinda* had their reasons."

The Spider-Dragon's head emerged from the mountain. Even just the corner they could see was several times larger than the *Untitled*. Where its eyes should have been were several crater-sized hollow scars seared into its slick, glistening black skull.

"Or one big reason, anyway," Cal said. "Stop up here, we should be far enough away."

Loren slowed the ship to a stop. They all watched in silence as the enormous creature heaved the rest of itself out of the volcano, sending molten metal slopping over the sides. The body was roughly the same length as the legs, possibly a little longer, but the way it was bunched up made it hard to tell for sure.

It only had six legs, so wasn't technically a spider at all, based on Cal's understanding of the word. Then again, the sheer size of each limb probably more than made up for the reduced number of them, so he wasn't about to argue semantics. Besides, even if he had been in the mood to do so, there was a *giant fonking spider* climbing out of a volcano right behind him, so now probably wasn't the best time.

The beast threw back its head and its mandibles parted, revealing a scrunched up sphincter of a mouth. It widened unpleasantly, and a screech tore across the sky. It echoed and rolled across the shimmering red landscape, and vibrated through the *Untitled*, making Cal's teeth rattle.

"Doesn't sound happy," said Loren.

"Hey, we don't know that," Cal argued. "For all we know, that was a positive noise. Sort of, 'hey, I'm a giant spider, I'm partially covered in lava, but I feel good nonetheless.' It could absolutely have been that kind of noise."

"It wasn't though, was it?" said Loren.

Cal sighed. "No. No, it's clearly furious and wants everyone dead."

Under normal circumstances, when confronted by a lava-sodden monster spider, Cal would have been among the first to run away. Anyone who *didn't* run away in that situation deserved everything they got, as far as he was concerned, even if what they got was eaten by a lava-sodden monster spider. Especially if that was what they got, in fact.

The *Untitled* was already out of its reach, unless the thing had some crack-shot web-shooting skills it was waiting to reveal. They could be in orbit around the planet in just a few seconds, far into deep space within a minute and a half. Less, if Loren didn't crash into anything. They could just go. Leave. The lava-sodden monster spider didn't have to be their problem.

But, sadly, it *was* their problem. It could be argued that Cal wasn't the most honest guy in the galaxy – his rap sheet back on Earth would attest to that – but he had an annoyingly straight-shooting conscience. Also, despite his best efforts, he had an unfortunate habit of usually trying to do The Right Thing. Even if The Right Thing was ludicrously dangerous, unfathomably stupid, and involved lava-sodden monster spiders.

He couldn't have just let Soonsho die. Even knowing what he now knew – that the Cantatorians weren't suffering from some shared delusion and did, in fact, have a Spider-Dragon living in their mountain – he'd have saved her. It was The Right Thing.

Annoyingly, though, saving the rest of her species from arachnid-based genocide was also The Right Thing. Like it or not, he'd caused this problem, and his conscience was going to make damn sure he helped clean it up.

"Cal!"

Loren's voice snapped Cal out of his thought process. "Hmm? Sorry, I was inner-monologuing. What's up?"

"What's...? What do you mean 'what's up?'" said Mech, pointing to the creature on screen. "That's what's up! What's the plan?"

"Why's it called a Spider-Dragon?" Cal wondered.

"Who cares?" asked Miz. "Let's just get out of here before it noticed us."

"No, but... I mean, I get the spider part." He gestured to the viewscreen. "Exhibit A. But... dragon? Where did that come from? Has it got wings or something we don't know about?"

As they watched, the creature snapped its head around and opened is puckered anus of a mouth again. A scorching jet of fire half a mile long flared from within its cavernous throat. As the inferno hit the clouds, they erupted in an explosion of red flame.

"Oh, it breathes fire," said Cal. "Of *course* it does. I mean, why wouldn't it?"

"Hold on!" Loren yelped. The clouds ignited around them, engulfing the *Untitled* in a fiery cocoon. Alarms wailed. Several new warnings appeared on screen, while the existing ones grew larger and more insistent.

"I'm not sure if you're aware, but it appears the ship is on fire," Kevin announced.

"We noticed!" cried Cal.

"Oh. I see. How did that happen?"

"What do you mean, *how did it happen?*" Mech boomed. "It was the fonking Spider-Dragon!"

"The Spider-Dragon, sir?" said Kevin, sounding rather skeptical. "Of Saktar, sir?"

"No, a *different* Spider-Dragon," snapped Cal. "Yes! Of course of Saktar. It's right there!"

There was a short pause.

"Oh my. So it is. Apologies, sir, there was a problem with the replicator which required my attention. One of the nozzles was quite badly jammed by a sweet, sticky substance I was unfamiliar with, but which I was able to successfully—"

"Kevin, shut up, we'll worry about that later," said Cal.

"No need to worry, sir. It's all taken care of. Emergency over."

"Kevin, you and I have very different definitions of the word 'emergency,'" Cal said.

"Shields holding," Mech announced. "We're good."

The flames fizzled away as the clouds burned themselves out. The screen cleared in time to reveal the Spider-Dragon springing from the mountain side, its legs thrashing as it hurtled directly towards the *Untitled*.

"I think 'good' might have been an exaggeration," said Miz.

"Loren!" Cal yelped.

"On it!"

She leaned on a lever and the ship shot forwards. The Spider-Dragon screeched furiously, narrowly missing its target. Sparks flew from the barbed tips of its legs as they slammed into the metal surface of Cantato Minor.

"Hit it with the thrusters," Cal said. Loren obliged and four jets of translucent blue energy blasted the monster right in the empty eye sockets.

The Spider-Dragon didn't flinch. "No effect," said Loren.

"The thing lives inside an active fonking volcano," said Mech. "You really thinking burning it's the way to go?"

"Good point, well made," said Cal.

"Incoming!" Kevin announced, with an uncharacteristic amount of panic in his voice.

A spider-leg scythed up and slammed into the side of the *Untitled*, sending the ship into a spin. Alarms screamed. Warnings flashed. A jet of steam or smoke or possibly even both *hissed* from a vent in the wall.

"Come on!" said Mech. "We just got this thing fixed."

Loren raised a foot and pressed it against the console, wrestling with the stick. She roared through gritted teeth as she frantically tried to stop the ship spinning all the way to the ground.

Cal gripped his arm rests, trying to ignore the cream, caramel, and half a plantation's worth of bananas currently churning around in his stomach.

The ground loomed on the screen, then the sky, then the ground again. It didn't help that a third of the screen was showing the exact opposite view, and that Cal's brain was trying to overlap them, forcing him to see in both directions at once. Either that, or he was having an aneurism. It was too early to tell.

With a yelp from Loren, a hiss from Miz and a, "Holy shizz!" from Mech, the *Untitled* tilted, turned, then levelled off. It was barely a hundred feet from the ground, and the Spider-Dragon towered before it, already moving in for the kill.

The concentric rings of the Cantato Minor buildings were behind the beast. This low, Cal could see people running for their lives. A few of the flying disks zoomed above them, but most of the citizens were fleeing on foot.

"Time to show this thing who he's dealing with!" said Cal. He grabbed the weapon joystick and took aim at the creature's sun-eclipsing head. "Eat this, you ugly piece of shizz," he snarled, before adding, "Pew! Pew!" as he squeezed the trigger.

They all watched two glowing red dots pass the viewscreen, headed straight for the Spider-Dragon. Despite its lack of eyes, it, too, seemed to watch the shots approach. It hesitated, as if waiting for them to arrive. They both hit just above the monster's left mandible. If it noticed, it did nothing to show it.

"And let that be a lesson to you!" Cal shouted. He raised his eyes to the ceiling. "OK, Kevin, I'll let you finish him off. Light this fonker up."

"As you wish, sir."

Two white beams burned past the viewscreen, targeting the monster's two front legs. Before they hit, the Spider-Dragon ejected another explosion of fire. It unrolled like a giant tongue towards the *Untitled*, forcing Loren to slam the ship into reverse.

"Did we hit it?" Cal asked, as the flames crackled and died away.

"Negative, sir," said Kevin. "The creature's fire-like ejaculation appears to have countered the attack."

"The fire-like what?"

"Ejaculation, sir."

Cal sniggered. "Yeah, I heard the first time. I just wanted you to say it again." He banged a fist on the armrest. "Hit it with the torpedoes."

"We don't have torpedoes, sir."

"Oh, right. Do we have something like torpedoes?"

"We have photon missiles, sir," said Kevin. "They're broadly similar, although the propulsion system varies quite markedly between the—"

"Just fire the fonking things!" said Cal.

"Well, technically we don't 'fire' them so much as 'launch'—"

"*Kevin!*"

"Very good, sir."

Four missile-shaped energy projectiles streaked away from the ship. The Spider-Dragon opened its mouth, but the missiles changed direction – two going wide left, the others swinging to the right. The jet of flame took down the two on the right, but the remaining missiles snaked through and exploded against the monster's side.

"Boom! Eat that!" Cal yelped.

"Direct hits," said Mech, checking the scanners. "But minimal damage. They barely made a dent."

"Shizz. What's that thing made of?" said Loren.

"Spider-Dragon," said Cal. "It's made of Spider-Dragon. Which, unfortunately, turns out is pretty tough."

"Shall I ready more missiles, sir?"

"Sure, why not?" said Cal. He spun in his chair. "Soonsho? Any advice on dealing with this thing?"

Soonsho stared at the monster on screen for a few lingering moments, then quickly moved her lips.

"She said you should let it take her," said Miz. "That's the only way to stop it."

"Not going to happen," said Cal. "Any weaknesses you know of? Tender spots?"

Soonsho shook her head. Cal winced, and spun back to the front. "This thing came from a lake of fire, right? What about cold?"

"What about it?" asked Mech.

"Well, if we had a load of ice, couldn't we, I don't know, freeze it?"

"That is a possibility, sir," said Kevin.

"Great! Go me!"

"And, do you have 'a load of ice,' sir?"

Cal stopped, mid-cheer. "What? Uh... no."

"Then I fear the point is rather moot, don't you?"

The Spider-Dragon swiped at the ship again. Loren scooted them sideways, narrowly avoiding the most ironic bug-swatting in history.

"If it's going to follow us, we should lure it away," said Mech. "Get it away from the city."

"Makes sense," Cal agreed. "Loren, let's back away, see if we can get it to stick with us. Once we've got it in the open, we'll hit it with everything we've got."

"Wait. What's it doing?" asked Miz, leaning forwards and peering at the screen. "Is that...?"

Behind the Dragon-Spider, something was scuttling away. Several somethings.

Several *hundred* somethings.

"Holy shizz, it's having babies," said Cal.

At around twelve feet high, each of the spider-infants was just a fraction of a size of its mother. On their own, they might not be especially dangerous – or no more dangerous than any other twelve feet high fire-breathing arachnid, anyway – but they were already spreading through the streets, and would overwhelm the city through sheer numbers alone.

"Estimated number of Spider-Dragon offspring, two-hundred and forty-nine," Kevin announced. "Estimated time for total eradication of Cantato Minor's native population, thirty-seven minutes. In case anyone was wondering."

"We have to stop them things," said Mech.

"But we can't stick around here, or Mommy Spider is going to wipe out the city," Loren argued. "We have to get it away."

Cal drummed his fingers on his armrest. Any second now, someone was going to ask him what to do. He wasn't really sure why.

Sure, he'd always insisted he was the captain. He'd always pretended to be in charge. But the fact was, he had no idea about any of this stuff. A month and a half ago, he'd been pretending to be an eccentric Russian billionaire having a quite remarkable run of luck at a number of casinos across the state of Nevada.

A fortnight before that, he'd been selling top of the range penis-extension sports cars to Wall Street traders. Top of the range penis-extension sports cars which A) he didn't own, and B) didn't exist.

He'd had an illustrious career as a conman. He'd met a lot of interesting people, and seen a lot of fascinating places.

Nowhere in there, though, had he gained any kind of experience that qualified him to lead a crew of intergalactic misfits in a fight against a giant spider. A number of giant spiders, in fact. Because, although the babies were far smaller than their mother, at a dozen feet tall they definitely still earned that giant tag, as far as Cal was concerned.

What would Captain Kirk do?

Something clever, that had been cunningly foreshadowed in the first act. Cal thought back over the past few days, hoping there was something there that would reveal itself to be the secret to saving the day. Other than banoffee pie, though, nothing came to mind, and if they were going to take this thing down, obesity-related arterial disease was unlikely to be effective in the short-term.

What would Jesus do?

Cal had no idea. Forgive it, maybe? Wash its feet? He was rusty on his Bible stuff, but he didn't remember anything which would be particularly relevant to the current situation. The bit about the dude who killed the giant, maybe, but even that was a stretch.

Which left only one question. What would Cal Carver do?

And there was only one answer to that. The same answer

as always.

His best.

"Cal?"

That was Loren's voice. He blinked, and realized everyone was gazing at him expectantly. On screen, mama spider was gearing up for another attack, while her offspring scuttled through the city streets, pouncing on anyone they encountered.

"What do we do?"

Cal took a breath.

"OK, Miz, Mech, you're going to have to get your hands dirty," he said, sitting up in his chair. "By which I mean, we're throwing you down there to fight the baby Spider-Dragons. Take out as many as you can, try to buy the Cantatorians time to escape."

Mech's eyes widened. "You're serious? Just me and her against hundreds of them things?"

"Come on, sounds like fun," said Miz. She flashed her claws. "Bet I kill more than you do."

"No, not just the two of you," said Cal. He took another breath, and forced the words to come out. "Take Splurt."

Down on the floor, Splurt straightened into an upright oblong, and rippled with excitement.

"Alright! Now you're talking," said Mech.

"But, I swear, you'd better not let anything happen to him," Cal warned. "You bring him back to me in one piece."

Miz jumped to her feet. She and Mech headed for the door, with Splurt flipping end over end like a Slinky behind them. At the door, Splurt stopped and looked back. Cal nodded. "I'll see you soon, buddy."

Splurt formed a head. It was the head of Dorothy out of *the Golden Girls* and Cal had zero choice in the matter but to laugh. Dorothy out of *the Golden Girls* returned the nod, stuck her tongue out, then became green goo and rolled out of the door.

"OK, here's what's going to happen," Cal called. "You guys tool up. You've got twenty seconds to get what you need. We'll drop you over the city, then we'll lead Big Momma's House out of here and – all being well – shoot the shizz out of her until she dies."

"Cal!"

The Spider-Dragon's mouth was opening directly above the *Untitled*. For a moment, Cal saw the darkness deep in its cave-like jaw hole, then a flicker of fire ignited deep in its throat.

"Go, go, go!" Cal cried, then his eyes were shoved back in his head as Loren launched them straight at the beast. She leaned on the stick, weaving between its teetering legs, just as the fireball erupted at their tail.

Cal craned his neck and looked up to the top of the screen, where the underside of the Spider-Dragon rolled by. He'd hoped to find some conveniently exposed soft tissue there, just crying out for a missile or two, but the thing's belly was just as armored as the rest of it. More so, possibly.

"Well, so much for that plan," Cal muttered, and then the bug's body became clear sky as the *Untitled* dodged through its back legs and sped towards the city.

"Coming up fast on the drop zone," said Loren. "We'll have to be quick. The big one's starting to turn. She's going to come after us."

"Guys, get ready!" Cal called. Beneath them, the streets heaved with the spider-creatures. A few of the bolder Cantatorians – women, mostly – were fighting back by screaming at the things. The sound waves forced the spiders to draw back, their mandibles gnashing the air as their soft insides quivered within their exo-skeletons. "And, uh, just so we're clear, there are a *lot* of spiders down there. Like, a *lot*. I feel I can't stress that enough."

"Shizz. Big one's coming!" Loren warned. "We need to drop and go now."

She jabbed the hatch control and the landing ramp lowered.

"What the fonk? We ain't even gonna *land* first?" hollered Mech from the back.

"No time," said Cal. "You'll have to jump."

"*Jump*?! And then what?" Mech cried.

"I don't know. You're an intelligent guy. Figure something out." He nodded to Loren and she jerked forwards on the thrusters. There was a brief shout from Mech, but it was quickly lost to the howling of the wind.

Cal raised his eyes to the ceiling. "Kevin, they all clear?"

"Indeed, sir. Master Splurt has transformed into some kind of parachute style device. Estimated touchdown in seven-point-one seconds."

"Does Mech look angry?"

"Exceedingly, sir."

Cal grinned. "This day is getting better already." He *cricked* his neck, locked his gaze on the monster ahead of them, and raised one eyebrow. "Now, let's go swat us a Spider-Dragon."

CHAPTER TWENTY-THREE

Seven-point-one seconds after being unceremoniously ejected from the back of the *Untitled*, Mech and Miz glided to the ground. The parachute fluttered down over their heads, before *twanging* back into a basketball-sized blob of goo.

"Thanks, man," said Mech. Splurt grew an arm and raised a thumb.

"There they go," Miz said. Above them, the *Untitled* sped straight for the Spider-Dragon, banked left, and curved around its mile-long torso.

From inside the ship, the monster had seemed enormous. Out here, it didn't actually look any bigger. It was more that they felt smaller. The bug could have squashed them in the *Untitled*. Down here, they felt beneath its notice.

What *had* noticed them, though, was one of the smaller arachna-beasts. Several of them, actually. They bore down on them from all sides, barbed feet *tik-tik-tiking* across the metal ground, mandibles opening and snapping in time with each step.

"I make six," said Mech, standing back to back with Miz.

"Half each?"

"Ha! Yeah. Try to keep up, grandpa," Miz snorted. She glanced back at Mech. He met her eye.

"Be careful, kid."

"Like… you, too," said Miz, then she curled up her lips, dropped to her haunches and lunged.

Mech adjusted the dial on his chest, diverting some of his brainpower to his hydraulics. He shuddered noisily as his strength levels increased. "That's what I'm talkin' about," he said, then he raised both his arms, took aim, and fired.

Unnoticed by either of them, Splurt inflated, becoming a colorful beach ball. He rolled off along the street, weaving between the legs of several other spider-things. He bounced around happily in front of them, looping in the air and drawing a figure of eight on the road.

Screeching, the spiders gave chase. Splurt rolled away, zigging and zagging down the road, always keeping just out of reach.

Two legs stabbed down at him as another of the bug-creatures pounced. Splurt stopped just in time, spun quickly, then jumped onto the monster's head. He bounced a couple of times, rolled down its back, then continued on along the road, a procession of twelve-foot tall insects teetering along behind him.

The *Untitled* finished its maneuver around the Spider-Dragon and straightened onto an even keel. "We're clear," said Loren.

"Good. Kevin, how are the ground troops doing?"

"Still alive, sir. Master Mech and Mistress Mizette are both in the process of battling the infant Spider-Dragons."

"And Splurt?"

"It appears he's running away, sir."

"He is?" said Cal, unable to hide his surprise. "That's... good, I guess. Safety first."

"Uh, we've got a problem," said Loren.

"Is it the god-sized Spider-Dragon chasing us?" Cal asked. "If so, yeah, I noticed."

"That's the problem. It *isn't* chasing us," said Loren.

Sure enough, the rear camera view showed the beast still looming over the city, its crane-sized mandibles snapping as it lowered its head towards the outer ring of buildings.

"I think it's going for Mech and Miz."

"Fonk!" Cal hissed. "Kevin. Blast that thing up the shizzpipe. That should get its attention."

"Missiles, sir?"

"Sounds good. Fire!"

"As I believe I previously stated, 'launch' would be a more appropriate—"

"Just do it!"

Four missiles launched, two from each side of the ship. This time they didn't swing wide, and instead hammered one at a time into the Spider-Dragon's bountiful backside. The creature squealed angrily and stumbled around on all six legs. A jet of flame ignited in its throat, scorching the air between it and the *Untitled*.

"Yeah, that seemed to do the trick," said Cal. The monster's legs twitched, launching it towards them.

"Little too well," Loren spat, lurching the ship to the left and narrowly avoiding being pinned.

"Now, let's take this ugly old fonk for a walk," said Cal. He glanced back at Soonsho. She was sitting with her back pressed against the wall, eyes wide, knuckles white on her chair's armrests. "Don't worry, we do this kind of thing all the time," he assured her. "I mean, you know, not *exactly* this, but broadly similar."

The Spider-Dragon screeched. Fire crackled past the viewscreen. Cal tried his best to look reassuringly calm. "Nothing to worry about. Just you try to relax."

He winked at her, smiled again, then turned back to the front. The shiny red landscape rolled past beneath them. In the rear view, the Spider-Dragon picked its way across the uneven ground, leaving the city behind as it followed the *Untitled*.

"That's it, baby. Stick with us," Cal whispered. "Then we'll see how tough you *really* are."

"Raaaargh!"

Mech's hand clamped around a leg that had been on a direct collision-course with his head. He yanked sharply, pulling the spider towards him, just as he drove a wrecking-ball uppercut into its jaw. It howled as the skeletal hinge that connected its mandibles together shattered.

Mech twisted, ripping the monster's leg off. As he spun, he hurled it at another of the things. The barbed end embedded deep into the second creature's side. It turned towards him, only to be met head-on by a series of armor-shattering laser blasts from Mech's arm cannons.

Its skull exploded in quite a pleasing way. The spider wobbled unsteadily on its six legs for a few seconds, then fell. By the time it hit the ground, Mech was already blasting a hole in his next target.

Man, this was fun. It actually worried him a little, how much he was enjoying it. Since the war, he'd always considered himself something of a pacifist. Not a very good one, by any means. He got into a *lot* of fights for one thing, and he suspected that very few other pacifists had military-grade weapons systems built into their forearms, or a dial on their chest that allowed them to kill more efficiently.

But *hypothetically*, at least, he considered himself a pacifist. Yes he'd hit, hurt, maimed and murdered multiple times, but he hadn't enjoyed any of it.

Well, some of it. He'd enjoyed some of it.

But never like this.

A set of mandibles pincered him around the waist from behind. Mech's top half spun, his elbow, then his fist both hammering against the spider's exo-skeleton shielded skull. It hissed sharply, then squealed when Mech wrenched the pincers in two.

"Bring it on, motherfonkers!" he cried, then he cranked his dial up another notch, and hurled himself into a seething mass of spider bodies.

A little further along the street, Miz was getting in touch with her animal side. Unlike Mech, she didn't lie to herself about being a pacifist. She knew exactly what she was, and she reveled in it.

It was rare that she got the opportunity to really cut loose. Her father had never wanted her to fight at all – it wasn't done for Greyx females to get blood on their claws, and especially not members of the royal family. But she was just so good at it.

For all her bluff and bravado, Miz never really thought of herself as gifted or talented. She wasn't funny like Cal, or super-intelligent like Mech, or super-strong, also like Mech, depending on which way his dial was turned. She could probably fly a ship as well as Loren, but then that wasn't exactly saying much. A short length of rope and a brick could probably fly a ship as well as Loren, provided someone pointed it in the right direction.

But this – this, she was good at. This, she could do.

She scythed her claws around, lopping off a leg and sending a spider staggering. Twisting, she pounced, her jaws snapping down on the back of the monster's neck, where it joined the head. There was a moment of resistance, then the exo-skeleton splintered between her teeth. The spider screamed. Miz howled in triumph.

Yes, this she could do.

Several miles away, Splurt had amassed a small army of spiders. He had stopped being a beach ball a little while back, and now took the form of a man. Specifically, 'Dan, Dan the Music Man,' a children's entertainer who had been the surprise guest at Cal's sixth birthday party, and who – for reasons Splurt wasn't clear on - was somehow still near the forefront of Cal's memory.

Several hundred Cantatorians hid in their houses, peering out the windows at the procession passed. Splurt – or Dan, Dan the Music Man, depending on your perspective – danced and jigged along at the front, skillfully keeping his distance from the spider-creatures, but never getting so far away that they lost interest.

Only he could hear the music – *Let's Hear it for the Boy* by Deniece Williams, from the soundtrack to the movie *Footloose* – as he was currently pulling it directly from Cal's subconscious. If any of the watching Cantatorians could have heard it, however, they would have no doubt been genuinely impressed by the way he ducked, dodged and darted along in perfect time to the beat.

With an army of baby Spider-Dragons following behind him, and wearing the face of a middle-aged kids party entertainer from the late 1980s, Splurt bopped and jived onwards through the city.

*　　　*　　　*

Cal leaned forward in his chair. The Spider-Dragon stood front and center on the viewscreen, the city of Cantato Minor a dim glow behind it in the distance.

"Fire!"

Nothing happened.

Cal sighed.

"Jesus. OK, fine. *Launch*."

"Launching, sir," said Kevin.

Four… eight… no, *twelve* photon missiles streaked towards the monster. Its puckered mouth opened, but the missiles all separated, curving wide like planets in a decaying orbit around a parent sun.

The Spider-Dragon spewed its fire in a wide sweep, igniting seven of the missiles before they could connect. The remaining five hammered its ribcage – or roughly where Cal imagined its ribcage to be, at any rate – and this time the monster took notice. It jerked violently and raced forwards, bucking its head like a charging bull.

Loren reacted quickly, firing the lift thrusters and propelling the *Untitled* upwards out of the creature's reach.

Cal sprayed it with a few quick blasts from his *pew-pew* gun, but they thudded harmlessly into the top of the armored skull.

"What was that white laser thing you fired earlier?" Cal asked.

There was silence for a moment. "Me, sir?" Kevin finally said.

"Yes, you. Who the fonk else would…?" Cal took a deep breath. "Yes. The white laser thing."

"The Phased Disintegration Blast, sir?"

Cal shrugged. "Could be. Let's see. Give it a taste of that."

"Very good, sir."

Two beams of white energy stabbed down at the Spider-Dragon. It hissed and wriggled as the beams carved two trenches in its armor – deep, but not deep enough to do any real damage. It raised its head and spat fire at them, forcing Loren to dodge again.

"Wow, this thing is fast," she grimaced. "That was close."

"Have we hurt it at all?" Cal asked. "Beyond its feelings, I mean."

"Hurt what, sir?" asked Kevin.

"The… what do you mean, 'hurt what?' The spider. The fonking Spider-Dragon."

"Oh, yes. That."

Cal made an exasperated gesture in the direction of the ceiling, but said nothing.

There was a moment of silent calculation.

"I'm going to be honest with you sir, we haven't hurt it *much*," Kevin announced. "We've put a few scratches on its exo-skeleton, and not a whole lot else. We appear to be getting on its nerves, more than anything."

Cal groaned. "What else have we got?"

"An impending sense of doom, sir?" said Kevin. "Or perhaps that's just me."

"Weapon-wise, I mean," said Cal. "Do we have anything else we can hit this thing with?"

"I'm afraid not, sir, it's… Oh."

Cal looked up. "What? What is it?"

"It appears we do have another weapon on board, sir. We have the Omega Cannon."

"That sounds more like it," said Cal, sitting up straight and rubbing his hands together. "What does it do?"

"I have absolutely no idea," Kevin admitted.

Loren shunted the *Untitled* sideways, avoiding a leaping leg-strike from the Spider-Dragon.

"You've forgotten?" said Cal.

"No, sir. It appears that details of the Omega Cannon have been kept from me on purpose. Its schematics are not available for me to access. What I can detect of its circuitry is... rather baffling."

Cal shrugged. "Ah, what the Hell? Let's try it."

"Are you nuts?" Loren yelped. "You don't know what it does."

"So? It's a weapon, and we need a weapon if we're going to stop that thing. Kevin, fire."

"Kevin, don't!" Loren barked. She turned in her seat. "You heard what he said, he has no idea what it'll do. It *might* blow that thing to bits, or it might wipe out half the planet. Half the galaxy, for all we know."

"Loren," said Cal.

"No! Just listen for once!"

"*Loren!*"

She turned back to the screen, only to find it filled from edge to edge in all directions by the head and mandibles of the Spider-Dragon as it launched itself towards them.

Its pincers snapped around the ship. Its head jerked sharply. Cal and Loren screamed – and Soonsho tried very hard not to – as the *Untitled* flipped through the air then slammed against the ground with an ear-splitting *bang* and a *screech* of grinding metal.

CHAPTER TWENTY-FOUR

Cal had been in space for less than two months, and had now officially been involved in his second spaceship crash.

Technically, he'd been in more than two, but the others were mostly just bumps, prangs, and the occasional drawn-out grinding scrape as Loren had failed to clear a docking bay properly, landed awkwardly on a platform or – on one memorable occasion – flown at warp speed through a grocery store.

What Cal would consider his first 'proper' spaceship crash had been a biggie – so big, in fact, that it had destroyed the ship, churned up a mile-long stretch of forest and, most depressingly, broken his guitar.

Man, he missed that guitar.

This latest crash wasn't so bad. Sure, it had started out pretty grim, what with being grabbed by an enormous spider and everything, but the *Untitled*'s shields had deflected the worst of the ground impact, and the hull seemed to have remained intact. That was the good news.

The bad news was that they were now upside-down, and the leg of the aforementioned enormous spider was currently pinning them to the ground.

The Spider-Dragon's sphincter-like mouth hung above them, dribbling a viscous orange-red liquid along the length of its mandibles. The thing might have no eyes, but it seemed to be gazing right at them.

"Kevin, Loren, someone get us out of here!" Cal instructed. The straps of his chair were holding him in place, stopping him plunging towards the ceiling below.

"Can't," said Loren. "Not while it's got us pinned. If we were the right way up…"

"Wait, what's it doing?" Cal asked, gawping at the screen. The Spider-Dragon's vast body was inching down towards the ship. It was so close they could make out the tiny hairs on the underside of its armored belly, each one barely the size of an exceptionally tall man. "Is it… is it going to have sex with us?" He looked anxiously to Loren. "Surely *this* calls for the Omega Cannon?"

"I suspect it's trying to crack us open, sir," said Kevin. "Rather like one might crack open the shell of one of your Earth coconuts, in order to get at the flesh inside."

"O-K…"

"You would be the flesh in that analogy, sir."

"I got that, thanks."

"And, to a lesser extent, the milk."

They could see almost nothing on the viewscreen now but exo-skeleton and a narrowing sliver of the world beyond. Any second now, the thing would be on top of them.

"How long can we hold up under its weight?" Loren wondered.

"I'm afraid I don't know, ma'am. Without having more

detailed knowledge of the creature's mass, I could only estimate."

"Then do that," said Loren. "Estimate."

"Very good, ma'am. I estimate hull integrity would remain intact for somewhere between three hours…"

"Oh, thank God," said Cal.

"And two-point-six seconds."

Cal groaned. "I rescind that last statement. Can you estimate *any* more accurately than that? Because – and no offense here, Kevin – that sounds like you're covering a lot of bases."

"Wait, look!" said Loren. On screen, the spider was rapidly rising. It began to turn, and the *Untitled* rocked as the leg was withdrawn from its exposed belly. "It's leaving. It's letting us go!"

"Alright!" cheered Cal. "See, Soonsho, I told you everything was going to be…"

He wiggled his chair around, which wasn't easy in his upside-down position. The chair where the girl had been sitting was empty. Soonsho was gone.

"Cal," said Loren, her eyes flitting to one of the many warning messages currently lighting up the screen. "The landing hatch." She looked back over her shoulder. "It's open."

Miz spun, slashed, dodged, snapped, then hurled herself at a spider-creature, ripping at its eyes with her claws. Her fur was thick with blood and gunge. Her limbs ached, but she fought on. She'd been too late to stop this last spider before it stabbed a hooked leg through the chest of a fleeing Cantatorian. All she could offer its victim now was vengeance, and she was serving it up as best she could.

The young Spider-Dragon hissed and opened its round

mouth. A jet of blue flame escaped it, forcing Miz to skitter back out of its way.

"OK, I sorta hoped you guys wouldn't figure that out," Miz said. Then she shrugged. "Still, guess it just makes the whole thing more exciting."

She ducked under the fire, twisted beneath it, then raked both sets of claws down the monster's now-exposed chin. The flesh split, spilling the spider's black, tar-like blood onto the ground.

Dropping to her knees, Miz swung both arms wide. Her claws found two of the thing's legs, carving out chunks right below the kneecaps. She rolled clear just as the spider dropped, then wrapped her arms around its head and twisted until its neck went *crack*.

"You totally deserved that," she spat, then she looked across to where the broken body of the Cantatorian lay, pushed down a pang of something like guilt, then turned to find her next target.

A leg slammed into her ribcage, catching her off-balance. Miz stumbled, already preparing to pounce on her attacker, but then a weight pressed on her from behind, knocking her to the ground. She spun onto her back, claws and teeth at the ready, only to find four more of the spiders crowding her, crawling over each other, fighting to get to her.

Barbed feet sunk into her shoulders and thighs, pinning her like a butterfly. She gritted her teeth, but refused to scream – yeah, like that was going to happen - as mandibles gnashed at her, spraying her with blobs of hot spider spit.

She struggled against the weight of the monsters, but each movement just dug the legs deeper into her flesh. A head lowered towards her. The puckered mouth expanded and a gust of warm air rolling down over her face.

"Ew," Miz told it. "Your breath *totally* reeks. Also," she added. "I hope you fonking choke on me."

She spat in its eye. Then quickly spat in the others, for good measure. She braced herself, but refused to look away as the head lowered and the mouth opened and a metal hand clamped down on the monster's skull.

Miz frowned. Wait. What was that last one?

The head was yanked back. A blast of laser fire exited through the front of its face, turning it into a gooey black paste.

The other spiders surrounding the lead one screeched furiously. Mech spun around, blasting them all at point-blank range in the head and throat. Two dropped instantly. The last remaining one stumbled backwards, no doubt giving some serious thought to this whole 'invasion' endeavor. Mech finished it with another few short blasts, then turned in time to catch the headless first spider before it collapsed onto Miz.

"Get it off me," she told him.

"But its legs. Ain't they hooked in?" Mech asked.

"Just do it!"

Mech got himself beneath the creature's lifeless body and pushed upwards, heaving it above his head. The legs tore free with a series of brief but unpleasant ripping sounds, and Miz allowed herself just the tiniest of pained groans.

With a grunt, Mech tossed the spider away. The area around them was clear now – provided you didn't count the corpses, limbs and gungy black blood – but that wouldn't last long. They had to move, and soon.

Mech dropped to one knee and extended a hand to the fallen Mizette. At first, she batted it away, but when he held it out a second time, she considered it more carefully.

She looked at the hand.

She looked past it, to the mash-up of metal and scarred flesh that made up Mech's face. He looked different from this angle. Bolder. More dynamic.

Hot, even.

Miz flicked her tongue across her chops, wiped a blob of spider's face from her fur, then took Mech's hand. He hoisted her to her feet with such suddenness, she was forced to throw her arms around his impressively broad shoulders.

"Hey," she said, her voice a low purr.

Mech's brow knotted. "Uh... hey yourself," he said. Her hands caressed the back of his neck and his frown deepened. It almost came as a relief when he heard the sound of approaching Spider-Dragons. The relief, however, did not last long.

There were hundreds of them, approaching along the street like an army. They hurried along, teetering on their ridiculous legs. It took Mech a moment to realize why they were in such a rush. They were chasing someone.

"Who," began Miz, peering along the street to where a man with a piano tie and a matching belt was jigging and dancing at the head of the spider conga, "is *that* guy?"

Cal swung down from his chair, dropped to the ceiling, and launched himself towards the door. "Get the ship the right way up and be ready!" he instructed.

"Ready for what?" asked Loren.

"Fonked if I know," Cal said, jumping up and catching the door lintel. His boots scrambled on the wall as he clambered for the opening above him. "Just be ready in general."

He heaved himself into the doorway, teetered on the lintel for a second or two, then toppled forwards and fell into the corridor. "Ow."

Too many seconds of climbing and scrambling later, he

made it to the hatch by way of the armory, lowered himself from the doorway, and dropped several feet to the ground.

Cal sprinted clear just as the *Untitled*'s thrusters propelled it along the ground in a shower of sparks. The scraping of metal on metal was piercingly loud, and he'd have clamped his hands over his ears, were it not for the fact he was holding two quite cumbersome hand grenades. A blaster rifle was slung across his chest, with a pistol tucked into the back of his pants for good measure. None of it was likely to hurt the Spider-Dragon, he knew, but he sure felt better for having it.

The scraping sound stopped as the ship lurched into the air. Cal raced up the side of a low metal hillock, his head back as he watched the monster above. It had blocked out most of the sky, casting the world around Cal into cold shadow. It was still in the process of turning, and backing itself up a little. From the way it moved, it seemed to be targeting a ridge a hundred feet or so to Cal's right. He set off towards it at speed, the grenades making a somewhat worrying sloshing sound as he ran.

"Soonsho!" he bellowed. "Soonsho, where are you?"

He skidded over the ridge, discovered quite a steep drop on the other side, and bounced twice on the way to the ground. He landed with a heavy *thud* on his back. The blaster pistol fired, scorching his buttocks and burning a hole in the seat of his pants.

After he'd recovered from that shock, Cal risked a glance at the hand grenades. Neither one showed any signs of being about to go off, so that was something, at least.

He struggled upright, considered getting rid of the pistol, then decided instead just not to fall from a height onto it again.

"Soonsho!" he hollered, then he almost screamed when

he turned to find her standing immediately behind him. "Jesus! Never sneak up on a man with explosives in both hands. That's, like, rule number one."

The Spider-Dragon's head hung over them, the tips of the mandibles just fifty or sixty feet from where they stood. Beyond the mandibles, its cavernous mouth was opening like a camera shutter, revealing a vast, moist blackness beyond.

Soonsho stepped forwards and put her arms out at her side, inviting the monster to come for her. Cal pulled her back, caught the pin of one of the grenades in his teeth, and pulled it free. Tossing it upwards with all his might, he dragged Soonsho away. They stumbled on, slipping and sliding across the smooth, shiny metal.

Taking cover behind a jagged outcrop, Cal watched the grenade soar up, up, up towards its target.

And then fall down, down, down to the ground. It bounced twice.

Several seconds later, it made a disappointing *pop* and burst in a flash of fluttering colors. "Well, that was fonking useless," Cal muttered, tossing the other grenade away. He swung the blaster rifle into one hand, and caught Soonsho's arm with the other. "Come on, let's get out in the open and hope Loren can see us."

He tried to drag her on, but Soonsho stood her ground. She pointed angrily to the approaching Spider-Dragon, then her face softened a little as she curved her finger back around to point at herself.

"No," said Cal. "No, you don't have to do that. It's not your job to stop that thing. You don't have to—"

Soonsho opened her mouth, just a little, and only for a fraction of a second. Cal didn't hear the sound she made, but he felt it. It hit him like a hurricane, huffing the breath from his lungs and hurtling him backwards through the air.

He crashed hard into a boulder-sized lump of metal and slid down it, his body completely ignoring his brain's instructions to get up again.

In a minute, it seemed to say. *Let's just lie down for a bit. Doesn't this rock feel nice?*

Cal watched, helplessly, as Soonsho turned away. He tried to call to her, but he had no breath left in him to make the sound. She opened her arms and tilted her head to the sky. An offering, to the monster.

Its head lowered. Its mandibles snapped open. Its mouth unpuckered.

Cal stared at the hideous thing.

He stared at the girl.

He remembered the rifle in his hand.

He pointed it at Soonsho.

His finger found the trigger.

And he squeezed.

CHAPTER TWENTY-FIVE

Miz limped clear of Mech and they both braced themselves for a fight. It was not, judging by the number of spiders approaching, a fight they had any hope of winning, but that had never stopped either of them in the past.

Halfway between them and the spider-creatures, Dan, Dan the Music Man jigged towards them, his short, flabby body gyrating in perfect time to *Come on Eileen* by Dexy's Midnight Runners, which only he could hear. Without the benefit of the music, the guy looked positively insane as he sashayed and slide-stepped the last few feet, then stopped just ahead of Mech and Miz.

"Who the fonk are you?" Mech asked.

Dan, Dan the Music Man smiled and winked at them, then he crisply about-turned until he was facing the approaching spiders. They were closing fast now — a few hundred of the things scuttling along on a few thousand legs.

Splurt shifted, changing his form from that of an ex-children's entertainer to something very tall and very wide, with a large, heavy hammer-shaped head.

"Splurt!" Miz gasped.

"Oh, man," Mech muttered. Even with his dial turned to the right, he was smart enough to realize what was about to happen. "That thing's a genius."

The spiders stopped scuttling and looked up. Splurt, despite having no face and a head made of ultra-dense neutronium, smiled. Much as he'd enjoyed the dancing, this had been the part he'd been most looking forward to.

He swung. His hammer-head smashed down on a bug, shattering its skeleton and spraying its guts across the street. By the time the monsters on either side of it had realized what had happened, it had happened to them, too.

Krik.

Krak.

Ksshk.

Splurt rifled remotely through Cal's subconscious until he found a suitable track – Phil Collins' 1981 debut single, *In the Air Tonight* – and, with the opening drum-beat pounding inside his head, he went to work.

The blast from the rifle clipped Soonsho on the underside of one outstretched arm, searing a perfectly circular hole in the flesh a few inches above her elbow. Whether it was the shock or the pain, it was impossible to tell, but the effect was instantaneous.

With a mile-long Spider-Dragon preparing to devour her, and her skin still sizzling from where Cal had shot her, Soonsho Sooss opened her mouth and – finally – began to scream.

The sound rose like a shockwave into the air. Even though he was several dozen feet behind her, Cal was forced to cover his head with his hands and grit his teeth as his eardrums collapsed and his skeleton tried to shake itself free of his body.

The Spider-Dragon's head snapped back, as if hit by an invisible uppercut. A web of cracks appeared on the glazing of the monster's exo-skeleton, fissuring and widening as Soonsho unleashed a lifetime of fear and worry and betrayal and regret in one long, drawn-out wail.

It rose from within her like an unstoppable force. All those horrors – all those years spent cheerfully preparing for her own agonizing death – were because of this creature. Because of this monster. Because of this thing.

The Spider-Dragon screamed, but Soonsho screamed louder. And as she screamed, the pitch rose and fell, becoming a song - a song of despair and destruction and death. For the first time in her life, Soonsho sang, and the world trembled at the beauty and the horror of it.

The monster's armor split open. Canyons raced along it, revealing the soft, pulpy flesh beneath. Soonsho sang. Fifteen years of silence – fifteen years of holding back – came to an end in a single flowing aria that ignited the clouds above her, scorching the sky in columns of flickering color.

And then, as suddenly as she had started, she stopped. Her piercing soprano became a croak, then a gasp, then nothing at all as her breath ran out.

The Spider-Dragon stumbled, its legs not quite its own, its armor falling away in truck-sized slivers. One of its mandibles hung limply and uselessly, while the other moved slowly back and forth, as if searching for its missing mate.

But the mouth. The mouth was opening. The head was coming down. And the Spider-Dragon, despite the damage, was hungry for one last meal.

"No!" Cal made it to his feet. He closed the gap between them in a second and a half, then hurled himself at Soonsho.

They connected just as four fiery red photon missiles slammed into the great beast above them. All four of the blasts pierced the thing's exposed, quivering flesh, then detonated deep inside its skull.

With a final shriek, the Spider-Dragon toppled sideways, and fell to the ground with a thunderous *boom*.

The *Currently Untitled* swooped above them, firing its landing thrusters as it came in for a landing.

"YOU OK?" Cal shouted. His eardrums had been completely obliterated - and he still had a hole in the back of his pants – but, all things considered, it could have gone worse. "SORRY I SHOT YOU!"

Soonsho nodded shakily and clutched her wounded arm.

"THAT'LL STITCH RIGHT UP! SERIOUSLY, IT WON'T EVEN LEAVE A..."

Cal's ears began to itch like crazy. There was a faint pop, a sharp ache, and suddenly the world became much louder. He jabbed a pinkie finger inside one ear and wiggled it around.

"What the...? Testing. Lalalala. Hey? HEY! Hey."

Yep, all good.

"Oh man." He grinned. "Forget Hannibal and Face – I am *totally* Wolverine."

The *Untitled* landed beside him in a swirl of dust and spider-armor fragments. "One sec, I have to check something," said Cal. Soonsho watched him run across the barren metal until he eventually reached one of the spider's legs.

He kicked it. He mumbled something too quiet for Soonsho to hear. He waited.

Then, he turned around and walked back. "Yep," he said. "It's definitely dead."

Cal gestured towards the back of the ship, just as the ramp lowered.

"Now," he said. "Shall we?"

Cal, Soonsho and Loren stepped down from the *Untitled* into a scene of utter carnage. Even from up in the sky, the scene spread out before them had immediately catapulted itself into Cal's top ten list of the worst things he'd ever seen, nudging his naked grandmother into eleventh place.

Now that he was actually standing knee deep in the sludgy black gore, though, it was rapidly closing in on the top five.

Mech and Miz sat on the back of a partially crushed spider creature. They waved at Cal as he sloshed through the flood of insect guts, both looking relaxed, like this was the most normal thing in the world.

"What the Hell happened?" he said, trying not to gag at the stench that swirled into the air with every step he took through the murk. "Did you guys do this?"

"Uh-uh," said Mech.

"We did, like five percent," said Miz.

"Then how did…?" Cal's eyes widened. "Splurt?"

A little green blob rolled out from behind Mech, squidged into a pancake shape, then *boinged* into Cal's arms. At least, that was the intention. Caught off guard, however, Cal missed, and Splurt vanished into the spider-slurry with a wet-sounding *shlop*.

"Ooh, shizz. Sorry, buddy," said Cal, then he jumped in fright as a long green tentacle wrapped itself around his neck, and Splurt leapt up onto his shoulder. Cal tickled him where he imagined the little guy's chin to be. "You did all this?" he asked. Splurt shuddered happily. "Well, way to go, you adorable fonking psycho. Good job!"

A number of floating disks swooped down over the buildings around them, ferrying The Conductor and

Conductress, Soonsho's parents, and a number of official-looking men in uniform.

"Oh. Here we go. Look heroic, guys," said Cal. "Space Team just saved the day."

"You idiots!" boomed the Conductor. "What have you done? *What have you done*?!"

Cal hadn't been expecting that. "Uh… saved the day?" he said. "Killed the Dragon-Spider—"

"*Spider-Dragon!*"

"Whatever. And all its little baby *Dragon-Spiders* so, you know, you can all live happily ever after." Cal broke out one of his best grins. "You're welcome."

"You have doomed us all," the Conductor seethed. He stabbed a finger at Soonsho, who drew back in fright. "*She* has doomed us all."

"What are you talking about?" said Cal, still working on the theory that his smile was bound to prove contagious sooner or later. "She – well, *we*, but mostly her – totally killed that thing. It's gone. Kaput. You don't have to feed it children any more, which I would consider a definite win."

"The Spider-Dragon of Saktar was our only defense!" The conductor roared, and the spider-slurry rippled in harmony with his tones. "For millennia, it was our protector. Our guardian. Resting, biding its time until it was needed. And now…"

He gesticulated towards the mountain-sized cadaver in the distance. "Now look at it! We are defenseless."

"You gotta have guns, right?" asked Mech.

"Ooh, great question," said Miz. "Even without your dial turned, you're super-smart."

"Uh… OK."

"No, we don't have guns! Why would we need guns?" the

Conductor spat. "We had the Spider-Dragon of Saktar!"

"OK, first of all," said Cal, "monster-spider based planetary defenses are *notoriously* unreliable. Seriously, it's a miracle you guys weren't wiped out centuries ago. We've totally done you a favor. And secondly, uh, *hello*? You've got something even better." He put an arm around Soonsho's shoulders. "You've got Soonsho."

Cal squeezed and Soonsho let out a sharp hiss as pain shot through her wounded arm. One of the uniformed men, who had been hanging back on his disk, looking vaguely menacing, was flipped backwards off it, and plunged into the gunk.

The Conductor and Conductress backed away slowly. Even Soonsho's parents watched her with fear in their eyes. Soonsho took a step towards them, but stopped when she saw them tense up in fright.

"She is powerful," the Conductor agreed, lowering his voice like he was scared he might startle the girl. "Of that, there is no doubt. But she cannot be everywhere at once. She cannot protect Cantato Minor forever. Without the Spider-Dragon of Saktar, we are all victims, just waiting to meet our fates."

Soonsho looked down at her feet for a moment, then tugged on Cal's sleeve. She glanced across to her parents. Neither of them could hold her eye.

Her lips moved silently. Miz's ears pricked up.

"What's she saying?" Cal asked.

"She's saying she's sorry," said Miz. She cocked her head a little. "And she's saying she has an idea."

"Are you sure about this?" asked Cal.

Soonsho nodded. Behind her, Dorid Tarkula – the real,

genuine, accept-no-imitations original – stood in the doorway of his castle. He was alone. His failed clones, he assured them, had been put out of their misery.

"I mean, this is a pretty creepy castle, even with all the freaks gone," Cal continued. "Look at it, it's *definitely* haunted. And I bet even the ghosts are a tiny bit creeped out by the place."

Soonsho's lips moved.

"She says she'll be OK," said Miz. "She says she wants to do it, so her parents can be safe."

"Not sure I'd bother with them myself," Mech muttered. "Didn't exactly strike me as a loving family."

"I guarantee the girl's safety," said Dorid. "My behaviour earlier… that wasn't me. I was desperate, but that does not justify my actions. Soonsho and I will develop the sonic shielding together. I will use it here and install it on Cantato Minor, also. Thanks to her – to her voice – her people will be protected. Always."

"And Zertex won't be able to steal your stuff," said Loren.

Dorid nodded. "Perhaps we can all stay out of the coming war, after all."

Cal looked to Soonsho, then made a clumsy waveform with his hand. "May your song carry long and carry far, kid."

Soonsho smiled shyly at Cal, then threw her arms around him and hugged him. She pulled away after a few moments, waved to the crew, then scuttled into the castle. "I will protect her. You have my word," he said.

"We'll hold you to that," said Mech.

"Yeah. We'll *totally* be watching," added Miz.

"We mean it," said Loren. "You don't want to mess with us."

"Especially him," said Cal, jabbing a thumb towards

Splurt, who pulsed on the landing ramp, watching on in cheerful silence. "Seriously, he has issues. You don't even want to know."

With a final warning glare from each of them, the crew turned and headed up the ramp. Cal stopped at the bottom.

"Oh one question, what's the Omega Cannon?" he asked, turning. But Dorid was gone, and the door was closed. Cal shrugged. "Ah, what the Hell? It'll be more fun to figure it out."

And then, he marched up the ramp, strode along the corridor and onto the flight deck.

"Captain on the bridge!" he announced, but no-one paid him even the slightest bit of attention, much less snapped to salute.

He slid into his chair just as Loren fired up the thrusters. The dark slate landscape lurched as the *Untitled* lifted into the air and headed for orbit.

"OK, so what's the plan, troops?" Cal asked. "We've got money in our pocket, a ship under our feet, and a whole lot of stars in the sky to choose from. Any suggestions?"

The screen flared a rainbow of colors as they left the atmosphere.

"I got one," said Mech. He picked an apparently arbitrary direction and pointed. "Head that way, and don't stop until we're waaay at the other side of the nebula."

"One suggestion," said Cal. "Miz?"

"I want to do whatever Mech wants to do," she said.

A flicker of a frown passed over Cal's face. "Uh, OK. What about your boat?"

Miz shook her head. "Mech doesn't like boats."

"That is true," Mech agreed.

Cal looked from Miz to Mech and back again, then shook

his head. "Loren? Any suggestions?"

"Picking up a transmission."

It took Cal a second to realize she wasn't making a suggestion and was, in fact, picking up a transmission.

"Is it Dorid? Soonsho?"

Loren shook her head. "No. Symmorium."

"Ha! Yeah, right, like we're going to fall for that one again," said Cal. "Nice try, Kornack."

"Not this time, sir. I have been able to establish a video feed with the Symmorium ship and, well, it isn't good news," said Kevin. "Certainly not if you're on board it, at any rate."

"On screen," said Cal.

A box appeared in the top right corner of the screen. It was black, and at first Cal thought the video hadn't started to play, but then sparks flew in the darkness, illuminating a heavily damaged corridor. One of the ship's crew – a particularly stocky and shark-like older Symmorium – lay sprawled on the floor, his body folded in such a way that it was immediately apparent he was dead. And not just a bit dead. *Top level* dead.

A wall had exploded beside him, filling him with shrapnel. When the damaged circuitry sparked, the light showed clouds of white air being siphoned through the hole in the wall, and out into the vacuum beyond.

"This is Commander Junta of the Symmorium," wheezed a voice.

"Junta?" said Cal. The crew and the commander had a short but eventful history together and one which, miraculously, had seen them part as friends. "Can he hear me?"

Loren shook her head. "This is a pre-record. It's one way."

"We are under attack. Half of my crew is dead. My daughter… Tyra… is gone. If you are within the sound of my voice, please… help us. We don't have—"

The transmission cut off.

"That's all there is of it, sir," said Kevin. "I have been able to ascertain the last position of the ship that sent the message. Putting them on screen."

"Zertex did this," said Loren. Her words hung heavily in the air.

"Like I said, ain't nobody getting out of this one," said Mech. "This war of theirs – of Zertex's – it's gonna tear the galaxy apart."

"So, like, what do we do?" asked Miz.

More silence fell.

Cal looked at the blinking red dot on screen, showing the location of the Symmorium ship.

He looked out at the stars, far off in the direction Mech had pointed, and the universe of possibility that lay that way.

They would all be looking to him, he knew. They would all be waiting for an answer. But he didn't know the answer to that question. Not the right one, anyway.

What would Cal Carver do?

Now that one, he did know the answer to. Right or wrong.

"Loren," he said, leaning back in his chair and gripping his armrests. "Plot us a course."

THE END

Space Team will return in

SPACE TEAM: THE GUNS OF NANA JOAN

To keep up to date with the latest from author Barry J. Hutchison, visit barryjhutchison.com

Made in the USA
San Bernardino, CA
06 March 2018